Praise for *The Good Wife*

"A deceptively simple style, confessional almost. Indeed, the tone here is so personal, so intimate, we feel like voyeurs, as if we're reading someone's diary. . . . It is in these quotidian moments that the novel reaches its lyrical height."

—*San Francisco Chronicle*

"O'Nan displays his astonishing ability to get under his diverse characters' skin and thereby draw us deeply into their lives."

—*Chicago Sun-Times*

"[O'Nan] depicts Patty's working class–milieu with rare and clear-eyed compassion."

—*Entertainment Weekly*

"Wholly engrossing and flawlessly crafted . . . Masterful."

—*Baltimore Sun*

"Grabs the reader immediately and refuses to let go . . . *The Good Wife* is a celebration of the bravery it takes to get from day to day to day when there's little to go on but hope."

—*The Hartford Courant*

"Forceful, oddly moving . . . O'Nan has completely captured Patty and her dogged determination to endure in this sad but strangely hopeful story."

—*Publishers Weekly* (starred review)

"O'Nan shows singular restraint; there is no preaching in *The Good Wife*. Instead, there is just one woman's story, quietly told. . . . Perfect."

—*The Denver Post*

"O'Nan has spun a taut, deeply affecting novel. . . . He has a pitch-perfect ear for dialogue, and especially for interior conversations. Indeed, the novel owes much of its power to the author's uncanny ability to inhabit Patty's mind."

—*Milwaukee Journal Sentinel*

W9-AXL-735

"O'Nan is a writer worthy of serious attention."

—*Chicago Tribune*

"[An] engrossing and heartbreaking novel . . . O'Nan has been named one of the best young American novelists by *Granta,* and it's evident here why."

—*Library Journal* (starred review)

"The overriding reaction O'Nan evokes for his heroine is awed sympathy. *The Good Wife* is a quietly devastating, thought-provoking examination of love and loyalty that can't be locked away."

—*Contra Costa Times*

"Have you grown tired lately of high-concept novels, full of flash and action but signifying nothing so much as our modern conceits? A wonderful antidote can be found in *The Good Wife,* a richly observed, eloquently executed working-class pastoral on an underappreciated human quality: endurance."

—*The News-Press* (Fort Myers, Florida)

"[O'Nan's] touch is deft with his plotline, his characters subtle and lifelike."

—*The Buffalo News*

THE
GOOD
WIFE

STEWART
O'NAN

FARRAR, STRAUS AND GIROUX

NEW YORK

THE GOOD WIFE. Copyright © 2005 by Stewart O'Nan. All rights reserved. Printed in the United States of America. For information, address Picador, 175 Fifth Avenue, New York, N.Y. 10010.

www.picadorusa.com

Picador® is a U.S. registered trademark and is used by Farrar, Straus and Giroux under license from Pan Books Limited.

For information on Picador Reading Group Guides, as well as ordering, please contact Picador.
Phone: 646-307-5629
Fax: 212-253-9627
E-mail: readinggroupguides@picadorusa.com

Designed by Gretchen Achilles

Library of Congress Cataloging-in-Publication Data

O'Nan, Stewart, 1961–
    The good wife / Stewart O'Nan.
        p. cm.
    ISBN 0-312-42501-5
    EAN 978-0-312-42501-2
    1. Prisoners' spouses—Fiction. 2. Separation (Psychology)—Fiction. 3. Mothers and sons—Fiction. 4. Married women—Fiction. I. Title.

PS3565.N316G67 2005
813'.54—dc22   2004053247

First published in the United States by Farrar, Straus and Giroux

10 9 8 7 6 5 4 3

its shell. Outside, the winter sky turns, Orion winking in the clear night air, a hunter's moon sculpting the drifts. Here, before it all begins, there's still time—time revolving along with the temperature on the display outside the Tioga State Bank in town, time ticking in the gears behind the lit face of the county courthouse belltower (quaint as a Christmas card), time circling like the sweeping red second hand of the dashboard clock in his truck, hidden in the turnaround down by Owl Creek.

Until now—until the phone rings—she's been happy, grateful to have him, and a place of their own. Their marriage, her first improbably successful campaign against her mother, is everything she wished for, and while her mother still considers him wild, with Casey on the way that topic's off limits. Now all her mother can complain about is Eileen living with her no-good boyfriend and Shannon not visiting. By default, Patty's the favorite again. She's the one their mother calls when she needs someone to bring extra chairs or make dessert, someone to drive her to the doctor. Except for marrying Tommy, she's reliable.

Miles away, the glass is broken on the carpet, the front of Tommy's shirt wet, though he doesn't notice.

The phone—no, not yet.

It's her bladder that wakes her. She mutters, surprised at the brightness. She gives up on her bookmark, sets the paperback on the headboard and clicks off the light. Her bottom sinks into the soft waterbed as she swings her legs free and levers herself out, pushing off the frame to lift her own weight. She's never been so ungainly—ugly, she thinks, and his stabs at reassuring her only make it worse. She doesn't turn on the light in the bathroom, just sits in the warm yellow glow, head bent, one elbow resting on the cool sink.

When she pads back to bed, she could trip over the phone, kick it open so the call will never come. But she doesn't. She goes all the way around, as if it would be a jinx to get in on his side. She lights the vanilla candle on the headboard, the flame doubled in the built-in mirror, then adjusts her peignoir and the covers to her advantage, but in a minute she's asleep again, snoring.

In the house on Blodgett Road, Tommy and Gary stand over the old woman, who's not moving.

"Jesus Christ," Gary says.

"I thought she was supposed to be gone," Tommy accuses him. "I thought the place was supposed to be empty."

"Shut up."

But this is invented too, a scene she doesn't want to watch yet is drawn to over and over. They could be saying anything to each other, or nothing, stunned by their own violence and bad luck. It's like watching a nightmare, the rising helplessness before the disaster she knows is going to happen.

It's happened. The two of them grab the state's evidence they've come to steal—the dead woman's dead husband's guns: a pair of beautiful his 'n' hers Ithaca ten-gauges with carved stocks, a vintage Colt buffalo gun, a brace of muzzle loaders. Gary has his hockey bag, and old towels to friction tape around the barrels. They go ahead as if the plan is working. At some point they'll have to stop and talk about the body, but not yet, not yet.

A draft snakes through the room and the flame wavers, dangerous. It's nearly two and she has to get up at six to be at work. It's supposed to snow tomorrow; she needs to leave time for the drive. She's been tired lately, nodding off over her circuit boards, the magnifying lens making her eyes go weird, the hot solder gagging her. She's been good, not smoking for the baby, only drinking Sanka. When she gets her leave, she'll make breakfast for Tommy in her bathrobe, kiss him goodbye, then crawl back in bed again, the morning sun warming the room.

By this time the call has come in on the truck. A neighbor on Blodgett marked it driving by with its lights off, dark figures walking out of the trees. A car from the sheriff's department is gliding cross-county to investigate the complaint, code two, silent approach. It's a slow night and the roads are empty, the traffic signals clunking unseen. The deputy slides through a red light. The bridge over the East Branch is slippery.

Gary's decided they have to burn the house down, and starts by lighting the drapes. The sheer fabric flashes, taking a snapshot of the body on the floor. Tommy can't stop him, and joins in. There's kerosene in the garage.

The fingerprints are his, she won't try to deny it. But she knows him too. She can't picture him sloshing the can around the house out of desperation, the carpet wet underfoot, fire leaping onto furniture, climbing the walls. She's imagined it happening to her, traded places with the old lady a thousand times. She could be the one picked up and repositioned under the covers, the one whose pillow burns, whose eyelashes curl.

Instead, she sleeps by candlelight—sleeps deeply now, plowing the hours toward dawn, work, the cold car again, scraping snow off the windshield while the tailpipe chuffs out clouds.

The windows are glowing when the deputy pulls up, the house pulsating like a spaceship about to take off. He blocks the road with his Fury and radios dispatch to send the fire department and the nearest backup—the night supervisor, who reads the situation and calls in the state police.

Inside, Tommy and Gary see the car and understand they're fucked. The only thing to do is slip out the back and get across the creek somehow. It makes sense for Gary—it's not his truck—but why does Tommy follow him? Because he does, down the steps of the back deck and across the sloping lawn, the crust crunching

underfoot, two sets of prints headed into the woods, easy to follow as a trail of breadcrumbs in a fairy tale. They splash through
the freezing creek, their boots filling, squishing as they scramble
up the long, contoured hillside, slipping, falling and going on, not
knowing another car is shuddering down the farm road right for
them. Its lights crest the hill and blind them, and then a spotlight
in their eyes.

If she dreams anything in these last minutes, she doesn't remember it, and she's tempted to see this as further proof that she's
a fool, no hints or intuitions, just completely clueless. Where did
she think the money for the truck came from?

They're handcuffed and shoved into different cars, driven the
silent miles to the Public Safety Building in Owego, fingerprinted
and interrogated separately, both of them standing on their Mi-
randa rights. Each is allowed one five-minute phone call.

The fire is pretty much out now. The Halsey Valley volunteers
stand around the yard, dousing a pile of melted vinyl siding. In
the bedroom, the county coroner leans over the old lady, who
rests on the smoking coils of the box spring, her arms curled in
front of her face as if to protect herself.

In these last minutes, Patty wonders, would she tell herself to
run? Take whatever money's in the house, throw her clothes in the
car and just drive? Would it even matter? Because what happens
next is inevitable.

THE SOUND OF LIES

SHE'S PREPARED TO HEAR THE HOSPITAL.

"I'm okay," he says. "Listen, me and Gary got in a little spot tonight. I'm in jail."

"What did you do?" she asks, afraid it's another DUI.

"I don't know, we haven't been charged yet. It's going to be a bunch of stuff, it looks like."

"What is 'a bunch of stuff'?"

"It's not as bad as it sounds."

"Tommy, what the hell is going on?"

"I don't really want to talk about it over the phone, if you understand what I'm saying. I need you to be here first thing in the morning, and I mean first thing. Call Russ and tell him I won't be in. Call Perry and find out who that lawyer was he had—wake him up if you have to."

"Jesus, Tommy, will you tell me what happened?"

"—and listen: whatever you do, do *not* call Donna. If she calls, don't talk to her."

"Why not?"

"Just don't. And see what kind of money we can put together for bail. There's a place in Elmira Perry knows, they're twenty-four hours. If you can't get Perry, try Shawn."

The lawyer is the most important thing, then bail. Sometime tomorrow she'll have to come in and get the truck.

She's wide awake but struggling to follow along. She needs to write all this down.

"Hon," he says, "I've only got a minute left. I love you."

"I love *you*," she says.

"I'm sorry."

"It's going to be all right," she says, but the line cuts off.

She hangs up, whacking at the base till it fits. It's four in the morning and cold in the house. She knots her robe closed over the peignoir and toes into her slippers, turns the lights on as she scuffs to the kitchen. The windows are black mirrors, the walls of a box. When she pulls out a chair, it sounds loud.

The first person she calls is Eileen.

"Okay," Eileen says, like it's no problem. "So it could be anything. And Gary's there with him."

"It sounded bad."

"It can't be that bad," Eileen says, "or else they wouldn't be setting bail. And don't go with the place in Elmira, they're shitheads."

There's no point calling the place in Waverly. They can't do anything until he's arraigned. The court has to set bond, and that depends on the charge and what judge they get.

"I don't know how any of this works," Patty admits.

"Want me to come over there?"

"No, that's okay."

"Right," Eileen says, "I'm there. There's no way I'm going back to sleep."

And like that the situation is under control. Together, the two of them can handle anything, just like when they were kids, teaming up against Shannon when she babysat them.

She still needs to deal with the lawyer. Perry's number is on the list taped to the wall. She thinks he'll be pissed but dials it anyway. She can always blame it on Tommy.

She *should* be calling her mother.

Perry's line is busy.

"That's weird," she says, and as she hangs up, the phone rings under her hand.

For a second she doesn't pick up, as if she's been caught.

It's Donna, though for a moment Patty doesn't recognize her. She's crying, her voice high and ragged with sniffling.

"I can't believe it," she sobs. "They fucking killed someone—do you believe that? They fucking killed someone."

"What?" One arm curls low around her belly. "What are you talking about?"

"This old lady, they were ripping her off—"

She remembers what Tommy said, and recovers. "Donna, I'm sorry, I can't talk to you."

"They tried to burn her house down."

"Not on the phone. Donna—"

"They're such assholes. Did you know they were doing this shit?"

"We're not supposed to talk on the phone."

"I'm not fucking stupid, Patty. The cops busted them right there."

Now she needs to know the details, but he told her not to talk with Donna—and right away she understands that if what Donna is telling her is true, then only one of them killed the old woman, only one of them is a killer, and it's Gary, and she'll do what she has to to protect Tommy from him.

"Donna, I can't talk to you. I'll see you tomorrow."

"I don't know what to do," Donna says.

Patty tells her to calm down, to start getting money together for bail and looking for a lawyer, the same advice Eileen gave her, and yet she feels like she's lying, withholding some crucial piece of information.

She doesn't hang up, just holds the button down for a second, then calls Perry. This time it rings.

"I heard," he says.

A decent lawyer's probably going to cost around ten thousand.

The number stumps her. They can't have more than a couple hundred in their savings, and she doesn't get paid till next Friday. Her mother has her father's insurance, and the house, but the thought evaporates before she can finish it.

After she gets off the phone, she turns on the lights and turns up the thermostat, unable to picture Tommy killing someone. The idea follows her around the house. All she can see is an old lady's bedroom, lamplight on a wall, shadows moving across dark woodwork—Gary and Tommy. But he was happy after the game; he finally scored.

She wanders through the house as if she's searching for something. She needs to get dressed. She needs to call her mother.

She blasts the shower, slapping the suds out of her hair. Toweling off, she rubs her skin red, and still there's too much time to think. The idea that he might have done it—that the two of them might have done it together—takes her over slowly, like a drug, paralyzing her. Obviously they've been lying to her and Donna all this time. And she's gone along with it. She thinks of all the poker nights he didn't get home till three in the morning, and the money he said he won (how could he never lose?). She keeps moving, to her dresser, where she hauls on a cold pair of stretchy jeans, the waist an equator around her belly. She piles on layers—a T-shirt and then a sweater—steals a pair of his wool hunting socks. The blow-dryer fries her bangs. It's not even five; she should be asleep, waiting for the alarm to go off.

The coffee fills the house, but she's afraid to put on the radio. In the driveway, a few flakes twirl down through the outside light. Where the fuck is Eileen?

She can't wait for her to save her. She digs her bankbook from her bag and sits at the kitchen table. The rent and the car payments are due around the same time she's going to get her check. He should be getting paid this week. Next week is Thanksgiving, and then Christmas right after that. She was going to get him new workboots, waterproof ones.

Her car is worth two thousand, maybe—but then how would she get to work?

If she has to ask Shannon for the money, she will.

She thinks if she just waits another hour, her mother will be up. That way she won't have to wake her.

She goes to his dresser and roots through the drawers, turning up a scuffed wallet and a dress belt she gave him last Christmas, still curled in its see-through box. She's digging through his shoes in the bottom of the closet when the doorbell stops her.

"Pats," Eileen says, taking her in her arms.

"It's bad, Leenie, it's so bad. I talked to Donna."

"What'd she say?"

"It sounded like they killed someone." She looks to Eileen as if to confirm how crazy the idea is.

"What did she say exactly?"

From the way Eileen concentrates, Patty understands that she believes it could have actually happened.

"Did you call Perry?"

"Yes."

"What about Mom?"

"Not yet."

Eileen clamps a hand over her mouth, then shakes her head. "We need to find out what's going on."

"Tommy told me not to talk to Donna over the phone."

"That's probably smart."

"What if we called the jail?"

"They won't tell you shit. You don't want to be talking with them anyway. We just have to wait till he's arraigned and see what they charge him with."

She's seen enough TV to know it will be murder. And it is like TV, it still doesn't seem real, except that Tommy's in jail and all they can do is wait.

"You should call Mom," Eileen says.

PROOF

HER MOTHER'S SILENCE STRETCHES BETWEEN THEM, GROWS UNTIL Patty has to fill it, spilling as little information as possible. She lies to her, says they don't know what the charges are.

Still no response. Patty paces, the cord reeling her back into the kitchen.

"We're trying to see what a decent lawyer will cost."

"Do you have the money for that?" her mother asks.

"No," Patty admits, and the answer hangs in electronic space between them. "I figured I might as well check. Otherwise we'll end up with a court-appointed one."

Eileen shakes her head at Patty, holds out an open hand to show there's no talking with her.

"That's all we know right now," Patty says. "I'll let you know if I hear anything."

Her mother doesn't offer to come over, just thanks her for letting her know. Not a word about Tommy and how he is. It's no secret: she's always thought Patty could have done better, and Patty's always held it against her, has held up their happiness as proof that she was wrong about him. Now it's her mother's turn.

They stumble toward a goodbye. "I love you, Mom," she says, stooped over the receiver so she can hang up.

"Pats," her mother interrupts—the first thing she's really said the whole call. "You know I'll do what I can."

"Eileen's helping me."

"God save us," her mother says.

MANNERS

THERE'S NO NUMBER FOR THE COUNTY JAIL. THE BLUE PAGES IS NO help; the operator says they show no listing. She tries the courthouse but it just rings. Finally she gives in and calls the sheriff's department, sure she's being recorded.

"I'll transfer you," the woman says.

"Can you give me the number in case I get cut off?"

"I'm sorry, ma'am, I can't. Please hold."

The guy at the jail sounds tired, as if she's interrupting his sleep. "What's the name of the prisoner you're looking for?" he asks, then says she's not allowed to talk to him.

He doesn't know what time his arraignment is.

No, he doesn't know who she could call to find out.

The courthouse opens at nine o'clock.

"Thank you," Patty says, as if being polite might help.

THE DIFFERENCE

THE PLOWS ARE OUT, SCRAPING THE MAIN ROADS, BUT THE SNOW'S falling hard and they can't keep up. It's a blowing snow, swirling, flying sideways, cars coming the other way suddenly bursting through the white curtain with their brights on and their wipers flipping. The clouds are right down on them, the hills invisible. The windows are steamed. She can barely see the trees at the far edge of the fields, just a dark band that follows them down the valley. Eileen's driving too fast, Patty thinks, because now she pictures the worst happening, disaster lurking everywhere. She's afraid they'll never get there, the Bronco overturned in a ditch or rammed under the back of a salt truck. She's afraid they'll be too late to save him.

She has her bankbook and her checkbook, for what little good it will do them. Perry's lawyer wanted a retainer of five thousand dollars up front. The only way she could raise that much would be to sell his truck, and that was just to look at the case, that didn't include the actual cost of the trial. When she started to cry, the guy told her that public defenders are better than most people think and gave her some names. The list is in her purse, along with the title to the truck.

She's called in sick—another thing to feel guilty about. Russ must have talked with Perry or Donna; he knew Tommy wasn't coming in.

At least her mother won't tell anyone.

They approach Owego from the west, snaking along the river with the railroad tracks, past the boat launch and the cemetery and the speedway. It's the heart of rush hour, a parade of taillights. West Main takes them straight downtown to the historic brick court-house, where the streets change to one-way, circling the square with its gazebo and Civil War statue and chained-off garden and empty park benches. The clock tower glows through the snow. The light poles are decorated with cookie-cutter bells and reindeer, tinsel bristling in the wind. Eileen nabs the last parking spot, gunning the Bronco across two lanes and cutting some guy off, slapping her signal on—and like that, they're right on time.

It feels like a trap, as if they'll arrest her once she steps out of the car, wrestle her to the ground. The Great American is lit, posters in the windows advertising the price of turkey and canned pumpkin pie filling. She's surprised to see the drive-thru of the Dunkin' Donuts where she sometimes stops is doing its usual business, as if it were any other day.

The courthouse is different too, no longer a beautiful antique, harmless and picturesque. She's driven by it thousands of times yet has never been inside. In third grade she missed the field trip to the mayor's office because she had chicken pox; when Eileen got busted she would have gone to her trial except Eileen pleaded guilty. It's as if the place has been waiting for her all these years.

"Ready?" Eileen asks.

She clambers down out of the Bronco. It's snowing, and her coat doesn't zip all the way closed. The footing's tricky; Eileen takes her arm. They put their heads down and trudge for the side entrance, jostling each other—tracked, she imagines, by every passing car.

The door's locked, and they check their watches. Any regular day, she'd already be at work. She's imagining herself in one of the cars smoking past, headed across the bridge, when Donna comes slipping and sliding up the sidewalk in her kneeboots and jeans and black leather jacket, her dark hair blowing across her face like a scarf.

Her eyes are a mess, her nose red. Patty thinks she's dressed wrong for the part but doesn't say anything, just holds her a minute before passing her on to Eileen. It's like their father's funeral; they don't know what to say.

"You guys hear anything?" Donna asks.

"No," Patty says, "you?"

"I talked to Lori. Her brother went out on a call last night around two-thirty."

"What else did Gary tell you?" Patty asks. She leans in close to Donna, almost whispers it. Eileen's part of the huddle.

"He said it was an accident. The old lady was supposed to be away. I guess she hit her head on something."

"What were they doing there?"

"What do you *think*, Patty?" Donna asks. "Don't pretend like you don't know."

"I don't," Patty says. "I swear to God."

"They were drunk and riding around. Things just got out of hand."

"No shit they got out of hand," Eileen says.

"The old lady freaked on them. I talked to a lawyer in Corning. He says because it was an accident they're probably looking at manslaughter."

Drunk, an accident. Patty clings to these facts as Donna goes on—and Donna can't stop talking, it's like they're the only people who'll listen to her. Patty feels sorry for her. It's unfair to blame her for something Gary did. They've never been close-close friends, but it seems wrong to treat her so coldly.

If it's not manslaughter, it's murder, and that's a lot harder to prove.

Inside, a shriveled security guard with a white shirt and a gold badge is walking up the hall, picking through his keys. The three of them turn to him, then wait as he fiddles with the lock.

He holds the door for them. Her shoes are wet and the marble floor is treacherous. She was so eager to get inside; now she realizes she has no idea where she's going. The old guy waves for them to follow him.

The courtroom resembles a bare church, the judge's bench a pulpit surrounded by high-backed pews, the dozen empty chairs of the tiered jury box a choir stall. The ceiling is vaulted; their footsteps echo. They hesitate in the aisle, not wanting to sit down yet, as if taking the front row amounts to a confession.

"I'm so tired," Donna says. "I swear I haven't sat down since I got the call." She can't stop babbling, her hands flapping like birds.

Patty worries that Tommy will be mad at her for sitting with Donna. She tries to think of a way to tell him they can't afford a lawyer, that they're just going to have to trust a public defender. She has the names in her bag, and knows she won't share them with Donna. It's selfish, but they're not married, Donna's not about to have a baby. She doesn't need Gary the way Patty needs Tommy.

"What is *taking* them so long?" Donna interrupts herself.

"I know," Patty says. "My butt's falling asleep."

From the hall comes a flurry, the clash of heavy doors closing, a herd of footsteps. They turn in time to see a team of cops tromp past. Beside her, Donna rises. It's Gary, his bowed head visible for

just a second in the throng, his dark beard. Patty uses the back of
the bench to push herself up on one knee, but the action's over.

"Did you see Tommy?"

"No," Donna says, still standing and staring at the open door
as if they might reappear.

"Just Gary," Eileen seconds.

Secretly, Patty's glad. She thinks it's a good sign that Gary's
first—as if his case is more serious.

Donna sits down, then gets up again and hurries to the door for
another look. She comes walking back, followed by a guy in a suit
who looks like a lawyer—wearing glasses, carrying a thick file of
papers. He notices them but passes without a nod, pushes through
the waist-high gate and takes a seat at a table.

A door opens in the paneling beside the jury box, and in wan-
der two cops and another guy in a suit. He goes over to the lawyer
and shakes his hand. The two of them stand there chatting like
old country club buddies. They're only a couple of feet away from
Patty but it's like the rail's a force field.

"Excuse me," Eileen says, to get their attention. "Excuse me?"
They both turn to her. "Is this the hearing for Gary Rooker and
Tommy Dickerson?"

The guy with the file has to look at his paperwork. "Rooker's
first, Dickerson'll be right after him."

Behind them, the doors to the hallway fall shut with a clank.

From the door in the paneling come two more cops, Gary shuf-
fling between them, his head bent as if he's trying to hide his face.
His hair hasn't been combed and hangs down over his eyes, and he's
wearing wrinkled sea-green hospital scrubs. Donna stands and
cranes over the rail, and automatically Patty and Eileen are up and
by her side. Gary finds her, gives her a look from under his hair that

Patty reads as resigned, then ducks his head again. The cops walk him to the judge's bench and stand there with their backs turned.

"All rise," one of the other cops announces, and the paneling behind the bench opens. The place is like a haunted house, full of secret passages and trapdoors.

To Patty's surprise, the judge is a woman a little younger than her mother, and tiny, child-sized in her black robe, her hair neatly pulled back, dark lipstick. Under one arm she has a yellow legal pad on a clipboard. She surveys the court like a queen before letting them sit down—all of them except Gary and the cops.

The lawyer takes a paper from his file and approaches the bench with it, hands it up to the judge, who glances at it—too fast to actually read it—then looks directly at Gary. For a second she doesn't say anything, just looks at him, and Patty knows the look. It's the look of her mother when she knows she's right, a look that dares you to even try to justify yourself.

Donna takes Patty's hand and squeezes. Patty feels Eileen doing the same on the other side.

"Mr. Rooker, you are charged by the State of New York with one count of murder in the second degree and one count of burglary in the second degree. You have the right to hire your own private lawyer in this matter. If you can't afford an attorney the court will assign one to represent you."

She runs through the words too fast. Patty's still catching up to "murder." Beside her, Donna is biting back tears.

"Do you understand, Mr. Rooker?"

"Yes, ma'am."

"Will you be hiring a private lawyer to represent you?"

"No, your honor. I can't afford that."

"All right then, I'll assign a lawyer to represent you. Please have them here with you for arraignment tomorrow, the twenty-second of November. In the matter of bail, I'll ask for a recommendation from the district attorney's office."

The lawyer stands up at his table. "The district attorney's office advises that the charge is a class A felony, therefore defendant must be remanded without bail."

"Defendant is ordered held without bail at this point."

The judge smacks the gavel, and that's it. The cops start hauling Gary away.

It seems too short, like they've skipped something. Gary looks back at Donna as the cops lead him out, and again Patty feels like she's eavesdropping on something private. And then the door by the jury box closes, and he's gone.

Donna gets up and heads for the hall. Patty's first reaction is to go after her, but Eileen reaches over and stays her.

She didn't notice anyone come in, but there are more people in the court than before, including two younger guys in suits a few rows behind them, both of them sitting alone and taking notes.

"I thought she said it was going to be manslaughter," Eileen whispers.

"That's what she thought. I don't know what the difference is exactly."

Patty's expecting the worst now. Donna's leather jacket slumps between them, and she thinks she doesn't really wish her any harm, she just wants things to be fair for Tommy. They both know Gary's an instigator, that after a couple of beers he can talk Tommy into anything. Tommy was just going along with one of Gary's crazy schemes. He probably just needed a ride.

She wonders if it would have happened if he hadn't scored that goal. If they hadn't won, there would have been nothing to celebrate.

It's going to be murder, she knows it the same way she knows she's going to have a boy.

Meanwhile, they wait. Donna hasn't come back. The lawyer is talking with the other guy again, jabbing at his tie to make a point. The judge straightens her papers like an anchorwoman. The tall radiators hiss. The snow from Patty's boots has melted to a dirty puddle someone will have to clean up, and she thinks of the building standing in the middle of town all these years, how she never suspected things like this went on inside it day after day. They were just stories in the paper or on TV, juicy rumors her mother brought home from the beauty parlor and unwrapped like gifts over dinner.

Donna returns. They're just getting settled when the door by the jury box opens again, followed by the scuff and clatter of footsteps. The lawyers separate, the judge looks over. Eileen takes Patty's hand and stands with her. So does Donna, and she takes back every selfish thing she's thought so far.

It's him, in the same scrubs, except his are far too small, stretched across the chest, tight at the biceps. Two cops hold his elbows like he might break free, and she wonders if they chose the shortest ones to make him look bigger. His hair's better than Gary's, but as she searches his face she sees they've hurt him. His left eye is nearly closed, a gash running up his cheek and ending on his forehead.

He signals her, palms down at his waist: Be cool, everything's okay. The cops lead him in front of the judge, then stand with their backs to her.

The judge fixes him with the same damning look.

"Mr. Dickerson," she announces, "you are charged by the State of New York with one count of murder in the second degree—"

She goes on but Patty hears none of it. She needs to get out of here and looks to the aisle, the quickest escape route, takes one step and crumples backward onto the bench, pulling Donna down on top of her.

"She's fine," Eileen tells a cop who comes over.

Patty sees the lawyer look back and then turn away again. Donna's rubbing the back of her hand. The judge is saying something. Patty's surprised the hearing is going on without her, as if it might stop for a pregnant woman fainting.

"Do you understand, Mr. Dickerson?"

"I do, your honor," Tommy says. "I'm going to use my own lawyer."

"All right, please have them with you for arraignment tomorrow," the judge says, and goes on before Patty can jump up and interrupt. What is he doing? They can't afford a lawyer. But he doesn't know that, she thinks; she hasn't told him. It's all her fault.

There's no bail—everything's a copy of Gary's, like they're the same person. The judge bangs the gavel and the cops hustle Tommy away. He watches her over his shoulder the whole time. She waves weakly, still sitting, then stops when he's gone.

Is that it? She doesn't know why, but she thought she'd get to say something.

Murder. She can't imagine telling her mother.

Eileen pats her on the back and leaves her hand there. Donna digs in her purse for her cigs. The rest of the court is noisily packing up. The judge has already disappeared through her secret passage, and the cops. Only the two reporters have nowhere to go. It's only when Donna stands and pulls on her jacket that both men slide toward the aisle and Patty realizes they've been waiting for them.

HANDS ABOVE YOUR HEAD

•

THEY TAKE SEPARATE CARS. BY THE SECOND LIGHT DONNA'S FIRE-
bird is right behind them, following them north through the run-
down side of town. It's still snowing and overcast. Patty watches the
gray scenery pass, darkened pizza places, empty storefronts plas-
tered with month-old election posters, bare trees and shabby blocks
of rowhouses, a torn couch on someone's porch. There's no snow
beneath the crumbling railroad underpass, and their tires whine,
then go silent again.

It's Wednesday; in all the confusion she'd almost lost what day
it was, and holds on to that fact now, though nothing sticks to it.
She'll call in sick the rest of the week as if she's come down with
something—and it's true: all morning she's felt sick.

It's not far out of town, a low brown box with a guy-wired antenna set off in a field like a radio station. The road leading to it's
been cleared and salted down to the asphalt. The windows in
front are mirrored so you can't see inside; as the Bronco ripples
across the silvered glass, Patty feels watched. They park away from
the line of sheriff's department cars and regroup, a team. She's
actually glad Donna's with her; it's like having another person
on her side.

As they near the doors, they both slow, and Eileen takes the
lead. She's been here before, for Blaine and then again for Cy—
misdemeanors. She even knows the lady cop at the front desk with

the blond bun, and Patty and Donna let her get the forms they need to fill out.

They sit in a row of connected chairs like in an emergency room, pressing hard through the carbons. A scanner blasts static above the chatter of electric typewriters. On the table there's today's Binghamton paper, the sections shuffled, sports on top. Patty tries not to write the headline. It's hot inside, and every cop that crosses the lobby looks them over. She wonders which one hit Tommy, and if his hands were cuffed.

Where it says previous convictions, she writes: *Speeding tickets*.

"She needs to see your license," Eileen says, and together the three of them take the forms up to the desk.

"Who wants to go first?" the lady cop asks.

Donna lets her.

"Leave your purse here," the lady cop instructs, and Patty has to retrieve the paper with the names of the lawyers right in front of Donna.

A heavy cop with a Wild West mustache arrives to guide her. He has to sign off on her paperwork before he leads her deeper into the building, opening locked doors as they go.

"You're not carrying any weapons or contraband of any kind, are you?" he asks casually—you don't want coffee, do you?

"No," Patty says.

The long hall he walks her down is normal and neat, yellow linoleum and a drop-paneled ceiling, overhead fluorescents, doors with officers' names on them. She expected something more dramatic—dank and dripping, cracks in the plaster. He opens a steel door at the end of the hall and the smell changes, the air sweaty and sharp, the vinegary, old-sock stink of a boys' locker room. Somewhere a radio plays a bouncy oldie. For the first time in her life she has to go through a metal detector. Patty worries that it might hurt the baby, but the cop says it's okay. She ducks as she passes through the frame. It goes off with a *ping*.

"Remove any metallic objects," the cop mumbles, and has her do it again without her rings.

Ping!

The cop takes a black plastic device like a sawed-off paddle and waves it over her like a magician until it makes a fuzzy noise just under her boobs.

"It's probably my bra."

The guy sighs. "We're going to have to get a female officer to verify that."

"What, are you going to strip-search me?"

"You want to see your loved one, you're going to have to submit to a routine check—simple as that."

He has her stand there while he makes a call. Finally the lady cop from the front desk takes her into a bathroom in the hallway. The woman treats her like an extra job she doesn't want. She asks Patty to lift her shirt and waves the paddle over her, leans down to inspect under her breasts and gestures for her to get dressed again, then hands her off to the guy cop outside—like a prisoner, Patty thinks.

The cop steers her past the metal detector to a windowless office with a big steel desk like the kind her teachers ruled from in grade school, a plain chair on either side, a foil ashtray. From TV she's been conditioned to expect a sheet of plexiglas between them, and a phone. The cop has her sit at the desk, her legs boxed in, then leaves, closing the door behind him.

She inspects the walls and ceiling for anything that might hide a camera. Maybe inside the light. They've probably got the room bugged.

She hangs her jacket on the back of the chair and smooths her

WITHDRAWN

front, combs her bangs with her fingers. She takes the piece of paper with the lawyers' names from her pocket and unfolds it on the desk.

The door opens. It's a different cop, and then Tommy, in scrubs and slippers, his eye puffed and purple. She pushes her chair back to stand and the cop shoots out an arm—"Sit down, ma'am." The heavy cop follows, a hand on Tommy's shoulder, making him sit, then clears off to the side, the four of them spread around the desk like a bridge game.

"Hey," Tommy says, trying to smile.

"Is it okay if we hold hands?" Patty asks.

The heavy cop nods. "As long as you're in your seat."

She reaches across the desk and takes Tommy's rough hands. His thumb brushes her palm, and she holds it still, finds his eyes to see if he's hiding anything from her—to see if he's the same Tommy she loves, the one who forgets what color his toothbrush is and uses hers.

"Pats," he says, shrugging, "come on," like the whole thing's a joke.

"I waited up for you."

"I'm sorry, you know? I didn't think I'd be that late."

"I guess not," she says, but then turns away. She doesn't want to fight.

His scrubs are short-sleeved and his arms look cold.

"Are you warm enough in that?" she asks.

"I'm all right. How are *you* doing?"

"I'm okay. What happened to your eye?"

"I ran into a tree. Seriously, it was my own fault. Listen, did you call Russ? He might call to borrow my tile saw. I told him he could."

She tells him about the lawyer.

"What about your family?" he asks, meaning her mother and Shannon. Besides Patty, he has no family of his own—another reason her mother doesn't like him. He was raised by his grandmother. She died his senior year. When her estate didn't cover the taxes on her house, he got an apartment downtown and supported himself by working at Longo's Carpet and selling weed on the side. It seems insane that anyone could think that that was the height of cool, but Patty remembers other kids pointing him out to her in the halls, envious of his independence. She was a freshman, and it had only been two years since her father had died. Even then, before she'd ever met him, she thought they had something in common.

"The guy said some of the public defenders are really good. He gave me some names." She takes one hand away to push the piece of paper toward him.

"You asked her," he asks, and in the silence that follows she's aware of the two cops listening in.

"Pats," he says. "I swear I didn't do it."

"I know," she says, and squeezes.

"I don't want one of their lawyers. I want one who's going to be working for me."

"I'll ask her again."

"I'm sorry, I was drunk. I know that's no excuse."

"I'll try," she says.

He reminds her to get the truck, but doesn't say anything about bail or Gary or Donna. They're not going to talk about last night, though it floats around them like a cloud. She deserves to know what happened before the rest of the world, but there's no chance here. He's eating, he's been running in place, he's trying to be positive. She must look awful, because he tells her she needs to get her rest. She needs to take care of Casey first, before anything.

"I love you, Pats," he says when their time's up. "I'm sorry I got us into this."

"We'll get through it," she says.

She doesn't get to hold him. After he's gone, the heavy cop walks her back up front.

Eileen quietly grills her while they wait for Donna. It seems she's gone a long time, and when she comes back she hardly says anything, just walks with them across the freezing parking lot, gets in the Firebird and drives.

"I wonder what Gary told her," Patty says as Eileen lets the Bronco warm.

"What did Tommy tell you?"

"He said he didn't do it."

"That's probably what Gary told her. The question is, what are you going to tell Mom?"

It's lunchtime and downtown is busy, the streets wet, brown slush in the gutters. They have to circle the courthouse.

The impound yard is across the river, off of Montrose Turn-pike. Half the cars behind the razor wire are smashed, windshields missing, snow capping the dashboards. The cop behind the chicken-wire glass is Eileen's age, and good-looking; Patty's seen him directing traffic at the Speedway. She slides the title to the truck through the slot and he checks a ledger.

They've got it, but he's sorry, the state police have put a hold on it.

"It's here though," she says.

"It's here," he says. He'll call when it's ready—just like a regular garage. He takes her name and number and gives her his card, apologizing again.

"He was helpful," Eileen says on the bridge, meaning he was cute.

"You want the card?" Patty asks.

They circle the courthouse and head back home. Spinning past the cemetery, Patty can't shake the feeling that she's abandoning

Tommy, leaving him behind. She needs to call the lawyer again, call her mother. The river runs beside them, black as oil. She watches the snow sift down and disappear into it.

"I read the paper," Eileen confesses.

"What did it say?"

"You really want to know?"

"I'm going to find out anyway."

Eileen waits, as if this is a bad idea. "It said she had a fractured skull."

"Because it was an accident," Patty says, even more sure now. "He'd never hurt anyone."

"Not on purpose."

"Not not-on-purpose either," Patty insists, and tries to remember him ever hitting anyone. Hockey fights, but he hasn't had one in years, the guys are always ragging on him about it. He wasn't a good fighter either. Every time he got locked up with someone she had to cover her eyes. Once when they were dating, a guy from IBM broke his nose and she had to help him pack it with gauze.

"He's a big guy," Eileen says.

"Cy's just as big."

"I'm just saying people are going to see him that way."

"Jesus Christ, what is he supposed to do—shrink?"

The silence that follows takes them into the hills. The fields are white and a caul of falling snow softens the trees in the distance. The plows have bulldozed a row of mailboxes. The houses with their empty driveways and blank windows remind Patty that she's playing hooky from work. It's not even one o'clock. She feels like pulling the covers over her head and sleeping.

"Thank you for doing all this with me," she tells Eileen as they make the turn onto Spaulding Hill—still not plowed, rutted with a dozen tracks.

"Pats, come on," Eileen says. "I'm not going to just drop you off."

Patty thanks her again, and Eileen chucks her in the shoulder. "Stop being a wiener."

As they round the curve, they both check out the sheriff's department car parked beside the Myersons' dog run.

"They'll say nice things about him. He helped put up the fence around their pool."

"That's good," Eileen says.

Who else besides her can testify that he's a good man?

Russ, but he'd have to do the same for Gary. Perry, but he's been in trouble, the same with Shawn, and the guys on the team aren't those kinds of friends.

She wonders what her mother would say on his behalf.

She's trying to think back to who his boss was on the road crew before Russ when they crest the hill and she sees her driveway lined with cop cars—some from the sheriff's department, some of them town cops, some dark blue state police cruisers—and way up by the porch, right by the open front door that people are going in and out of, her landlord's piece-of-shit van.

MENNEN

■

THEY TAKE HIS ROLLAWAY, THE TIERS OF FIRE-ENGINE-RED TOOLBOXES still locked—confiscated. They take the brand-new chainsaw and the Skil saw and the electric hedge trimmers, copying down the serial numbers. They take a dirtbike and a spiderwebbed ten-speed from under a green tarp; they take his new deer rifle and his compound bow and his grandmother's old shotgun—all stolen, according to the warrant.

She's never seen the dirtbike or the ten-speed before, and she's not sure of some of the power tools, but she was with him at Ben's Den when he bought the bow. His grandfather's initials are carved into the stock of the shotgun, all they have to do is look.

It doesn't matter; the warrant lets them take anything. They have pages of property claims, long lists of descriptions.

They take his weight bench and his dumbbells. They take the eight-track player and the quad speakers he wired up in the corners of the garage so he could listen to Little Feat and Lynyrd Skynyrd and the Allman Brothers while he lifted. They have to back up a truck with a hydraulic gate to take the tile saw, and she can't stop them, can't say that Russ needs it for a job.

Eileen deals with the police, makes sure to get a receipt while Patty guards the bedroom, glaring at the invaders with their cotton gloves searching her dresser drawers, pawing through her bras. While she's busy shadowing them, Mr. McChesney climbs in his van and takes off without a word to her.

The house is occupied, a dozen cops tromping snow through the rooms, blackening the yellow bathmat. The head detective assures her they won't be much longer. There's nothing they can do but wait, so Eileen makes lunch for her. Patty sits at the kitchen table slathering their peanut butter and jelly sandwiches and imagines splashing the detective with the potful of hot chicken noodle soup.

It's impossible to talk with all the cops around. She and Eileen huddle at the table, spooning up noodles, taking patient bites of their sandwiches. The soup tastes good; it used to be her favorite when she was little. She used to keep a kind of food diary, a faithful record of what they ate for every meal. The cops would probably think her shorthand was some kind of code.

What the stolen property means about Tommy—if it's actually stolen and they're not just hassling them—she doesn't want to contemplate. That he was lying to her the whole time. That he thought she was too stupid to notice.

The detective comes through and says they're finished with the back of the house. Eileen does the dishes while she fixes the bedroom, digging under the corners of the waterbed to fit the sheets on—tough, since she can't bend at the waist. The cops have knocked over her perfumes and haven't bothered to set them upright. She's surprised they didn't take her jewelry box just on principle.

She's going to have to wash the bathroom rugs, there's no way around it. As she's straightening the shelves by the sink, she stops, his deodorant in hand. She pulls the cap off and rubs the lime stick on her wrist, sniffs it with her eyes closed. The scent is nothing at all like him. She caps the stick and puts it back, glad no one saw her.

The detective says they're all done. She has to sign a list of everything they've taken, Eileen double-checking it over her shoulder. The detective turns his clipboard sideways and carefully tears off a copy for her.

"When will I get everything back?" Patty asks.

"That depends on the outcome of our investigation."

"Is that a week, a month, what?"

"That's as soon as we can, ma'am."

She chains the door after him, shoots his car the finger as it eases down the drive, then stands there, making sure he leaves.

"Well," Eileen says, "at least they didn't take the TV."

"Yeah," Patty says, "great."

They clean up, going room to room. The garage looks empty without his weights and his toolbox, like they've broken up and the cops have helped him move out. She wishes she could remember seeing the dirtbike before. Outside, snow coats the pines. The drive is a switchyard of tire tracks. She should scrape off her car and bring it in, but just rolls the door closed and goes upstairs.

IN A HEARTBEAT

SHE HAS TO CONSCIOUSLY PREPARE TO CALL HER MOTHER, TO PSYCH herself into the right frame of mind, as if she has only this one shot. Eileen understands, and offers to run out to the P&C and grab something for supper. She won't take the twenty Patty shoves at her, and then she's out the door and the house is finally quiet. For the first time today, Patty's totally alone.

She gathers what little information she has on the lawyers and squares a pad and a pen with her chair at the kitchen table before bringing over the receiver and sitting down. She can't get too emotional or her mother will turn cold and logical on her, as if Patty's incapable of dealing with this rationally.

She stands and hangs up, circles through the living room and the kitchen and the bedroom and then back again, pausing at the front window to stare at the bare trees crossed against the sky, trying to find an answer that will satisfy any questions her mother might ask. Because she can't just give her the money, that would be too easy. Patty's fear is that she'll say it's just not possible, meaning Patty's being unrealistic.

She looks at the estimate she scratched down last night and thinks it won't be good enough. Her mother will want to know exactly how much this is going to cost her, to the penny. She'll ask Patty to come up with a number before she makes any decision, and they don't have time for that.

She wonders how much she could really get for the truck.

The fucked-up thing about it is that Shannon would have the money.

She brings the phone over again and stabs at the buttons before she can think. For the hundredth time today she wishes for a cigarette.

"I was wondering when you'd call me back," her mother says.

"It's been kind of crazy here."

"I can imagine."

"I saw him. He's doing okay." She gives her mother a chance to interrupt, but the line is silent. "They're saying he broke into this house with Gary—"

"I heard," her mother says. "Mrs. Tuthill was good enough to call me and tell me all about it."

"He didn't do it. I know he didn't."

"But he was there?"

"He was with Gary. They were drunk."

"That makes me feel better," her mother says.

"Mom, come on."

"Are you aware that you knew her?"

"I haven't been listening to the news."

"Patty, it was Mrs. Wagner."

Her mother waits. Patty's so overwhelmed by the idea that she can't place the name.

"Elsie Wagner's mother. You remember. Elsie used to lifeguard at the Y when you girls were little. Tall blonde, freckles, wore her hair in a ponytail?"

Patty doesn't completely remember her, but she can't say that.

"Her mother went to St. Ann's with the Tuthills. They're going to have the funeral there on Saturday."

She mentions this as if Patty should go.

"I didn't know" is all Patty can say.

"So, how are *you* in all of this?"

"Okay. Tired. I'm still trying to find a lawyer."

"What have you found out?"

"They're expensive."

"That goes without saying."

She mentions the five-thousand-dollar retainer.

"That's highway robbery," her mother comments. "How many of them have you talked to?"

"He's the one everyone recommends."

Patty registers her silence.

"The police have the truck. I figure if we sell it—"

"I know what you're asking. Do you honestly think I have five thousand dollars just lying around? I wish I did. I'd give it to you in a heartbeat, Patty, I would."

"I wasn't asking. I just wanted to let you know what we're doing."

"Then I apologize. It sounded like you were building up to something. I didn't want you to get your hopes up."

"Don't worry," Patty says, "I'm not."

She barely listens after this, drawing a fat black X through the numbers in front of her. Her mother won't let her go, offering to come over. She saw a show about burglars taking advantage of women in her situation; the way she says it, it's like Patty has a terminal disease.

"Eileen's here," Patty says.

"Eventually she's going to have to go back to work. You really shouldn't be there by yourself.

"Let me know if you need help," her mother says as they say goodbye.

"Thanks, Mom," Patty says. "I will."

EASY

SHE TALKS WITH THE PUBLIC DEFENDER'S OFFICE, THEN MAKES A second trip to the jail. He takes it better than she expected, and she understands that she's let him down. The sun is setting over the hills as Eileen drives her home. Patty's glad to see it go, and at the same time worries about him spending the night there by himself. The day is finally over, but the feeling that she's forgotten something nags at her.

Eileen makes dinner, their mother's chicken casserole with the swiss cheese and boxed stuffing mix. It smells good, but they've both been awake too long, they're shaky from running on raw nerves, and neither of them feels like eating. Patty rakes hers over her plate, wondering what Tommy's having. She's supposed to drink milk for the baby, and gags a glass down, tipping her chin up to help her swallow. What she could really use is a double shot of Jack to punch her into a different frame of mind, but that's at least three months away. She takes her vitamin at the sink and starts to do the dishes.

"I'll get those," Eileen says.

"I've got to do something, otherwise I'll go nuts."

So Eileen dries, squatting and craning to fit the pots and plates into the cupboards.

They don't dare watch TV, and the stereo's a trap, all the songs that belong to him. Eileen votes for gin, and Patty gives in to her. They sit tailorseat on the couch, facing each other, wrapped in sleeping bags, a supply of soft dutch chocolate cookies within reach.

"This is like a slumber party," Patty says.

"Except there's not popcorn all over the floor."

"And Mom's not screaming at us."

They pick up and discard from a pillow set between them.

"That was stupid," Eileen tells herself when Patty nabs the queen she just dumped.

They don't keep score, but it seems to Patty that Eileen wins almost every hand. She wonders if it's too early to go to bed.

Eileen wins again.

"It's just not my day," Patty says, and they quit. She finds the jokers and folds the flaps closed. "Are you going to be okay out here? You can watch TV if you want, it won't bother me."

Eileen's fine.

"Thank you," Patty says, and leans down to kiss her forehead the way she did when she used to babysit her. Now Eileen's taking care of her; it's like they've changed places. Like always, their mother and Shannon are nowhere.

She brushes her teeth and pees, the bathroom all hers, unnatural. Dropping her clothes in the hamper, she sees one of his tube socks under yesterday's jeans, the butterscotch dye of his workboots worn into the heel. For an instant she's tempted to rescue it, but doesn't.

She circles the bed and gets in, her skin absorbing the chill of the sheets. She's too tired to read, and the book seems stupid now, bad luck; she'll give it back to Eileen. She settles in, then decides it's too cold and levers herself out, gropes the three steps to his dresser and hauls on his favorite Bills T-shirt and a pair of wool socks. They don't help right away; she just has to stay still and let the bed warm, like an engine. All day she's wanted to crawl under the covers and surrender; now, with the house fallen silent around her, it doesn't feel like an escape. She rolls over and curls around the body pillow.

She's seen the beds they have in jail on TV—steel bunks with thin mattresses and scratchy blankets. She's afraid he'll be cold. He needs two pillows; sometimes when he doesn't sleep right his neck hurts and she has to rub Heet into his muscles.

She feels herself concentrating, focusing her closed eyes as if she can see his cell. She needs to relax and see nothing, an empty screen. She thinks of Casey, floating warm inside her, his heartbeat slowing, echoing hers. Sometimes at night she feels him flutter or turn, a dolphin swimming, but right now he's quiet. He's probably as tired as she is.

Outside, a car motors by, a jetlike rush of wind, then nothing.

The bed warms, and she drifts into a pleasant half-sleep, a dream of summer on her grandmother's farm when she was eleven—the old metal seat of the tractor, the barn that smelled of musty hay and cow dung. She's happy there, peeking over the rough boards of the stalls. The cows look up at her with milky eyeballs but don't stop chewing. Their gums are a mix of pink and black like a dog's.

When the phone goes off, it's like a memory, the ring calling her back to the present. Immediately she knows it's about him, someone from the jail. It's past midnight, the time reserved for bad news. She slaps at the phone, grips it.

A man asks if this is Mrs. Dickerson—older, serious, official.

"Yes," she says, "this is she."

"Mrs. Dickerson," he says calmly, "do you know how easy it would be to kill you right now?"

A FAIR
AND SPEEDY
TRIAL

LOVING YOU

ISN'T THE RIGHT THING TO DO

FLEETWOOD MAC

HEART-SHAPED BOX

SHE CAN'T EVEN CALL HIM. HE CAN CALL HER, BUT ONLY AT PRE-
arranged times and only collect. She's taking unpaid leave, so
there's no paycheck coming in where there used to be two.

"We better get off," she says.

"Yeah," he says, and then they stay on.

Their calls are taped, his letters to her opened. She's not allowed
to bring him any food or money or cigarettes, not even a blanket.
Sometimes she gets to kiss him hello and goodbye when she visits,
sometimes not, depending on the guard, depending on the guard's
mood. Her doctor says the metal detector won't hurt the baby as
long as she doesn't go through it four or five times a day. Some days
she goes through two or three times and then worries.

The first time she meets their lawyer she wishes she'd tried
harder to come up with the money. He's young and looks nervous
in his skinny tie, a college kid dressed for an interview. She's supposed to call him Andy.

To start, he says he believes Tommy's not guilty, then goes on to
talk about the problems of the case as if that doesn't matter. They
can place him at the scene, so there's no way to prove he's *completely*
innocent. Luckily they don't have to. The DA has to prove he's
guilty beyond a reasonable doubt, that's their one advantage. The
first thing they have to do is ask for severance, make the DA try the
cases separately. If they can do that, he wouldn't be surprised if

both of them walk on the murder charge, the evidence isn't there. If not—and the DA's not going to want to do that, it makes things a lot harder for him—they could be in trouble. Either way they're definitely going to see time for the burglary. The danger in a case like this is the other guy taking a plea and testifying against him to get his charges reduced. They'll have to keep an eye on that. Patty doesn't ask how.

That's the problem—she doesn't know what to ask him. She thinks she should do more than just sit there and nod like an idiot.

She understands why Tommy doesn't squeal on Gary, but if they're such good buddies, why is Gary hanging him out to dry like this? He should stand up and be a man. Instead, the two of them are acting like little kids. Their strategy is to shut up, say nothing. The lawyer says it's actually the best thing they can do at this point.

The cops still have the truck, and Mr. McChesney wants her out by the end of the month. Eileen says she can stay with her and Cy for a while, but for how long, and where's all of their junk supposed to go? On top of that, her mother's invited everyone for Thanksgiving, including Shannon and her family.

Her mother comes over to see her. As always, Patty can sense her grading her dusting, the contents of the refrigerator. They talk about Casey mostly, avoiding the real subject. "I've always said Gary was bad news," her mother huffs, then finishes her cup of coffee and heads off to the library before it closes.

Eileen goes back to work, and Cy expects her home at night, so Patty's alone most of the time. She wanders around the house, wrapping their breakables in old *PennySavers*, deciding what she needs and what can go to storage. She's learned to not stop and moon over the wedding pictures of him without his mustache or the heart-shaped box she kept from the chocolates he gave her one Valentine's Day. The pile that's going to Eileen's grows. And still, she can't attack his closet. It will all come with her—she can use it. Already she's wearing his flannel shirts to stay warm, using his sweatpants as pajama bottoms.

She sleeps late, and still she's exhausted. He can't always tell her when he'll call next, so she's always waiting. All morning the snow light reaches through the windows, warming her hands. She walks by the phone, willing it to ring. She packs and packs, taking breaks to rest her back, kneading her kidneys with a fist. Lunch comes. The soap operas are on, but they no longer tempt her, full of murders and hollow plots. The afternoon passes, icicles glinting in drips, birds skirmishing at the feeder, making it swing. The sky fades to gray above the trees and the cars flying by outside turn on their lights. She can't get used to cooking for herself, and ends up with leftovers. Normally she'd watch TV, but she's afraid of the news. At seven she's ready for bed. Some nights he calls around nine and they stay on until she's sleepy, tucked under the afghans on the couch with her eyes closed, the two of them murmuring the way they do in bed. When they hang up, the day's over. After ten she won't answer the phone, lies still, listening between rings, as if someone's in the house.

It's strange not having to get up for work in the morning, a luxury she knows she'll pay for later. She goes to the jail to visit him, then comes home and feels trapped inside the house. She doesn't go out, speaks to no one except Eileen and her mother and the lawyer. Donna hasn't called, and none of his friends. The Myersons don't look in on her, so she doesn't bother them. If she needs something—packing tape, more boxes from the liquor store—she drives to Elmira to get it. She gasses up at the self-serve, treating herself to a Snickers bar, humming as she chews. She's never liked the idea of living in a city before, but now she can see the two of them taking the top half of a duplex and parking on the street, going to work and coming home, completely anonymous.

Taking apart the rooms she put together, she imagines Mrs. Wagner's house sitting empty and half-burnt. The man who called could have been a neighbor, the police said, or maybe it was just a nut. Patty thinks she should go over there, take some flowers to say she's sorry, but it's not on the way to anything.

She unplugs the TV. She takes apart the stereo and tapes the gathered cords to the backs of the speakers, tapes down the arm of the turntable the way she's seen Tommy do it. The records are too heavy; she can barely lift the cinder blocks the shelves rest on. She's already done most of the dishes. She can't box up the toaster oven yet, and the tapestries she's saving for last—their bright patterns the only relief from the white walls.

She's never done self-storage before. She drives by one all the time on her way to work. It's new-looking, rows of prefab garages surrounded by high fences topped with barbed wire—a prison for their stuff. The ad in the Yellow Pages lists the different sizes. The only really big thing is the couch; the waterbed comes apart. She figures it'll take five or six trips; they can probably get away with the small. There's the tarp in the garage if the weather gets bad— at least the cops didn't take that. She should put it over everything, in case the place leaks.

When she calls to reserve a unit, the price seems high and the guy has all these questions. Does she want heated or unheated? How long of a lease is she going to need? Long-term, short-term, the price is different. What about insurance? How much are the contents worth, ballpark?

Without Tommy there to ask, she can't answer the man. She says she'll have to check and get back to him and hangs up feeling the same way she does when the lawyer tries to explain the difference between the arraignment and the preliminary hearing.

There's so much she doesn't know.

THE CONDITION OF THE
DECEASED

THE LAWYER HAS TOLD HER OVER AND OVER THAT THE PRELIM means nothing, so why do the TV people have their lights set up outside? She circles the courthouse, trolling for a parking spot, hoping they don't know what her car looks like. It's the middle of the morning, the Tuesday before Thanksgiving. She expected downtown to be quiet, everybody working, getting ready to call in sick tomorrow—the only reason Eileen's not here. She would have taken off if Patty asked.

She finds a spot on the far side of the building and struggles out from behind the wheel. There's another entrance here, the same arched vestibule like a church. Climbing the stairs, she thinks she might get away with it, then finds the doors are locked. She can see cops and lawyers far down the hall and knocks on the glass, but no one hears her.

She tries taking the back way, skirting the frozen garden and the Union soldier's statue, screened by the building. At the last second she gathers speed and rounds the corner, walks straight toward the crowd as if everything's normal.

They have their backs to her, mobbing someone else—not Donna but a tall woman hiding behind Jackie O sunglasses, her hennaed hair freshly done under a purple scarf. A guy wearing oversized headphones notices Patty and points, and they all turn. A flash dazzles her, makes her raise a hand, but she keeps walking, meeting them head-on. The reporters are two deep, the ones in back shoving their microphones over the front line.

"Mrs. Dickerson," one calls out, "do you have anything to say to the family of the victim?"

"Excuse me," Patty says, trying to push by. She bounces off the wall of people and barely stays on the sidewalk. Can't they see she's pregnant? She shoulders into them like a running back. "Excuse me, let me through. Ex*cuse* me."

"Mrs. Dickerson, did you know that Mrs. Wagner was legally blind?"

She ducks her head to watch the steps, her lips clenched in a hard line.

The cameramen push through the door with her and flare out, running ahead, walking backwards, blasting away like she's Patty Hearst. She didn't think they were allowed inside. She ducks into the ladies' room to get away from their lights, taking a stall and blowing her nose with the stiff toilet paper.

Blind. She closes her eyes to imagine it.

A steel catch slaps open—she's not alone. She waits for the other woman to finish washing her hands, leans forward and peeks through the narrow gap of the door and sees the purple scarf.

The woman carefully lifts it off and checks her hair in the mirror. Without the sunglasses, her face is narrow, doll-blue eyes, a long jaw and horsey front teeth Patty remembers even without the whistle on a shoelace and the navy one-piece with the Red Cross patch and the chlorine-blond ponytail. Elsie Wagner. She looks old, her cheeks sunken and rouged.

Patty waits until she hears the door swing open and the noise from the hall. In the mirror, she looks like she's been smoking dope.

The cameramen are waiting. She keeps her head down as if it's raining and scurries across the hall. She knows they're not allowed in the courtroom. The same elderly security guard shepherds her through, as always, without a word.

The court is fuller today. She sees faces from the arraignment, including the two reporters. Elsie Wagner sits alone in the front row behind the DA's table, and for a second, walking up the aisle, Patty thinks what it would mean if she sat down beside her and offered her her hand.

Donna's saving a place for her. She's had her hair cut short, a neat shoulder-length swing. She's not wearing any makeup and has on a dowdy flower-print dress.

"What's with all this?"

"It wasn't my idea," Donna says.

"You're not wearing your rings."

Donna holds up her hands. "I know, I feel naked. They tell me it's supposed to help. You're lucky, you don't have to worry about that." She tips her chin at Patty's belly.

"Yeah, I'm real lucky."

"You know what I mean."

Patty wants to ask her why she didn't call this week, but knows Donna could say the same thing.

As they're waiting, the door by the jury box opens and in walks a round woman in her forties with what looks like a makeup case— the court reporter. She takes the table in front of the judge's bench and sets up her equipment while the lawyers file in, the DA first. Tommy and Gary must be sharing the defendants' table, because her lawyer and Donna's both come over, lean across the rail and shake hands with them.

The lawyer's already told her it's a show. All the DA has to establish is reasonable cause, and he will. Patty doesn't understand. They're supposed to lose, and that's okay?

Across the aisle, the DA is consulting with Elsie Wagner, and Patty feels foolish for ever thinking she could have apologized to her.

"Here they come," Donna says, and the cops bring in Gary and Tommy in their prison scrubs. At least they let him shave and comb his hair this time. She hears a camera click and whir behind her, though she knows they're not allowed either.

Tommy's face looks better, the swelling down to a mouse, the scratch a scabbed line. As the cops maneuver him to his chair, he nods as if everything's under control.

"All rise," the bailiff calls, and the lawyer turns him away from her.

Across the aisle, Elsie Wagner is staring at Tommy and Gary.

It's the same judge, the woman with the tight hair and dark lipstick. She leans over the edge of the bench to say hello to the court reporter, then settles herself. The whole courtroom waits while she messes with her papers. She finds the one she wants and holds it up, reads the case number into her microphone, then instructs the DA to call his first witness.

It's a man named Ayres, Mrs. Wagner's neighbor from Blodgett Road. Patty tests his voice against her memory of the late-night caller, but it's not him. The DA takes forever to get his address and the exact location of his house with respect to Mrs. Wagner's place, the day, the date, the weather, the moon, the visibility. Tommy's lawyer scribbles notes on a yellow pad, and Patty wishes she'd brought something to write on. With the reporter tapping away and the courtroom nearly full, the proceedings seem more official, as if everything counts now. She wants to challenge everything he says, tries to remember back to that night, the moon on the fields, what time she got to bed. She listens intently, waiting for him to make a mistake.

"You said in your statement that something outside caught your eye," the DA feeds him.

The questioning is a slow form of torture. Blodgett Road is a dead-end. Mr. Ayres can see the dead-end from his window, and the creek. Mr. Ayres saw the truck's brake lights down in the dead-end. Mr. Ayres stood at the window for maybe ten minutes. Mr. Ayres could see the shadow of the truck in the moonlight; it had its lights off. Mr. Ayres saw two figures get out of the truck. Mr. Ayres saw the same two figures walk back up the road toward Mrs. Wagner's house. This is when Mr. Ayres telephoned the sheriff's department—the DA has the exact time of the call.

This part is new to Patty, and she realizes how little Tommy has told her about what actually happened.

That's all the DA has for Mr. Ayres.

"Does defense wish to cross-examine?" the judge asks.

Andy lets Gary's lawyer answer. "No, your honor."

The next witness is the deputy who responded to the call. The DA wastes a half hour asking him about the day, the date, the time of the call, the visibility, the road, the truck (caught in his spotlight, a dark color), the location of the two houses, what time the fire company arrived. Beside her, Donna shifts positions. Patty realizes she has her arms crossed tightly on top of her belly and folds her hands in her lap.

"When I entered the residence there was a strong smell of gasoline," the deputy testifies. "I also noticed a red metal gas can on a table in the dining room."

The DA is taking them through Mrs. Wagner's, leading the deputy to the bedroom, and Patty can't help but think of her mother, alone in their old house out on Tinkham Road, the key under the mat for anyone to use. She doesn't want to hear what comes next, and focuses on Andy's hand needling his pen across the page.

"I would say the fire damage was basically confined to the rear hallway and the master bedroom where the deceased was discovered," the deputy says.

"And where was she discovered?"

"On what was left of the bed."

"What was the condition of the deceased?"

"She was burned over a good portion of her body."

"Were there any other indications of foul play?"

"Her face was bruised and cut."

"Cut how?"

"She had a gash under her left eye." The deputy points to his own.

Their lawyer objects to this, since he's not a medical professional. Across the aisle, Elsie Wagner is dabbing at her eyes with a wad of tissue.

The deputy discovers the guns in the hockey bag with Gary's name on it.

"Let's go back to the truck you saw parked at the bottom of the hill," the DA says. "Did you have a chance to examine this truck?"

"I did," the deputy says, and identifies Tommy's truck as if it committed a crime.

Again, there's no cross-examination. To Patty, it feels like they're just letting the DA win.

The third witness is another deputy, maybe her age, who goes through the whole day, date and time deal and then describes seeing Tommy and Gary running up the hill on the other side of the creek, their jeans soaking wet. "At that time I placed the defendants under arrest and advised them of their rights."

"Thank you," the DA says.

And that's it, no cross-examination, no further witnesses. It's not quite lunchtime.

The judge sums up: "The court determines there is reasonable cause to believe that the felony of murder in the second degree was committed, and reasonable cause to believe the defendants committed such felony. Defendants are ordered held without bail for action of the Tioga County grand jury." She raps the gavel, and everyone starts talking.

The cops come to take Tommy away. He says one last thing to Andy, then turns and looks back at her and winks. Donna stands there with her, watching as they file through the door in their slippers. When they're gone, Patty sees that Elsie Wagner is watching her. Patty turns away.

"Well that sucked," Donna says, oblivious.

"It doesn't mean anything," Patty says.

She keeps her back to Elsie Wagner, takes her time pulling on her coat and then fishing a Tic Tac from her purse. When she's finally ready to go, she sees that it worked—she's gone.

They catch up to her in the hallway, surrounded by TV cameras and wearing her sunglasses. She's reading a statement from a piece of paper, something Patty thinks she and Donna could never get away with.

Outside there are more reporters, more lights. Donna's parked behind the Great American, so they split up. Patty doesn't hide this time, just keeps a closed, concerned face as the pack bombards her with questions. She takes the back way, and once they realize she's not going to say anything, most of them give up. Only one photographer follows her to the Dart, clicking as she turns the key and fastens her seatbelt, then checks her mirrors and pulls into traffic.

On the way home, she feels even more deeply that they've lost something. From the evidence—and now that evidence is official—one of them did it. She's not a lawyer, but she doesn't see how they're going to beat the charges if they're tried together. It's clear to her, though Tommy's not going to want to hear it: he's going to have to testify against Gary.

FOR THE RECORD

"WHY?" SHE FINALLY ASKS HIM, NOW THAT SHE'S NOT GIVING ANY-thing away. "That's what I want to know."

"I don't know," he says. "Money."

"We don't need any money."

"Everybody needs money."

"That's crap." She sits back from the table to see if he'll take it back.

He shrugs like there's no good answer.

"You know, you're an asshole," she says.

"Now I am. I wasn't before."

"Yes," she says, "you were."

SAYING GRACE

■

SHE'S NOT SUPPOSED TO BRING ANYTHING, AT LEAST THAT'S WHAT her mother's been broadcasting all week. It's a dance: she doesn't really expect Patty to show up empty-handed, even in the middle of moving. It's Thanksgiving. She'd be disappointed, though she'd never say a word. At the same time, Patty's not allowed to upset her plans by duplicating a dish she's assigned someone else, so Wednesday after lunch Patty has to check in and warn her that she's baking a pie.

"Not pumpkin," her mother says. "Shannon's doing pumpkin."

"Is anyone doing apple?"

"Apple's fine."

Patty agrees to this before she realizes she doesn't have any apples, meaning a trip to the store.

She cheats, driving cross-country to Iron Kettle Farm, where she doesn't have to stand in line and face the racks of accusing newspapers. The big-boned girl in the apron who bags her apples asks if she's having a boy or a girl. Do they have a name yet? Patty chats with her, then walks back to her car, humming in the bright air.

The feeling's brittle, though it returns as she's rolling out dough for the crust and slicing the apples. It's sunny and the house smells of flour and cinnamon. Finally she's doing something useful. And then she thinks how she'd make Tommy all of his favorites if they'd let her bring food in.

The pie turns out nicely. Eileen admires it as she drives Patty the next morning. Eileen's the only one of them that doesn't bake. Her assignment, like every year, is the sweet potatoes, impossible to ruin. Patty has no lap, and traps the slippery casserole dish against her legs as she cradles the pie plate. The Bronco reeks of Eileen's cigarettes, a smell that nauseates Patty even as she craves one. It'll be worse at her mother's, everyone drinking, sneaking peeks at her as they cook and watch football.

"How does Cy get out of going again?" Patty asks.

"It's his folks' year. *I'm* getting out of going."

"I'm sorry."

"Hey, don't apologize," Eileen says. "They're no picnic either."

"I wonder if Marshall will bring his olives again."

"How much you want to bet Mom bought him some special."

"Watch, they won't be the right kind."

She wishes she and Eileen could just keep driving like this, never get there, but the county's only so big. When she looks out over the open fields and pines and miles of gray sky, she thinks of Tommy locked in his cell, and the day seems unreal and pointless, an empty ceremony. They'll waste the whole afternoon trying to ignore the obvious—and she has so much to do for the move.

Here's the hump where the culvert runs under the road, and ahead on the left, the dark box of the house, Marshall's custard-yellow boat of an Eldorado nosed up against the garage.

"I can't believe I'm really going to do this," Patty says.

"What are you going to do, sit home by yourself?" Eileen says. "Besides, it's not like you're flying solo."

Her mother's oversalted the walk; pellets crunch under their feet. They come bearing gifts, each carrying their own dish. The front door's not locked, but Patty rings the bell anyway, then stands back.

"Maybe no one's home," Eileen jokes, just as they hear the

tread of footsteps in the hall. The knob crunches, the door opens, and there's their mother, her hair just done, wearing an apron patterned with holly and candy canes.

She holds the door for them, waving them inside. "Come on, don't let the cold in. You're just in time for Santa Claus."

She takes the pie from Patty, and Eileen follows her to the kitchen. As Patty hangs her jacket in the front hall closet, shoving her scarf into one arm, Shannon appears with a glass of wine, her little black dress too sexy for Thanksgiving. She gives Patty a bony hug. She's deeply tanned, her chest freckled from some vacation. Beside her, Patty feels pasty and dumpy with her egg of a belly.

"How *are* you?" Shannon asks. "Mom's been telling me about Tommy and what's happening."

All Patty can do is shrug and nod.

"If there's anything we can do," Shannon says, waving a palm across the space between them, erasing a word on a blackboard. "I mean it."

Patty thanks her, already moving toward the living room and the brassy clatter of the parade.

Marshall stands up to kiss her skimpily, his mustache brushing her cheek. He's neat—perfect dry-look hairstyle, blue blazer, cologne. Even on a holiday he's dressed to make a sale with his creased slacks and Italian loafers.

"How's it going?" he asks, subsiding.

"Good," she says, and that's the extent of their conversation.

She has to bend down to kiss Randy and Kyra, both too absorbed in the TV to get up from the couch. Patty tickles Randy just to bug him, but Santa's coming, and she flees to the kitchen and sits at the table sipping a Tab while her mother frets over how there's no space left in the refrigerator. Shannon and Eileen try to help but just end up getting in the way.

"If you want to do something useful, stay out of my hair," their mother says, then asks Eileen to run downstairs and grab a new milk for her. Shannon takes the onions and the cutting board to the far end of the counter.

It could be any year, except that Patty's allowed to sit and watch it all play out.

Randy and Kyra cruise through, bored and lobbying for sodas.

"Why don't you go up to your mother's old room and see what kind of toys you can find."

"It's all girl stuff," Randy mopes, but goes, clumping up the back stairs after Kyra.

"The game's starting!" Marshall calls from the other room, but there's too much work to do. Patty snaps the green beans while Shannon assumes her usual job peeling the potatoes. Eileen checks the turkey, pulls it out, the fat crackling in the pan. Their mother runs a finger down a recipe, her lips moving as she wipes her floury hand on the holly and candy canes. At one point all four of them are working quietly, the kitchen warm, the window on the backyard fogged.

"Think he's okay out there all by himself?" their mother asks, meaning Marshall.

"He's fine," Shannon says, then goes out to check on him. She comes back with an empty tumbler and pours him another gin, forking out three olives from a tall jar in the fridge door. Eileen gives Patty a wink.

"You taking orders?" Eileen asks, holding up her empty Genny Cream.

"Don't overdo it now," their mother coaches—a sore spot, because Eileen defends herself: "It's my second."

"She's pacing herself," Shannon says, handing her a cold one.

"I'll make a fool of myself later," Eileen says, "I promise."

"I didn't say that," their mother says. "Did I say that?" and Patty thinks nothing has changed except her own situation. Shannon's still the success, Eileen still the wild girl. Patty's always been the quiet one. Now what is she?

Pitied. A family embarrassment.

It must be the old house that's making her feel this way, the memory of her teenage misery and eagerness to leave, her belief that life had to be better away from their mother, and somewhere in there, hiding like a ghost, their father and the happy Thanksgivings of her childhood, the laughing black-and-white movies they'd play on the living room wall.

She excuses herself to go to the bathroom and then sits on the cold ring of the seat with the door locked, her face buried in her hands.

At the sink she splashes water on her face, pinches her cheeks, and still she looks like shit. She's always been the least attractive of the three (a worry to her mother through high school), and her old insecurity returns, fresh as ever.

In the living room Marshall's talking to the players the same way Tommy does. On top of the TV leans the sepia, almost formal portrait of her father in the tooled gold frame, looking out at them like a kindly minister. It's been there since Patty was fourteen, a never-changing shrine she's always hated, as if her mother was using him as an excuse.

Her mother sets out the chips and dip, and the kids magically reappear, making Marshall turn up the volume.

"How many sodas is that for you?" he asks Randy.

Shannon drifts in, then Eileen, taking a break. Her mother comes in without her apron, lifting a glass of wine.

"Who's winning?" she asks, as if it matters.

For a few minutes they're all together and Patty thinks she should use the opportunity to say something—to thank them—but the game has their attention. She'll have another chance at dinner when they go around the table and everyone says what they're thankful for.

Halftime clears the room, all but Marshall, who seems bent on watching all six hours of football. Her mother finishes her wine and ties her apron on again. The stove is smoking more than the fan can handle; Eileen props open the back door so the cold pushes in. Patty wants to help but there's nothing to do.

"Go sit and relax," her mother says.

"How about setting the table?"

"That's the kids' job."

The first game isn't close; the second's the Cowboys, who Tommy despises. Marshall swears at the set. In his gold frame, her father smiles, unconcerned.

Outside, a front is moving in, darkening the room. Patty gives up on the game and stands at the picture window, warming her hands over the radiator, gazing at the vine-choked thicket of trees across the road, waiting for the first flakes. No one drives by; there's no motion but a crow gliding down to inspect a dark blotch in the snow. From the kitchen comes the whir of a mixer and the creak of the oven door—someone whipping the potatoes and checking the turkey. They must be getting close.

She's surprised she's made it this far. She's tempted to slip upstairs and poke around their old room, but resists. Even in the best of times the view of the lone dogwood in the front yard is enough to send her into a tailspin.

The easiest thing is to concentrate on tomorrow, when she'll see him again. He'll ask how her Thanksgiving was.

It was all right, she'll tell him. It was good.

SELF-STORAGE

■

SATURDAY PATTY MOVES—A PERFECT DAY, BRIGHT AND DRY, THE ditches sparkling with melt-off. The storage place opens at eight. All morning they drive back and forth in a convoy, Patty leading in her car, Eileen following in her Bronco, then Cy in his truck with the big stuff. They do it room by room, moving from the rear of the house to the front, saving the garage for last. Patty can't lift anything, and stands aside as Eileen backs Tommy's old recliner through the door.

She springs for lunch, ordering subs, thinking this may be the last call she makes from this number. They sit on the swept floor of the bedroom to eat, the sun warming the bare wood. Without furniture, the place looks the way it did when she and Tommy first saw it, excited to finally find something they could afford. Compared to his apartment, it was palatial—and no more roaches. They didn't mind that it was in the middle of nowhere, or that the hill it perched on might be trouble in winter. They even liked Mr. McChesney in his overalls and his clunker of a van. It seems so long ago, Patty thinks; it's only been three years.

After lunch, the house empties out. The waterbed drains, a hose running to the tub. Cy slides the heavy lettuce crates full of records into the bed of his truck. Patty crams her trunk with odds and ends from the kitchen. When she sets the toaster oven on the passenger seat, it spills three years of crumbs.

"I think we can get the rest in one load," Cy says.

"I think so," Patty agrees. She thought it would take a lot longer, but all that's left are some stray free weights and oil cans and Tommy's softball gear; the old snowshoes and bamboo rods on the wall came with the place.

They don't even need Cy's truck for the last load, and leave him to sweep out the garage.

At the self-storage, she takes a last look before pulling the corrugated door shut. She's twenty-seven, she thinks, and this is everything she owns.

WISH LIST

"SO, WHAT DO YOU WANT FOR CHRISTMAS?" TOMMY ASKS OVER THE phone.

She laughs. "What, are you going to run out to the mall?"

"Seriously. Pretend everything was normal. What would you be asking me for?"

"I don't know," she says. "Nothing."

"Come on."

Whatever it was, she can't think of it.

"Remember that little crib thing at Babyland?"

"We don't have the money for that."

"You still want it, right?"

"I don't want anything," Patty says, and realizes how negative she sounds. "How would you get it anyway?"

"Leave that to me," he says.

"Okay," she plays along, "what do *you* want for Christmas?" and now it's his turn to laugh at her.

SHOPPING DAYS

THEY HAVE TO WAIT FOR THE GRAND JURY—SIX WEEKS. THE LAWYER says it's normal. Both sides need time to put their cases together, and they're both waiting on the coroner's report. If Mrs. Wagner had a heart attack, they're looking at a whole different ballgame. He's got someone checking her medical history. It helps that she lived in the county her entire life; all of her records are in one place.

It seems cruel to Patty, wishing the woman a bad heart on top of everything else, but it opens up the possibility of manslaughter. The lawyer says they could plead and get away with six to ten, meaning—*worst* case—Tommy would serve three to four years. Patty can't imagine three years without him, and wishes the lawyer would concentrate on proving that Tommy's innocent.

The next six weeks is the hardest part of the year, the start of deer season and then the hysterical countdown to Christmas as the days darken and give way to the long, tree-cracking nights. She sleeps in Eileen and Cy's guest bedroom, no phone of her own, watched over by half-unpacked boxes. She's so used to their water-bed that it's like sleeping on a rock; in the morning she has to crack her spine and roll her shoulders. She's not working, and some days she doesn't get up until ten, wanders into the gray kitchen in Tommy's sweats and hunting socks for cereal and Sanka and the handful of vitamins her doctor recommended. From the woods out back, she can hear the distant crackle of rifle fire.

Every morning the sink is piled with dishes. She opens the dishwasher and puts the clean ones away. Eileen refuses to charge her rent, so this is a way of repaying her. Plus Patty can't stand the mess. For years she's listened to their mother complain about the way Eileen keeps house; now she's experiencing it firsthand—scummy clots of hair dried to the side of the shower stall, the sink dotted with blue blobs of toothpaste.

Her nemesis is the refrigerator, the sticky shelves stuffed to the edges with fuzzy jam jars and lumps of flesh wrapped in tinfoil. Since she's been pregnant, Patty's nose is extra sensitive, and she has to hold her breath when she opens the door. Though she knows better, she'll go out and buy fresh burger rather than trust the stuff in the freezer.

One thing she has now is time to cook. Some nights when she makes dinner for the three of them, the grease and heat turn her stomach and she ends up not eating. And still she's growing. She'll skip lunch and then drink glass after glass of milk with Ritz crackers and peanut butter, going through a whole sleeve before capping the jar and licking the knife clean. And then an hour later she finds herself digging through the cupboards, looking for something sweet.

No wonder she feels fat—lolling on the couch like a walrus, reading Eileen's *TV Guide*, trying to pick something mindless. Mornings it's game shows, then soap operas after lunch. She stretches out, pulls the afghan up to her neck and nestles warm into the cushions. It's like when she was a kid, missing school with the flu, time crawling in half-hour blocks, waiting for everyone else to come home.

And then at night she's tired, falling asleep beside Eileen and Cy during *The Rockford Files* or *The Night Stalker*, when they're the ones who've been working all week—and snoring. Eileen elbows her, tells her to go to bed. Patty brushes her teeth and wipes the sink down with a wad of toilet paper, then quietly shuts the door to her room. She says good night to Tommy, kisses his pillowcase and closes her eyes.

She visits Tommy every chance she gets and calls the lawyer so much she's afraid she's bothering him. They both tell her she just has to be patient. Meanwhile Casey turns inside her, urgent, a sudden kick leaving her breathless. They're running out of money. She waits till the last possible day to send in the final bills from their old place, then replenishes their account with her paycheck, but she's only postponing the inevitable. Mr. McChesney hasn't coughed up their deposit, and the cops still have Tommy's truck at the impound lot.

She needs to buy Christmas presents for everybody. She'd bake them pies if she could get away with it. If she had another month she'd crochet them all scarves.

"You don't have to get me anything," her mother insists, then asks if Patty wants to borrow some money.

"Is two hundred enough?"

Patty wants to laugh: how fast her mother wants to give her money when it's Christmas that's in trouble. She can hear, years from now, her mother hauling this act of charity out as evidence of her support, and though Patty's almost broke, she needs to say no while she still has the ability.

"Suit yourself," her mother says. "The offer stands."

The house is a dirty cage she paces. She hasn't been out all day, and she's thinking she should just go to the mall and get it over with when she stops to look out at the birds weighting the mulberry tree in the side yard, her breath fogging the windowpane, and she realizes what she can make for them—ornaments.

Not for Tommy or the kids, but everyone else. She remembers seeing some in *Good Housekeeping*, Styrofoam snowmen with changeable faces like Mr. Potato Head, a team of matchstick reindeer pulling a sleigh. There's a craft store at the mall that would have magazines full of ideas.

She gathers her ChapStick and her purse and takes off before the plan has time to cool. It's only in the car, after miles of silence, that she doubts herself. She'd have to make them a dozen apiece, and who knows if they'd be any good, she's never made them before. It's too late to turn back, and soon she's caught in mall traffic, a double line stretching up the exit ramp. At least there's an Arby's. When she and Tommy picked up their waterbed, they hit it for lunch on the way home, Patty steering for him while he unwrapped his second sandwich. That will be her reward—a Big Beef on an onion roll, sure to upset her stomach.

The lot at the mall is ridiculous. No one would complain if she took a handicapped spot, but she cruises row to row like everyone else, following people with keys, signaling hopefully. She has to walk a long way (she hates the way she waddles), then rests inside, reading the directory.

Upstairs, the lady in the Craft Barn who helps her find everything asks, "Boy or girl?" Patty chats with her, and coming down on the escalator she finds herself admiring the oversized tree and humming along with "Good King Wenceslas." She drops some change in the Salvation Army pot outside—just enough to make her feel part of the pageantry around her. Walking to her car, she shakes her keys at an old guy searching for a spot, and he waves back.

It's the middle of the afternoon so there's no line at the drive-thru.

"You want Horsey sauce on that?" the woman on the speaker asks.

"I better not," Patty says, and when she pulls around, the woman sees her and understands.

"Take care of yourself," she says.

The sandwich is salty and juicy, even better than usual. She hums as she chews, driving along with the sun flooding in the windows.

The next morning she gets up as soon as she hears Eileen and Cy leave for work. While the water for her Sanka heats, she turns on all the lights in the kitchen, spreads the table with old *PennySavers* and lays out her materials. The house is quiet. She cuts green and red strips of felt and pins them to a Styrofoam ball with fancy upholstery tacks, then paints on lines of glue, sprinkles glitter over them until the design appears, and finally adds a green pipe cleaner to hang it with before setting it aside to dry. It's not exactly how it looked in the magazine, but not bad for a first try.

The next one turns out nicer. She puts on an Eagles album to keep her company and makes another three before switching to spangles. Her fingers are crusty; she has to palm the edge of the record to flip it. There's a way to make an elephant with a pipe cleaner trunk, cutting the top and bottom of the ball off and using them for ears, but she doesn't want to risk it yet. She does these easy patterns, getting faster with practice, recycling the spangles until she runs out in the middle of one.

After the Eagles it's Dylan, then Neil Young. The finished pile grows; by lunchtime she's up to a dozen. Which one should she save for Tommy? It can't have tacks in it—probably not a pipe cleaner either.

She has to get him something, but they won't tell her what's allowed. She's already tried to bring him a blanket.

And she still has the kids to shop for.

She's hungry but knows there's nothing in the fridge but baloney and leftovers. She's out of spangles, and eventually she's going to need more glue. It's a flimsy excuse, but she's been good this morning, getting up early, getting so much done. For once she's not going to feel guilty for treating herself.

Traffic is just as bad as yesterday, and parking. Linda—the woman at the Craft Barn—remembers her and asks how they turned out.

"Good. I think I'm going to try the elephant."

"I'll give you a tip," Linda says. "Use toothpicks to keep the ears in place."

"Thanks," Patty says, too grateful, as if she's saved her.

Downstairs she browses the windows, hoping to stumble across something for the kids. A telescope would be good, but it's too much. Everything's expensive. She ends up on a bench in a sunken jungle of plants and fountains, resting her feet, watching people to the music. She knows she should be at home, learning the elephant, but it's nice just to sit and let the world turn around her. She can do the elephant anytime.

Like yesterday, she sees couples shopping, guys tagging along from store to store, loaded down with bags. She recalls all the Saturdays she and Tommy came here, eating lunch at the Ground Round, the mugs frosted so cold their beers turned into Slurpees and gave them brain freeze. And then the long Sundays fixing things and lounging around the house. It feels like she could go home right now and he'd be there.

She said she wouldn't feel guilty, but how can she escape it, walking around free while he's locked up? By now it's a familiar feeling, like being pregnant, a weight she's used to carrying. Since it would be the same anywhere, it doesn't ruin the mall, it just intrudes for a minute, bringing her back to reality. She sits a while longer as if to prove she can do it, listening to the voices milling, the water splashing, then rocks herself up off the bench.

At Arby's a kid in a Lynyrd Skynyrd shirt's doing the drive-thru. Her Big Beef's dry, in need of some Horsey sauce, but her curly fries are hot. She gobbles it down like a trucker and has to use her last napkin to wipe the grease off the steering wheel.

It's not even three when she gets home, the school bus stopped farther down the road, unloading. She parks alongside the house, by the garbage cans, where she always does. By the time Eileen and Cy pull in, it'll be dark, her tiretracks dry, the only evidence against her. She buries the Arby's bag deep in one can, goes inside and turns on the lights and sets to work again, as if she never left.

Overnight it snows, at daybreak changes to rain, the trees candied. She spends the morning baking Christmas cookies, spooning on the bright icing. She takes a paper plate of them over to the jail, knowing they'll never let her bring them in. They don't, and even though it's no surprise, she's angry, and then, driving home, hurt.

The next day she's back at the mall, not at the Craft Barn but downstairs, window-shopping, wandering the halls. She sits by the North Pole and then in the food court, watching. It's an addiction. The doors don't open till ten, and by nine-thirty she's antsy, dying to get out of the house. She's got enough ornaments for everyone, and she can't bring Tommy anything. The kids are her only excuse, and that won't last. As soon as she finds something for them, she'll have no reason to be here.

She stalks the mall, she visits him. There's nowhere else to go. Her mother calls to talk, but that's all; she doesn't drop by or ask

Patty over for lunch. Patty's not imagining it, her mother doesn't mention Tommy, as if he's already gone, no longer part of their lives.

She goes to the doctor alone. Everything's on schedule, everything looks good. He's not concerned about her weight gain, it's typical. Rest is more important. Has she been sleeping well?

Ten more shopping days till Christmas. Nine, eight. She feels herself inching them along, taking naps in the afternoon to waste the hours. She comes home from a bad visit with Tommy and plops on the couch, sits there in her jacket, staring at the crack on the wall behind the TV. She's done with her elephants—not that they have a tree to hang them on. She's already called the lawyer once today, and it's too late to go to the mall. She has to force herself to start dinner. Stirring in a bag of egg noodles, she pictures her things in storage frozen in a solid block, a black scab of ice covering the floor. She hasn't been back to check on it and thinks that's something she can do tomorrow.

Once Eileen and Cy get home, they'll distract her. She used to dream of having time like this. It used to be that work took up the entire week.

As she's draining the tuna fish, Casey kicks her, a sharp knee in the gut. She groans and drops the can, doubling over. She has to lean her arms against the sink to catch her breath. She worries that it's something wrong. But she just saw the doctor on Tuesday. She waits to feel the telltale trickle of blood, stays still an extra second to make sure. The tuna's okay—still compressed tightly inside the can—and she's fine, just winded, her heart thumping from the surprise. She thinks of blind Mrs. Wagner, the shock seizing her, knocking her to the carpet, and Tommy and Gary freaking, not knowing what to do.

That's as far as she'll venture into Mrs. Wagner's house, just deep enough to imagine something other than murder. She wipes her hands and turns on the radio to drown out the other versions that crowd in—and gets Carole King, *You just call, out my name, and you know wherever I am.* She turns it up so it fills the kitchen. When Eileen finally opens the back door it's a surprise.

After dinner, their mother calls to discuss Christmas plans. They're having ham, so could Patty make her cheesy potatoes? Oh, and that pea casserole that was so good last year. Eileen waits patiently for her assignment—applesauce and crescent rolls.

"Gee, do you think I can handle it?" she asks when they're off.

Patty wants to offer her the pea casserole but knows enough to shut up.

She hasn't asked Eileen yet if they're going to have a tree; no one's mentioned getting one and Christmas is a week away. She used to have to badger Tommy about it. Eileen and Cy are the same way—practical, not like her. If worse comes to worst, she'll buy one and decorate it herself.

The next day she sees a place on her way to the self-storage and almost stops, then figures they'll be open over the weekend.

The unit's the way they left it—dry, the tarp in place. She resists the temptation to move one of the concrete blocks and check.

At the mall she finds a gift for the kids, a nature kit with a floating lens that lets you see underwater. It's perfect for the goldfish pond in their backyard that Shannon's always bragging about, and Patty hasn't seen anything else. It's expensive, so she skips Arby's and goes straight home. She wraps it on the coffee table, taking her time, watching *GH*, then during a commercial she adds it to the pile of presents at the bottom of her closet. And like that she's done. It's stupid, she thinks, but somehow it feels like another loss.

So why is she surprised when the lawyer calls and tells her the coroner's report is in and that Mrs. Wagner died of a blow to the head? She's known it the whole time.

BEST CASE

THE GRAND JURY'S SECRET. SHE'S NOT ALLOWED IN, OR THE MEDIA, only Tommy and the lawyer, and the lawyer can't object to anything. It's basically the DA's show. Patty doesn't see the difference between the prelim and the grand jury; it seems like they're trying him over and over, each time nailing down his guilt a little more. Now the DA's tacking on extra charges in case he can't get the murder conviction.

"Just to prepare you," the lawyer says, "and I told your husband this, he's going to see some time on the burglary no matter what, unless he testifies against his friend."

"He's not going to testify against Gary," she says.

"At some point the DA's going to come sniffing around. I don't want Tommy to get caught on the wrong side of that, because that's worst case."

"You don't think we can win."

"Not if they're tried jointly. If we can separate them, we get our reasonable doubt back. I'll tell you what I told your husband. I think you need to hope for the best and prepare for the worst."

Patty says that's exactly what she's *been* doing, but on the way home, winging through the frosted fields with the sun warm on the dashboard, she thinks it's a lie. He's right. She's so messed up over what's happening now that she doesn't see how things could get worse.

SECRET SANTA

∎

CHRISTMAS MORNING SHE WAKES UP BEFORE EILEEN AND CY. THE house is quiet around her, only the furnace blowing in the basement, sending a rush of dried air through the floor vents, herding the dust bunnies along the baseboards. She takes her shower and gets dressed by the cold light of her window, the brown trees crowding in on the backyard, shriveled weeds poking from the snow.

She pulls the box for Eileen and Cy out of the closet and carries it into the living room, where their tree fills the far corner in its brand-new stand. The silver bulbs are new too, and the single string of colored lights like the ones around the mirror at the Iroquois, all for her. She kneels to slide the box under the lowest branches—the only present so far. She wishes she had something else to give them besides the ornaments and hopes they haven't gotten her anything too nice.

She can't wrap her gift for Tommy. It sits in a manila envelope on the card table she uses as a desk—a picture of the two of them from Perry's Fourth of July party, blown up. The store put it in a cardboard frame with a cellophane cover special for her because glass isn't allowed. Tommy's tan in his yellow muscle shirt and has his hair tucked under his bandana. He's sitting on her lap in a lawn chair with an arm around her neck, kissing her cheek. They're both toasting the photographer with their beers. A couple seconds later the chair fell over and they both got soaked.

She's too impatient to wait for the teapot to boil, and pours herself a lukewarm cup of Sanka, takes a couple slugs and ditches it in the sink. She needs to leave if she wants to get there before the doors open. She grabs her bag and the envelope, pulling her jacket on as she pushes through the side door—which bangs against something solid and knocks her in the head when it won't open the whole way.

For a second she thinks she's forgotten to take the chain off, but there on the stoop sits a huge cardboard box with THIS END UP on the side and a red bow stuck on top. She has to muscle the door open and squeeze through to inspect it. There's a torn orange plastic pocket where an invoice should be, but she knows what it is just from the size of it.

It's too heavy for her to move, and she needs to go. She can't just leave it out here.

She squeezes back into the house and pads up the stairs. Their room is gray, the blinds letting in slices of light. She has to push Eileen's shoulder.

"Hey."

"What?" Eileen grumps.

"Merry Christmas," Patty whispers.

UNAPPROVED ITEMS

SHE PULLS UP AT THREE AFTER NINE. DONNA'S FIREBIRD'S OFF IN A corner by itself, and she swings the Dart in right beside it. She doesn't bother to lock it, just grabs the envelope, flings the door closed behind her and heads across the lot.

Donna's sitting in the hospital chairs, made up for a night out and wearing a white silk blouse, open to show off her throat. In her lap, on top of her folded leather jacket, she holds a shoebox.

"What's up?" Patty asks, because she should have been processed and inside by now.

"There's like nobody working, and there's a big fire up in Candor."

She goes to the empty desk and stands there, a customer looking for some service, but it's no use. She takes the clipboard back to the chairs and fills in the blanks mindlessly, then has to scratch out their old address. She clips her license to it and leaves the whole thing on the desk.

"I do that too," Donna says.

"Where are you now?" Patty asks, though she's heard from Eileen that she's moved in with Gary's folks—into the separate apartment they kept for his grandmother.

"It's not like I eat dinner with them every night. I've got my own entrance, I come and go when I want. They've been really great."

"Good," Patty says. She points to the shoebox. "What'd you get him?"

Donna takes the top off to show her—a tape recorder, the kind you lay flat on a table, with a square silver grill and a row of big plastic keys. There's an adapter wrapped in its cord, a pair of headphones, some extra batteries, a couple of tapes.

"It's cheaper than the phone, and it's easier than writing letters."

"I hope they let you take it in," Patty says.

"What'd you get Tommy?"

She opens the envelope and shows her the picture.

"That's sweet," Donna says, giving it back.

Patty tells her about the bassinet waiting outside the door.

"So you got it okay. Tommy was all worried it might get snowed on."

"You knew."

"Who do you think picked it out? You think I'd let Russ go by himself?"

"Thank you," Patty says.

She keeps the rest of her questions to herself, waits until the lady cop comes back and processes Donna and then her one at a time.

She can't take the picture in. She can mail it to him, the lady cop says.

"It's Christmas," Patty argues. It takes her a minute to recover. She's not going to let this bitch ruin the visit.

She thinks there's no way Donna got the tape recorder in.

Inside, the guard lets her kiss Tommy. She lingers, pressing her belly against him, smelling his hair—newly shampooed, fruity and chemical—before they have to sit down. She tells him about the picture.

"So Merry Christmas," she says.

"It sounds nice," Tommy says. "I'll make sure they don't lose it in the mail."

"Thank *you* for the nice surprise."

"I knew you wanted it."

He's pleased, so she's happy, but no matter how many times she visits, it's always awkward, the guard standing in the corner, the stale, windowless cube of a room as if they're miles underground. After a couple minutes the conversation stalls like a bad date.

"It was nice of Donna to help out."

"I figured that was the best way."

It's a special day, and they want this visit to be a good one, so they stick with safe topics. Neither of them mentions the security deposit, or his truck. They don't bring up anything having to do with the grand jury, or Gary.

"So what are you doing the rest of the day?" he asks, and she tells him about her mother's.

"How's she doing?"

"You know how she is. She never changes."

"Say hello for me," he jokes.

"I *will*," she threatens. "No, you're lucky. It's going to be a repeat of Thanksgiving, except Cy's coming."

"Cy's a good guy."

"Yeah, I feel bad for him," Patty says. "He's going to have to watch football with Marshall all day."

"Tell him I'm sorry."

They riff back and forth, sleepwalking through these old routines. The guard turns his wrist to look at his watch, and she tries not to check hers. She thinks they have to give her and Donna the minutes they missed earlier, fears that they won't (they don't *have* to do anything), and yet, in the middle of Tommy talking to her, she's already gone, dicing the potatoes by the sink, running water while she chops the onions. She needs to find a dress that will fit her and iron it. She fades back in, and he's still talking, saying something about his grandmother's mincemeat pie, she hasn't missed anything. She wants to reach across the table and take hold of his face, but she knows the rules. All she can do is give him her complete attention, and she does, searching his eyes the whole time, as if she can pour herself into him, absorb him into her, the two of them changing places right under the guard's nose, the perfect jailbreak.

They're back on their favorite topic, Casey, when the guard rocks himself off the wall and says, "Time."

Patty checks her watch and sees she was right. "We're supposed to have an hour and a half. The guys in front let us in late."

"Visiting hours end at ten-thirty."

"We're supposed to have an hour and a half."

"C'mon, man," Tommy says, "it's Christmas."

"Sorry," the guard says, and turns his back on them to open the door.

"Thanks a lot," Patty says.

"It's all right," Tommy tells her, his voice low and serious. The new skin over his eye is pink, and she realizes there's nothing she can do to protect him except shut up.

She's allowed a goodbye kiss, a last touch of his cheek.

"I love you," she says, and then the lady cop takes her away, through the metal detector and back into the world. The light through the windows is blinding.

She gets her picture back at the desk. Donna's waiting for her out front, smoking in the cold, the shoebox under one arm. "You believe those assholes?"

"They always treat us like shit," Patty says. "Why should Christmas be any different?"

"How'd he like your picture?"

Patty pulls it out of her purse.

"Jesus."

Donna's finished and flicks the butt onto the cops' sidewalk. They walk together across the lot, and as she has so many times since this whole thing began, Patty feels like she should invite Donna for lunch or just coffee, but the situation makes it impossible. She already feels like she's lying just saying goodbye at their cars.

"Hang in there," Donna says.

"You too," Patty says.

GOOD NEWS

IT'S A NEW YEAR, BUT IT DOESN'T FEEL LIKE ONE. THE NUMBERS look strange on the sign-in sheet, as if she's been transported to the future.

The grand jury meets and nothing happens for a week. The DA's people have to draft the indictment, the lawyer explains over the phone.

"*If* they indict him," Patty corrects him.

"I'm actually glad they want the manslaughter. It means they're prepared to get the lessers and hope the judge maxes them out at sentencing."

"I thought we didn't want the manslaughter."

"I'd rather have that than assault one. Combine that with the burglary one and we're looking at a minimum of eight years."

Holding the phone, Patty wonders if he says shit like this to scare her. She clearly remembers him saying they didn't want the manslaughter; it backs up the murder charge if the jury's not completely sure.

"What about the arson?" she asks.

"They'll probably get that."

"It sounds like they're getting everything they're asking for. Is that right?"

"We won't know till the indictment comes back, but that's how it usually goes."

"I don't see why they even *have* a grand jury if that's how it works."

"I understand how it can seem that way, but you have to remember, it's just an intermediary step. It doesn't prove or disprove a thing, and it lets us see what the DA's thinking. That's the most important result of a grand jury, and we've got that, we can see he thinks his case is weak. I think that's good news. Murder two—*minimum*—is fifteen to life."

Patty can't see how any of this is good, but doesn't argue. She knows by now that half of what he says is bullshit. He says things not for what they really mean but like moves in a game, strategy that she has to guess at. Right now he's probably just softening her up so she won't freak out when the grand jury returns the indictment.

The next time he calls, two days later, he has news. The court clerk has sent him notice. The indictment's officially in.

"Okay," she says.

"Now remember what I said the other day," he says, and she thinks: You fucker, you fucking bastard.

CONTEMPT

∎

THEY'RE ARRAIGNED TWO DAYS LATER. THE BENCHES ARE FILLED; the room buzzes like a farm auction. Elsie Wagner reappears with her Jackie O sunglasses, sitting in the front row opposite them with an older man Patty thinks must be her husband. Patty's mother has said she'll attend the trial itself with her and Eileen, as if these hearings are just dress rehearsals. Neither of them mentioned Shannon.

There's a different judge today, a man with a greasy comb-over and bushy eyebrows who wears a permanent scowl. The lawyer's already talked to Patty about him. "He's not the worst we could do," he said.

The charges are murder two, manslaughter two, burglary one, arson two and criminal mischief two. Bail is a half million dollars, cash.

"Gimme a fucking break," Donna says out loud.

She'll never get used to seeing Tommy in his prison scrubs. He looks back at her as if he's sorry, this is all his fault. It is—*and* Gary's—but when they're face to face she can't be angry with him, only when she's alone.

The lawyers enter not guilty pleas and they take him away. The courtroom clears out, the hall all noise. Elsie Wagner is doing interviews. With Eileen at her side, Patty walks a gauntlet of cameras, and finally they're outside and then in the car, driving, free of the insanity.

At Eileen's she retreats to her room, lying on the hard bed, facing the wall as if she's sick. Eileen looks in on her and then leaves her alone, pulling the door behind her till it clicks. Patty tries to be quiet as she cries, covering her mouth with a hand, cradling her stomach with the other. She didn't really think they'd make bail, but now there's no way he'll be out in time for the baby. That by itself doesn't worry her; it's the fact that—she realizes only now, afterward—she's been holding on to some slim, hidden hope that he actually might.

SEVERANCE

THEY HAVE FORTY-FIVE DAYS TO FILE MOTIONS; SO DO GARY AND HIS lawyer. Usually they'd try to get the worst of the evidence suppressed, but in this case it's all solid. The cops caught the guys and Mirandized them right there, the truck falls under probable cause, the house was on fire. A suppression hearing would just repeat the same basic testimony they heard at the prelim. The thing to do now is go ahead and file the best motion for severance they can and hope the judge grants it.

"What if he doesn't?" Patty asks, because by now she knows to question everything he says.

"If he doesn't and nothing else happens, I'm not going to lie to you, we're probably looking at manslaughter."

"Probably or definitely?"

"Eighty-twenty, seventy-thirty. I can't give you exact odds."

She watches him as he says this, trying to see if he's lying.

"What else could happen?"

"There are two possibilities. One, your husband turns his buddy. Two, his buddy turns him."

And she doesn't see why he can't make the trade—Gary for her and Casey. This is how the cops want her to think. They want her to turn him the same way he's supposed to turn Gary. The lawyer would go for it; it's a hell of a lot easier than doing his job, which is proving Tommy's innocent. They don't even talk about that anymore.

"So we go for the severance," she says, like they're a team.

She's eight months and it's harder to get around now. It seems the only time she leaves the house is to visit Tommy. She thinks she's getting strange, wearing the same Bills sweatshirt of his, mumbling to herself as she lumbers from room to room, watching for the mail jeep and then swearing when there's nothing but flyers.

When she's two weeks away from her due date, her mother comes over during the day so Patty won't be alone, the two of them watching soap operas and leafing through Eileen's magazines. *Search for Tomorrow, The Edge of Night.* Her mother makes her Lipton chicken noodle soup and toast, brings a platter in as if she's sick. It's the most they've been together since right after her father died. Patty stayed with her then, keeping the household going, making sure she ate. It was easier, having a job to concentrate on, and Patty appreciates her mother doing the same for her. And there's a bonus;

her mother has no problem seizing the opportunity to give the whole place a good scrubbing, for the baby's sake.

They've already turned her room into a nursery, the bassinet at the head of her bed. Patty thinks she should have a place of her own, though she knows that's not possible. And besides, she reminds herself, to plan anything beyond the trial is pointless. She needs to just wait and see.

The days go slowly—like anything watched. She can't stand sitting there while her mother buzzes around the downstairs in her rubber gloves. She calls Mr. McChesney and lets it ring ten times, waits and tries again, then calls the lawyer and asks if he can send him a letter about the security deposit. She calls the impound yard and bugs the guy about the truck.

She hates to look at the checkbook. She has enough for another month, a month and a half. After that, she has no idea. Her mother's offered her her old room at home. When Patty confides this to Eileen, Eileen says she can stay as long as she wants.

Even Shannon surprises her one night, calling in the middle of *Hawaii Five-0* to see if Patty can use a hand after she has the baby. She's got the time, and she knows Eileen's working. Patty doesn't think she's serious—their mother probably thought it would be a nice gesture on her part—but thanks her anyway.

"I've still got all of Randy's baby clothes if you want to look through them," Shannon says. "There are some really nice outfits. If you don't take them they'll just go to Goodwill, because we're done."

Patty thanks her again—she knows how expensive those clothes are from her trips to the mall. They set up a time to meet as if this is a regular thing.

"That was weird," she says when she gets off the phone, and replays their conversation for Eileen.

"That's fine if she wants to come up, but she's not staying here."

"I don't think she's coming up, she was just offering."

"She can if she wants," Eileen says, as if she doesn't care.

"I wouldn't ask her to," Patty reassures her, out of loyalty. "There's going to be too many people here already."

They watch the show in silence for a while—cops in suits chasing a sniper across a hotel rooftop, a blue sweep of ocean in the background. She almost wants to ask Cy to change the channel, but it's so stupid that it doesn't bother her. The guy stops at the edge and shoots at the cops. The cops shoot the guy and he falls over the side, all the way down to the parking lot.

"I'm surprised she remembered my number," Eileen says.

The next day, when Patty feels her mother out about Shannon's call, her mother acts like she had nothing to do with it. "Are you going to take her up on it? I think it would be nice, all four of us together."

"I don't know," Patty says. It's a battle she's spent most of her life trying to defuse. The last couple of years she's succeeded in avoiding it altogether, living with Tommy. She feels guilty—she needs her family but doesn't want to have to deal with them, at least not all in one place, and not now. She wishes she could file a motion for severance against them.

She calls the lawyer, hoping for news on the motion. He's still putting it together.

"How long is it going to take?" she asks, and he explains that they normally use whatever time the court gives them. He's been talking with Gary's lawyer.

"Right now the thinking is we're going to ask for relief from prejudice on the grounds of the two defenses being irreconcilably antagonistic."

"What does that mean?"

"It means they're going to try to prove it was your husband, and we're going to try to prove it was Mr. Rooker. We're not actually going to *do* that—we can't, short of one of them testifying—we're just using it as a basis for severance. Without solid evidence against one or the other of the defendants, a judge will usually go for it if he thinks the two defenses could end up confusing the jury."

"So you think it'll work," Patty asks.

"I think it's what we have to do. You can never tell, especially with this particular judge. I'm going to say fifty-fifty, so who knows. How are *you* doing?"

"Okay," she says. She's not used to him asking her anything personal. She tells him she's ready to have the baby.

"That's going to be at Robert Packer?" he asks, because he should check in with her, even if nothing's happening. She almost doesn't want to tell him. It feels like he's making it part of the case. When she puts down the phone, she's bummed, but covers it up, with her mother right there.

At least she can tell Casey how she feels, lying on her side in bed with the door closed, the eggshell wall so close her eyes can follow the brushstrokes, even in the muted light from outside. She curls up like a child wishing the rest of the world would go away and hums made-up lullabies to him, quietly, a murmur cupped in her throat and the ear pressed against the pillow.

He's more active now, as if he's trying to get out. She has trouble sleeping at night and can't nap in the afternoon the way she used to. Her mother says it's her body getting ready for midnight feedings. The doctor says it's normal, but he always says that. She could walk into his office on fire and he'd say that's to be expected.

She's a week away. When it's time, her mother will call Eileen and then take Patty to the hospital. Eileen will call the lawyer, who'll call the jail and let Tommy know what's going on—unless it happens at night, like it did both times with Shannon. Everyone tells her to relax, that everything will be fine. She pictures the delivery room and her imagination takes over—gloves and scalpels, a baby with eyes like bloody fried eggs. She's been so frantic these last months; it has to be affecting him somehow.

Tommy calls at the same time every night after supper. She runs the phone cord under her door for privacy. "You've been careful," he reminds her. "You're eating right, you're taking your vitamins. There's nothing else you can do."

The joke around the house is that her mother's the slowest driver of them all.

"I hope you're ready to have it in the backseat," Eileen teases.

Secretly she hopes it happens at night so Cy can drive her and Eileen can hold her hand.

Patty's only half interested in the Super Bowl. The Steelers, who eliminated the Bills in the playoffs, completely shut down Fran Tarkenton and Minnesota. "Hell, the way they played we coulda beat 'em," Tommy gripes over the phone.

It's the last day of January, it's the first day of February. Her due date is the day after Groundhog Day. It comes and goes.

The doctor won't admit he was wrong. He brings her in and measures her, weighs her, checks her cervix to see how dilated she is.

"Any time now," he says.

She sees it as another thing that's gone wrong, and then, late the next afternoon, she feels a cramp in her side and presses a hand to it, only to have the pain regroup and move, circling her whole belly while she holds her breath against it. It could be a false alarm, so she sits on the couch until a second wave takes her before reporting the news to her mother.

"Okay," her mother says, one hand out to stop her from getting up. "Where's your jacket?"

PLACE OF BIRTH

IT TAKES HER EIGHT HOURS, WITH DRUGS AND A PAIR OF SHEARS.
The doctor has to sew her closed, but by then Casey has been tested
and placed on her chest. She's weak and afraid he'll slide off. He has
a cap of dark hair, but what impresses Patty most are his fingers,
perfect all the way down to the tiny nails. In her Demerol-softened
exhaustion, she credits this workmanship not to herself but to God,
someone she normally ignores.

They take Casey from her and make her sleep. By the time she
wakes up, it's four in the morning. There are roses on her night-
stand, and Eileen's sleeping on a cot. Patty doesn't want to wake
her, but she needs to know if someone told Tommy.

"Who do you think the roses are from?" Eileen says.

It's impossible, for a bunch of reasons. They're probably from
the gift shop downstairs; Eileen probably bought them herself, to
cheer her up. Patty doesn't question it, just leans over, bends one
to her nose and breathes in the clean scent.

A RESPECTABLE FAMILY

CASEY MAKES VISITING EASIER. THE GUARDS TREAT HER DIFFER-
ently, suddenly sentimental. Tommy's allowed to hold him at the
beginning and the end. In between she props the carrier on the
table and they try to read his mind. His eyes never settle on anything long, as if he's searching for a way out.

"He's thinking, No way," Tommy says, "I just did nine months."

The silences that used to separate them are filled with making
faces and baby talk. They can't resist being ventriloquists.

"'Daddy thinks Mommy should tell Aunt Shannon to go
fly a kite.'"

"'Mommy thinks Daddy should take a look at the checkbook,
yes she does.'"

For minutes at a time they're happy here, the three of them together. That's what's real, she thinks, not these bars and walls.

And she's busy now. For the first time in her life, her mother's
advice is actually helpful. She shows Patty how to bathe Casey in
the sink, how to wrap him snug in a cocoon so he can't scratch his
face. He takes to her breast immediately, and she feels supremely
useful. There's a satisfaction she takes in watching him sleep. It's
like a crush—she can't get enough of him.

She trails him into sleep and wakes to his demands. Cy's fitted
the window with cardboard so no light from outside disturbs
them. When Patty pads to the bathroom, she's not surprised to

find her mother making lunch for herself, or Eileen and Cy getting high. It's like she's a dreamy visitor in their lives, a bleary, bad-breathed ghost. Time only takes on a shape when Tommy calls, or the lawyer.

He's finished drafting the motion and submitted it. The next step is the hearing itself. After that, the judge has two weeks to rule.

"You definitely want to be at the hearing," he says. "You and the baby and whoever else you can get. From now on we need to show what kind of support he's got. How many people can you bring?"

"I don't know," Patty says.

"That's okay, the baby's the important thing. And wear your Sunday best. This guy likes to see a respectable family. Pretend you're going to church."

She spends the week before the hearing trying to find something to wear. She's flabby and slack, in between sizes. Eileen's too small, and doesn't wear those kinds of clothes. Her mother wants to lend her an old Easter outfit, navy with cookie-sized white buttons and piping. Patty can't say it's horrible, but manages through her silence to communicate that fact.

"Well I'm sorry," her mother says. "I thought I was trying to help but obviously not."

There's only one person in their family who would have what she's looking for. A couple of diplomatic phone calls and Shannon drives up for the day, bringing a cream pantsuit and a blouse with ruffled cuffs. The unspoken rules of her visit are as rigid as the county lockup's. Eileen's at work and out of the house, but Patty still has to take Casey over to their mother's.

She recognizes the suit from an old Christmas card, the airbrushed family standing by the mantel. Shannon has to give her its whole history. She bought it when she was pregnant with Randy, she couldn't have worn it more than three or four times. It sounds like a warning, as if Patty might ruin it.

Patty tries the suit on in the privacy of their old room ("Come on, big butt"), cinching the built-in belt over her mushy stomach. The jacket smells of mothballs; a dry cleaning tag's still pinned through a buttonhole. It's a little tight in the boobs and the hips. She checks herself out, craning back over her shoulder. She looks like one of the fat-assed secretaries from work.

She comes down to the living room and models it for them, trying to muster a smile. They watch her parade around the coffee table.

"I like it," her mother says.

"How does it feel?" Shannon asks.

"The jacket's a little tenty around the boobs."

"It's not the jacket," her mother says, tugging it down in back. Shannon pulls the collar free.

They stand back, examining her like a statue.

"I believe she'll pass," her mother says.

"I think so," Shannon seconds.

Patty has no vote. All she can do is thank Shannon, say she's a lifesaver. But upstairs she's glad to get the suit off and back on the hanger, as if it's been strangling her.

They go through the bag of baby clothes, Shannon reminiscing about each piece.

"I remember that," her mother says, cooing over a jumper as if it's an infant. She makes a show of reading the labels, impressed with Shannon's taste (though most of the clothes came from her mother-in-law, who their mother is desperately jealous of). Everything is cute and expensive. Patty's glad she can smoke now. That and two cups of real coffee get her through the afternoon. She thanks

Shannon again, pecking her cheek goodbye, then tucking her bag of loot into the backseat. It's only on the way home, with Casey's carrier belted safely beside her, that she lets out the storm of profanity she's been keeping in.

At dinner, Eileen asks how Shannon is without looking at her.

"You're not very subtle," Eileen says.

"She's helping me out," Patty says, hoping that will be the end of it, but of course there is no end when it comes to the three of them, no neutral ground. No matter what she says, this defection will be held against her. A couple of months ago she would have just said fuck it and the two of them would have stopped calling each other for a month. Now, since she's living there, she's supposed to show her allegiance.

"Look," she says, "I'm not exactly in a position to choose who helps me, I'm just glad they are. You are—Cy, you are too."

"You don't think it hurts me that she won't set foot in my house?"

"I'm sure it hurts," Patty says, "but it's not new. You're acting like it's a big surprise."

"I'm just surprised you let her get away with it."

"I'm not the one who told her she's a crappy mother."

"She *is*! And I never said that. I said she should keep a better eye on her kids after Randy broke the fucking *mirror*."

Cy keeps quiet, cleaning his plate. Patty should apologize just to be done with it, but she doesn't. Because she's not wrong. If Eileen doesn't understand, then tough.

They make up later, watching TV. Eileen says she's sorry she jumped down her throat. Patty says she's sorry she wasn't honest with her. There's no winner, only a truce—and absolution: they agree that it's Shannon's fault for being Shannon.

And like that they're back to normal, which blows Cy's mind. It's why she's at Eileen's.

There's no question that Eileen will take the day off to go to the hearing. She even convinces Cy to get a haircut and wear his powder-blue suit.

When Patty asks her mother point-blank if she's going to come, her mother presses a hand to her chest as if she's having a heart attack.

"Of course," she protests, shocked that Patty could ever think otherwise, and instead of letting loose with her stockpile of evidence to the contrary, Patty holds back.

She spends that night calling around town, trying to scare up a crowd. One by one, the team begs off, wishing Tommy luck. They're guys; some of them don't even have phones. She doesn't bother calling Perry. Shawn's girlfriend says she'll let him know. Russ she has hopes for, but he says he's got to work, and she doesn't shame him with her silence, just hangs up and keeps going down the list. It's no surprise; she's known all along that they're alone in this, but she can't give up. She finds the next number and dials, closes her eyes and waits.

In the end it's just the four of them. That morning her mother comes over early to help her get ready, swaying with Casey as Patty pinches in her earrings. Only Cy feels like eating; the rest of them get by with coffee and cigarettes. They're quiet as they leave the house, solemn as bank robbers. It's a bright day, springlike. The school buses are running, people going to work. No one talks for a while. It reminds Patty of following the hearse at her father's funeral, the gloom reinforced by their separateness.

"Thanks, everybody, for coming," she says. "I'm making dinner tonight, okay?"

"You don't have to," Eileen says. "It's worth it to see him in his suit."

"What are you making?" Cy asks from the back.

"Whatever you want."

The vote goes to her chicken parmesan, an easy dish, quick.

"Look how high the river is," her mother says, because they're free to speak now.

"It's the snowmelt," Cy guesses.

Patty's stomach clenches. She can't disarm her body with small talk. It's only a hearing but it's the most important one so far, and she's begun to fear the courthouse. It's like stage fright, it hits her as soon as she thinks of Elsie Wagner sitting across the aisle.

They're early enough to get a decent parking spot. She holds Casey to her shoulder while Cy lugs the carrier. The photographers hustle into position, clutching their cameras, kneeling to shoot like soldiers. She has to shield Casey from the flashes. Again, he's magic; for the first time the reporters part for her. "Mrs. Marion," the ones who've done their homework call out, and she thinks it was a mistake asking her mother to come.

"Is it always like this?" her mother asks inside.

"Pretty much."

In the courtroom she recognizes faces among the spectators. Donna's already taken her place in the front row—all by herself in a white turtleneck and dark wool skirt Patty's never seen before— leaving room for her behind Tommy's chair. Elsie Wagner's bench is empty. After they say hi to Donna and get settled, Patty keeps looking back at the doors, expecting her and her husband to come bursting through at the last minute.

The procession begins without them—the DA and the lawyers, the court reporter, the deputies herding Tommy and Gary along. Tommy's gotten his hair cut, and shaved, but he's still in his scrubs.

He tips his chin at her mother, smiles at Eileen and Cy all duded up. *Thank you*, he mouths, and she wonders if the lawyer's coached him to do this. The whole time, Casey sleeps beside her, snuggled into his carrier, a bubble on his lower lip. He only stirs when the bailiff calls the court to order, shuddering and curling his hands as everyone stands.

As the judge comes out, her mother leans across Casey and touches her on the arm. "I *know* him—that's Ronald Sherman. I went to school with his sister."

Patty just nods and sits down again. Is that piece of trivia supposed to help them?

Tommy's lawyer goes first, reading a brief outlining the motion point by point. He speaks precisely, as if reading instructions, explaining the rules of a complicated game. "We ask the court to grant relief from prejudice as it is anticipated that our defense and the defense of the codefendant will be irreconcilably antagonistic. I believe my client will be denied a fair trial by reason of the greater quantum of evidence to be adduced against his codefendant. As a result, the trier of fact will not be able to render a fair decision by inability to reconcile the two defenses and to separately consider evidence relevant to each defendant."

"He seems to know what he's doing," her mother whispers.

But the judge interrupts: "Mr. Rosen, you mention in your affidavit 'competing factual allegations.' Can you be more specific?"

He lets Tommy's lawyer flounder, sitting back and watching him but not responding. "Thank you. Mr. Tatum?"

Gary's lawyer gets up and folds his glasses into his jacket pocket and basically says the same thing—the pointing fingers defense.

The judge asks him the same question about evidence, then waits for him to sit down.

"Mr. Atkinson?" he says, and the DA rises behind his table.

"The district attorney's office considers there is a valid allegation of combined participation, therefore joinder is proper."

A long minute passes after he sits. The judge shuffles his papers as if he's lost the one he needs. Finally he leans over his microphone and reads the case number and their names, the purpose of the hearing—a flat recap—and Patty understands that, though it will take a week for the court to respond officially, it's over.

STRATEGY

THE TRIAL'S SCHEDULED FOR EARLY MAY. WHEN SHE MEETS WITH the lawyer, he says there's no way a jury will go murder two on both of them, as if the manslaughter charge would be a victory. Each time she speaks to him she comes away even more discouraged. She replays those first few days after the arrest and thinks she should have done things differently, starting with hiring their own lawyer. She doesn't see how she could have pulled it off, but is hounded now by the idea that she didn't even try.

Since their motion for severance failed, their lawyer has to craft an overall strategy with Gary's. Neither of them will take the stand. Both lawyers will hammer the fact that Mrs. Wagner's death was an accident, the result of a fall. They've lined up an expert witness to question the coroner's report. That way it still comes down to reasonable doubt.

As the date grows closer, Tommy swears to her that he didn't do it. He says it in the visiting room where the guards can hear and over the phone they know is being taped, as if he's trying to find a blameless way to inform on Gary. Patty doesn't tell him to cool it.

She doesn't tell him he can still make a statement either. He knows how she feels about that.

Instead, they concentrate on getting him a suit to wear. The lawyer has a tailor he recommends, but Patty has to pay for it. To her surprise, her mother comes through without any hesitation, and Patty's grateful, moved by her honest generosity. The suit is beautiful, charcoal gray with thin lapels. The tailor has to visit Tommy to make alterations. He's a little round Greek man who talks to himself while he measures and marks with his chalk. Twice he's supposed to have the suit ready for them and then postpones at the last minute, saying he's got a wedding. There's less than a week. The lawyer tells her not to worry, he always cuts it close.

When she gets a call at nine in the morning three days before the trial, she thinks it's him, that the suit's finally done.

It's the lawyer. "I'm glad I got you," he says. "I just got some news. You better sit down for this."

"What?" Patty says, thinking he's being dramatic.

"He's pleading out," the lawyer says. "Your husband's buddy."

"He confessed?" Because this is what she's been waiting for, for Gary to step up and tell the truth.

"Just the opposite," the lawyer says. "He's gone state. He's giving the DA a statement right now."

INNOCENCE

WHEN SHE CALLS DONNA, DONNA SWEARS SHE DOESN'T KNOW WHAT'S going on. She says she's sorry.

"Why is he doing this?" Patty asks, because she needs an answer, while another, uglier part of her wants to trap Donna, to make her say something incriminating, since the phone's probably tapped.

"I don't know," Donna says. "But I know he wouldn't lie."

"Not even to save his own ass."

"I know him. He wouldn't."

"I don't care," Patty says. And she doesn't. "He should have kept his fucking mouth shut. And you can tell him that from me."

EXHIBITS

NOW THAT THEY'VE GOT GARY, THEY WANT TOMMY TO PLEAD TOO. It's neat and clean that way; the DA gets both convictions and the court avoids having to try the case. The lawyer's not sure what they'll offer, but with Gary's testimony, it won't be less than the murder two as charged, which is fifteen to life.

Patty rejects it out of hand. Gary's lying.

It's possible, the lawyer says, but the way he says it makes her understand that at this point it doesn't matter.

He asks her to go over the statement to see if she can disprove the smallest part. As Patty reads about their earlier burglaries, she recognizes things Tommy brought home—the chainsaw, the ten-speed—all the evidence numbered and catalogued right in front of her. The feeling sinks in as she reads on, the heat of shame gathering in her cheeks. Maybe it's the strangeness of seeing her fears laid out on paper, but she's even more certain now that he didn't kill Mrs. Wagner, as if there has to be a limit to her cluelessness.

She can't picture him hitting her, or spinning her, or flinging her against the dresser, though she can see him laying her gently on the bed.

Patty gives him back the statement.

"Nothing?" he asks, and she wishes she could lie and make it stick the way Gary has.

"So," the lawyer says, "what we need to do is figure out which way we want to go here. We turn down the plea, odds are the DA's going to recommend the maximum, which is twenty-five to life. So you're looking at a ten-year difference there."

Patty's thinking of the fifteen years, not the ten. To life. And Gary's lying. This whole thing was his idea, Tommy just went along with it. She knows Tommy.

"There's still room for interpretation, I think," the lawyer says, "between murder and manslaughter. Depending on how much leeway they give us on the old lady's frailty. And they may give us none—that may actually work against us. The arson will, regardless of the fact that it didn't really do anything. So there's a number of unforeseeables."

He talks like a doctor laying out the dangers of surgery, letting her know everything that can go wrong, so that, whatever happens, his ass will be covered. In the end, he wants her to know, it's her decision.

THE PROBLEM OF CAUSATION

THE TRIAL GOES AHEAD AS SCHEDULED, EXCEPT NOW TOMMY AND the lawyer have the table all to themselves. The new plan is to discredit Gary's statement, then attack Gary himself, which is fine with Patty. The lawyer's turned up some previous B&E convictions—not the felony count they wanted, but enough to make him look shady, while Tommy's record is clean. The cops also took a bundle of money when they raided his and Donna's place. The lawyer's trying to find a way to make everything admissible. If they can convince the jury that Gary was the brains behind the operation, they're halfway there.

Tommy still can't believe Gary would do him like this. On the phone he sounds down, like he doesn't care what happens. In the courtroom, he slouches in his suit, and the lawyer has to nudge him to sit up straight. Like a bad actor, he doesn't know what to do with his hands, and keeps rubbing his nose.

Donna doesn't come anymore, doesn't call. And Patty used to feel sorry for her, that's how big of a fool she was.

At home, her mother and Eileen pretend they still have a chance. Cy avoids the subject, tries not to get caught alone in the same room with her.

The trial's like going to a job she despises. Every morning she gets Casey ready, stuffing his diaper bag full of cloths and bottles and wet wipes, then hands him off to her mother so she can get dressed. She doesn't fit into her old clothes yet. Her mother's taken her on an emergency shopping spree at Penney's, but still, people who watch the news must be sick of Shannon's pantsuit. Patty's learned to bring extra pads after soaking through one of her new shirts.

Every recess she expects her mother to go over and introduce herself to Elsie Wagner and her husband, but she stays with her, taking Casey when Patty needs her hands free.

And Casey's good, Casey's easy. When he fidgets, she walks him on her shoulder in the women's room, cooing to him and pacing in the mirror. The reporters leave her alone there, as if they've agreed it's safe, home base.

Most of the time she sits still on the hard bench behind Tommy, trying not to show her emotions. It's surprisingly easy. The trial is mesmerizingly dull, an endless church service. She's heard so much of the evidence already that she's not shocked. The neighbor, Mr. Ayres, returns to tell his version of events, and takes all morning, placing the truck in the turnaround, verifying that Mrs. Wagner was legally blind. It seems to Patty that every sheriff's deputy testifies. The DA's just being thorough, her lawyer says; it's a big case for him.

Does he even listen to himself? It's a big case for her and Tommy, not the fucking DA.

The worst part is listening to the coroner describe what might have happened to Mrs. Wagner. Patty can handle the diagram of the room with the body on the bed, the location of the broken glass and the capsized night table; it's only when he starts making guesses that she has to grip her own leg to keep from flinching. Elsie Wagner raises her tissue to her face like a white flag.

The injuries sustained by the deceased are consistent with a blow to the head with a heavy object such as a lamp or telephone receiver.

"Isn't it also possible," their lawyer cross-examines him, "that she could have received these injuries by falling and striking her head on a hard surface like that of a dresser or a doorframe, maybe even a plaster wall?"

"It's possible," the coroner concedes, and for the first time since Tommy was arrested, Patty thinks they've scored a victory.

Afterward, in the lawyer's office, she asks him what kind of time Gary's going to see. He says he doesn't know what the agreement is. But something; he's definitely not getting away with probation in this type of case. For an instant she savors a vision of poetic justice: Tommy walking and Gary going to prison for turning on him.

When they leave his office, the TV vans are gone, the sidewalks empty, the courthouse doors locked. It's only when they're driving home that the rest of the world returns—the steamy heat of spring with its sun and thunderstorms, bright backlit clouds riding the green hills. On Hunt Creek Road the tidy houses all fly flags. Her mother gazes directly ahead, her face slack under her makeup. The car makes Casey sleep. In these empty moments Patty's mind wanders to harmless places, memories of a better future, Casey growing up, Tommy playing catch with him in the backyard of their new house while she makes dinner, as if all this—the last six months, today—is in the past and can no longer touch them.

After dinner she waits for Tommy's call. They go over the day's testimony and preview what's coming up tomorrow. He asks about the bumps on Casey's arm—gone, thanks to the cream the doctor prescribed. They've gotten better at not wasting their expensive minutes, hopping from topic to topic like talk show hosts. *Happy Days* is on at eight, then *Welcome Back, Kotter*; they'll watch it as if the TV can magically connect them, a place where they meet in secret. It gives them something to share next time.

When their shows are over, she gets Casey down and says good night herself. She has to get up to feed him and then again at six to be at the courthouse, but of course she can't sleep, and wakes up with a headache.

She's busy; there's not a lot of time to sit around and feel sorry for herself. Plus—she never forgets—she's not the one in jail.

The trial grinds on, the firemen taking the stand. The DA props blown-up photos of the house on an easel. Patty has to be careful not to stare at the jurors. She sneaks peeks to see what interests them, the way they lean forward to absorb a witness's testimony. She can't help but see them as the enemy, the same as the judge and the DA and the reporters. She's even come to resent Elsie Wagner for being there.

The only person on her side is her mother, and she says almost nothing about the case, as if she'd rather not get involved. She critiques the trial like a movie with a faulty plot, but gently, as if she's afraid of upsetting her. "I'm surprised he didn't question that second guy more," she'll say in the car, and that will be it.

The DA's saving Gary for last, hoping he'll clinch the deal. The rest is buildup, putting things in place. The forensics expert from the state police barracks testifies that both Tommy's and Gary's fingerprints match those taken from the gas can and that traces of accelerant were found on the bed. The jury's interested in his diagram showing the trail of gas winding through the furniture; though Patty can see it from halfway across the room, the DA has them pass it along both rows for a closer look.

"I was afraid of that," the lawyer says in his office.

Then why didn't you do something about it, Patty wants to ask, because now it just sounds like an excuse.

Gary can't surprise them. By the terms of the plea agreement, he has to stick to his sworn statement. What they have to do is hammer his record and then trip him up on cross.

But first the DA wastes a day nailing down the burglary charge, introducing Gary's hockey bag and the guns into evidence, then going over the long list of property confiscated from their garage, bringing in a sheriff's deputy to recap their other robberies to show they're professionals. Their lawyer scores a point, asking the court to acknowledge the exact sum of the wad taken from Gary and Donna's apartment. Patty's strangely embarrassed, and angry at the way they used Tommy: they kept the money while he got stuck holding a bunch of junk.

What bothers her is how methodical and bloodless the process is, the steady accumulation of tape from the court reporter's machine, the folders full of typed pages the lawyers take out of their briefcases every morning. The whole thing is just words, so why is it so expensive? And anyway, the most important ones are lies. From the beginning, no one's been interested in the truth.

She knows what Gary's going to say, so that when he finally gets up on the stand in his fake suit and tie, his answers seem rehearsed, which of course they are. His story's familiar to anyone who's been following the news. He and Tommy go into the house, thinking it's empty. Tommy struggles with the woman and knocks her down; after that, she doesn't move. Tommy decides they have to set the fire and gets the can from the garage.

Gary recites his lines so matter-of-factly—dipping to the microphone so he has to look up at the DA—that Patty can't believe the jury will buy it, and yet they're paying attention to every word he says. Question after question, the DA keys on the violence of the struggle, the size of Tommy, "a hockey player," against a bony old lady. One woman in the front row raises her hands in self-defense as Gary describes how Tommy poured the gas on Mrs. Wagner. Patty contains herself, jaw clenched, staring directly at Gary, daring him to look her in the eye.

On cross, their lawyer nails him on his previous convictions and the bundle of money. He asks whose idea it was to target Mrs. Wagner's in the first place, then quotes from a list of property reported stolen from their earlier jobs, including a dozen rifles that are still missing. He tries to tie the guns to the money, but the DA objects, and the judge sustains it.

Patty wishes they could call Donna to the stand and make her tell the truth. That would prove that all of this was Gary's doing. But they can't, by law, as if that makes any sense.

And the lawyer can't make Gary take back his statement. It's admitted as evidence, testimony given under oath, meaning now the jury will have to find out that he's lying by themselves, and she's not sure they're that smart.

The judge dismisses Gary, who's escorted out the side door by the bailiff like a special guest. It's past four, and Patty thinks they'll just adjourn for the day, but the DA steps forward and asks to introduce one last piece of evidence.

He brings it out on an easel, hidden behind a black shroud. It's probably another diagram of some kind—or a photo of Mrs. Wagner, burnt.

He circles it, recounting Gary's testimony of the struggle between the defendant and the victim. "She realizes she's fighting for her life," he says, "but her opponent is too young, too strong. And yet she doesn't give up. She *can't* give up. In her final minutes, Audrey Wagner does everything she can to stay alive. It's the most basic human instinct, self-preservation." With that, he lifts back the veil.

It's a blowup of Tommy's mug shot, his hair wild, the bloody slice across one eye.

"Ob-*jec*-tion!" their lawyer yells, and the judge orders the DA to cover it up and calls a conference.

The picture isn't admitted, but it doesn't matter, the damage is done.

"He told me he ran into a tree," Patty says. "*I* think the cops beat on him."

"I don't think we want to argue either of those. It was a cheap shot, we just have to move on."

What he's really saying is that they have to play by the state's made-up rules, but the DA can do whatever he likes.

That night, Eileen informs her that she and Cy are coming tomorrow. Patty wonders what their mother told her. She half expects Shannon to call and try to cheer her up.

The next morning the court is packed to hear the lawyer and the DA make their closing arguments, but for Patty the trial's over. If that's all the evidence the state has, she isn't convinced, not beyond a reasonable doubt. In the end it comes down to Gary's word, and it's obvious he testified to save his ass. As she listens to the judge give the jury their instructions, she thinks they have to see that.

She tries not to imagine what the jury's saying as they deliberate—the way she willfully ignores a Bills game on TV in the other room, afraid to hear something bad happening, wanting only the relief of the final score. She plays with Casey in the lawyer's office, pressing his nose like a button. There's not enough room for all of them. She's told Eileen and Cy they can go home, but they won't, filling the chairs, staring out the window at the street below, the reporters smoking in the gazebo. The lawyer says they want the jury to stay out as long as possible, which makes the afternoon drag. Every time the phone rings, Patty holds Casey still, as if the slightest movement could jinx them.

At five, there's still no word.

"That's a good sign, right?" Patty asks.

"Usually," the lawyer says.

He checks with the court clerk, and it's official, the jury's sequestered for the night. She might as well go home.

In the car, she thinks the phone will be ringing when they pull in.

It isn't, of course, and it doesn't ring—as she fears—just as she's walking past it, a land mine set just for her.

Eileen and her mother try to distract her with dinner and TV. Casey picks up on her nerves and cries, and she can't calm him. That's never happened before, and after a while she has to hand him to Eileen and close the bathroom door to compose herself. It's been eight hours, and they couldn't have spent much time on the burglary and arson charges. Or have they already quit for the night?

She splashes water on her face, comes back out and takes her place on the couch. She can feel herself vibrating inside, a tremor in her skin that makes her want to swallow. If she could just stop thinking, but it's impossible, and the TV's no help, flashing pictures of airports and convertibles at her, a dog running across a yard in slow motion. It's almost like being stoned, the way her mind flies around, bouncing off things, never landing.

In the middle of a bad *Streets of San Francisco*, her mother stands up and says it's getting late if she's going to wake up at a reasonable hour. Everyone agrees. They see her off, and by then Casey's head is heavy on her shoulder, a spot of drool on his cloth. Patty's in their room, changing him into his jammies, when the phone rings, making her turn toward the door.

"Do you want me to get it?" Eileen yells.

"Yes," Patty calls, then stops trying to fit his bottoms on and heads for the living room.

"I do," Eileen is saying stiffly, officially, then holds the phone out to her. "It's Tommy."

"Jesus, you scared us," Patty tells him.

"I told you I was going to call."

"I'm going a little nuts here, if you can imagine that."

"I know, I'm sorry," he says, so they don't squabble, but as they fall into discussing what might be happening, she thinks she should get off in case the lawyer's trying to call.

Eventually, their pauses grow longer, and it's time to get off.

"Pats," Tommy says. "Listen. Tomorrow . . ."

"Whatever happens, we'll get through it. I promise you. Okay?"

It's that promise she comes back to after they hang up and she lays Casey in his bassinet. She doesn't know if she's strong enough to keep it. She'll have to be, because she knows—even if deep down she can't quite admit it to herself right now—that, no matter what, he *is* going away. It'll just be her and Casey for a while.

The phone doesn't ring, meaning nothing. She watches TV with Cy and Eileen until a special comes on about the fall of Saigon, then says her good nights. She knows she won't sleep, but it's easier to just lie in bed by herself and listen to Casey breathe.

Somehow she does, because hours later she wakes in the dark to Casey complaining. She feeds him and rocks him to sleep again, changes pads and crawls between the sheets, all of it dreamlike.

In the morning he's her alarm clock, crabbing at her, the room stark. She paws through her wardrobe, the few choices. It's going to be hot, Eileen warns.

They have to wait for their mother so they can all go in together.

Patty wants to call the lawyer but figures he won't be at the courthouse yet. Driving, she tailgates, then catches herself and backs off.

The lawyer's waiting for them with coffee and doughnuts. No news yet, but it could be any minute. County juries are pretty quick.

The phone rings, and they all look at it.

It's just another client.

The phone rings, the phone rings. The lawyer's busier than she would have thought—more people who can't afford a real one. They've grown so used to false alarms that when it rings around ten-fifteen, they're more annoyed than anything.

The lawyer covers the mouthpiece with a hand and turns to her. "It's in," he says.

Shouldn't a hung jury take longer?

"Not necessarily," he says, gathering up his papers. They're supposed to reconvene immediately.

They take the elevator down and make it a couple of steps into the hall before the photographers spot them. Cy shoulders in front of her, brandishing the carrier, clearing the way.

The crowd is back as if they never recessed, the benches filled. The only empty seats are theirs in the front row. Elsie Wagner and her husband watch them process up the aisle like a bridal party, and, too late, Patty understands: they can't do this without her. She should have just stayed away.

The ritual begins, the ceremonial entrances, the actors taking their places. She tries to read the jury. They're tight-lipped, grim. None of them will look at Tommy. They all rise for the judge, then settle again.

"Mr. Foreman," the judge asks, "have you reached a verdict?"

"We have, your honor."

Patty wants to run, except she's boxed in, Eileen and her mother holding on to her as she cradles Casey, as if they all might be swept away. She braces for pain like at the dentist, knowing it's coming, hoping it won't.

"On the charge of murder in the second degree," the foreman reads, "we find the defendant guilty."

Behind her, the room erupts so she can't hear what comes next. The foreman's still standing, the lawyer leaning into Tommy like he's giving him advice. The judge calls for order. She listens, squinting to filter the noise, because that can't be it. There has to be something else—a correction, an explanation.

There isn't, only further convictions on the burglary and arson charges.

It will be weeks before she believes it, and even then not completely. Because she can't accept their verdict. She won't. She's not exaggerating when she swears she'll fight this decision the rest of her life, no matter how many appeals it takes. Like Mrs. Wagner's death, it's just a terrible, terrible mistake.

25 TO

LIFE

AND IF YOU DON'T LOVE ME NOW

YOU WILL NEVER LOVE ME AGAIN

FLEETWOOD MAC

ESCAPE ATTEMPTS

THE LAWYER'S ONLY HALF RIGHT ABOUT THE SENTENCES. THE JUDGE gives Tommy the maximum, just like he said. Gary gets off with five years' probation and time served.

When Patty hears this, she calls Donna.

"We're sorry," a recorded voice answers. "The number you have reached is not in service at this time. Please check that you have dialed the number correctly."

"Fuck you!" Patty says, like it might get through anyway.

She's twenty-seven, meaning she'll be fifty-two by the time he gets out—*if* he makes parole on the first try. There's no time off for good behavior like in other states. Her mother's only fifty-one, and look at her. Patty can't imagine him wanting that.

When she goes to see the lawyer about their appeal, he shows her a Department of Corrections map of the state with all the different locations. She's surprised at how many there are, and the different kinds. Because it's murder, Tommy will be assigned to a maximum security facility. The lawyer points them out, marked with black triangles like state parks. She remembers seeing cops in riot gear storming Attica on TV, firing their rifles into clouds of tear gas, and later the bodies laid out on the ground. There's one right in Elmira that would make visiting easy, and another in Auburn about an hour away. The rest are down near New York City, and one place upstate, way the hell up by Canada.

"How do they choose who goes where?" Patty asks.

"It's whoever has room."

The way the system works, they won't know where he's going until he's already there. The state keeps it a secret so their people don't get ambushed when they're delivering prisoners. Patty hadn't thought of that, and sees it as a missed chance, standing in the middle of the road with a shotgun and flagging down a van, like something from a bad movie.

He gives her a pamphlet from a place called Prison Ministries with a cross on the front and an Elmira address rubber-stamped on the back. "It helps to be in touch with folks who know the ropes."

She accepts it to be polite, and to get back to the real reason she's here.

The appeal's pretty much automatic in a case like this, he says. He can file a notice this week and write up a formal brief as soon as he has time. It would go to the Appellate Division in Albany, but the earliest they'd hear the actual argument is around eighteen months from now. He says all this offhand, as if he doesn't think it will work.

"And you'd be doing it," she asks.

"Unless you have someone else in mind."

"Like who?"

"You can ask the appellate court to appoint you a lawyer if you want to claim insufficient counsel, that's your choice." The way he says it, it's more than a question.

All she wanted was the information; she didn't think he'd be part of the appeal. There's no way she'll ever trust him again, not after how badly he fucked up the case, but she doesn't want to say that, just sits there taking notes like she's catching up. She wonders if he knows that's what she's going to do, because he basically tells her how, and as Patty jots it all down she realizes the bastard's quitting on them.

the way Tommy likes it, the strawberry blonde fan setting off her freckles. She reads with her mouth slightly open, showing the pointed canines he calls her fangs. She could almost pass for a sexy vampire, except she's wearing the gold-framed Ben Franklins she's had since high school, very Jan Brady.

In the book, two of the characters are fucking in a cramped airplane bathroom, something Patty—who's never been on a plane—finds impossibly glamorous and unlikely, but which makes her even hornier.

It's been a while. The truest test of love, she's always thought, is making love, and while Tommy still comes to her now, he's too careful, too quiet. She misses their first crazy days together, when he'd come out of the bathroom naked and walking on his hands, as if daring her to knock him over or pin him against a wall.

She figures he'll be late. They'll close the Iroquois and he'll come in humming, bumping into things. She waits for the chug of his truck, the swish of the storm door, the shock of his hands on her, waits, warming, resting her eyes now, the book still propped on her stomach, until she slips all the way under, splayed beneath the heavy comforter.

For a while *The Other Side of Midnight* lies tented on her chest, then capsizes, her place lost, the Kleenex bookmark somewhere in the tangle of covers. She's snoring, a rhythmic click in her sinuses and then a long praying draw that would embarrass her if she knew. The night-light is on in the bathroom, glazing the sink. In the kitchen the faucet drips into a sponge.

She has no idea that as she sleeps he's in another woman's bedroom; that a few miles across the fields he and his best friend Gary are fighting with this woman, who's woken from her own solitary sleep and attacked them with the first thing at hand—a glass of water. The phone sits on the floor by his side of the bed, alive inside

THE OTHER SIDE
OF MIDNIGHT

She goes to Tommy's game to see him play. He scores his first goal of the season, but she's pregnant and can't drink, so there's no reason for her to go out with the rest of the team after. She's tired, her back hurts from work and sitting on the hard bleachers, and she uses that as an excuse. It's why she brought her car in the first place. She teases him in the parking lot, saying she might have a surprise for him when he gets home. "Be good," she says, and kisses him, the ends of his wet hair needling her cheek.

It's freezing in the Dart, the steering wheel burning through her gloves. The defrost doesn't work, and all the way home she swipes at the windshield, tries to breathe lightly. Farms sail by in the night, the snowy fields ghostly, chore lights showing a corner of a barn door, a skeletal gas pump. The muddy ruts of the drive crumble under her tires, hard as chocolate. When she slides into bed the sheets are chilly on her skin.

The waterbed is huge and new, the one real piece of furniture they own. She lies propped in the middle, reading *The Other Side of Midnight*, a novel her mother has already declared trash. Instead of her flannel nightshirt, she's wearing a sheer black peignoir that shows off her impressive new breasts. She's brushed her hair out

ARRESTED

AND IF YOU SEE MY REFLECTION IN THE SNOW-COVERED HILLS

WELL THE LANDSLIDE WILL BRING IT DOWN

FLEETWOOD MAC

"Good luck, Mrs. Dickerson," he says when she leaves, and from reflex, she thanks him.

PENDING TRANSFER

TOMMY ALREADY FEELS FAR AWAY IN THE COUNTY JAIL. ONCE HE'S IN the system, she's afraid he'll disappear completely.

At home, she takes care of Casey, waking early with him, then waiting for visiting hours to roll around. Her mother's retreated, leaving her alone most of the day, and when she does come, she says things like, "You really need to think about what you're going to do." She makes it clear that Patty's throwing her life away if she sticks with him.

Patty can't make plans. The truck's still in custody, and she hasn't been able to pay the hospital bill. She notices she's smoking a lot; she has to bum from Cy when she runs out, and his Camels are harsh. When Casey goes down for his nap, she gets stoned and sits on the back stairs, watching the ants zigzag at her feet, letting the sun warm her bare arms. Birds flit from tree to tree. She doesn't know what she's going to do—go back to work, ask her mother if she can watch Casey during the day. It won't solve anything, but she needs the money. It's what they want for her, a regular life.

"Too late," she says to the sky.

Father's Day, she makes a card for Tommy, wraps Casey's

hand around a magic marker and shakily signs his name. They spend their hour together playing with a rainbowed, oversized ring of plastic keys and dreaming aloud about the appeal, the promise of a better lawyer. Leaving, she hangs on to him too long, and the guard tells her to step back. In the parking lot she's teary, blowing her nose in the hot car. From his carrier, Casey watches her, and she stops. "It's okay," she says. "Mama's just sad."

At home, the monthly bill from the self-storage is waiting for her, the only one she absolutely has to pay. Her checkbook says she can just cover it. She tries to think of something she can sell, but the cops took everything worth pawning. She wedges the bill into her checkbook and sticks it back in her purse where she won't have to look at it.

She doesn't mention money when she visits. They only have so much time together, and there's nothing he can do about it. It's like everything else: she just has to deal.

Her biggest fear is that they'll send him upstate, the place way up near the Canadian border. The last week of June, he hears rumors. The guards are talking about the first of the month as a transfer date. When it comes, nothing happens. The Fourth of July annoys her, all the patriotic crap, like it's the bicentennial already. And then the next Saturday when she goes to see him, he's gone.

HIGHWAY MILES

■

ALL THEY CAN TELL HER IS THAT HE'S IN PROCESSING. SHE IMAGINES what they're doing to him. All she can think of is army recruits going through boot camp, getting their heads buzzed, putting on starchy uniforms.

Now there's really nowhere to go. After two days of wandering around the house, she invites herself to her mother's for lunch.

"It's like when your father was in the war," her mother says. "I'd get a letter, but he wasn't allowed to say where he was. I swear, sometimes it looked like swiss cheese."

Patty's mystified by her sympathy, even if it's unintended, comparing Tommy with her father.

They talk about summer coming on, and the groundhog that's living under the shed in the far corner of the garden. It feels normal, the two of them taking turns cradling Casey—as if she's free for the afternoon while Tommy's off at work.

"Oh honey," her mother says, reaching over to comfort her, because suddenly Patty's crying.

"It's all right," her mother says, hugging her sideways. "Things will get better. They have to."

Her mother's right, or partly, because a few days later a letter comes from the sheriff's department saying they're finished with the truck. They'll release it to her even though her name's not on the title, but they want three hundred dollars for impound fees.

Even after she borrows the money from her mother, before Patty can sell it she needs Tommy to sign it over to her.

At least she has the truck. She sits in it, breathing in his smell, remembering nights at the drive-in, or the time it rained when they were camping up on Seneca Lake and they stayed warm in the cab, playing cards all weekend. His cigarette butts are still in the ashtray, his work gloves and a Nerf football in the toolbox. There's an extra pair of cruddy boots shoved under the driver's seat for rainy days. Sunglasses, change, a bottle opener, a fluorescent orange bobber, a dozen Juicy Fruit wrappers—even the dust and pebbles in the floor mats are his. She'll have to vacuum it before she parks it out by the road with a sign in the window, but not yet. She can't do anything until she hears from him anyway.

Cy says she should drive it. Sitting idle for so many months isn't good for the engine; the seals dry out. Patty waits till Eileen gets home to run it around the backroads. It hasn't been a week yet, but she doesn't like to leave the phone unattended, in case.

She turns the radio up and the green hollows fly by, the dips and creeks and eroding stone bridges, the clumps of skunk cabbage and elephant-ears. The gearshift is familiar under her hand, and the bright asterisk of the crack in the windshield. She rumbles over railroad tracks, downshifts to climb the winding hills. Compared to the Dart, it's got power, and she likes riding high and being able to see. It's newer than her car—plus it's his. It would be wrong to get rid of it, though she knows Tommy would tell her not to be stupid. She can hear her mother: she needs to think about Casey, not just herself.

But she can't sell it until she hears from Tommy.

Little things are starting to get to her, things people say. Cy gives her shit about smoking O.P.s and Patty whips the unlit butt back at him. Eileen opens the fridge at breakfast and asks where the milk went, when all Patty had was the last little dribble in her coffee.

"Look," Patty says, "I'll buy you a whole gallon, all right?"

"That doesn't do me any good now," Eileen says.

When they've left and she's alone with Casey, she coos to him, walking her fingers up his breastbone, tapping his nose: "Aunt Leenie is being an asshole, yes . . . she . . . is!"

And then she scrapes together some change and belts his carrier into the truck and races cross-country to Iron Kettle Farm—leaving the phone—to buy the goddamned milk, which Eileen doesn't even say anything about until right before bed, a grudging thank-you that Patty knows Cy is behind.

Sometimes it's not a fight with anyone, it's just Patty being mad at herself. There doesn't have to be a reason. With no warning, a needling feeling of frustration rises and takes control of her. She can be doing anything—washing dishes, changing Casey—and her hands clench. She wants to scream or hit something or both.

Some of it's sex. It's been seven months. She's given in to her hands, pretending they're his, but they only make her miss him more. She swears off touching herself, then surrenders and feels slutty, a vicious circle. It doesn't help that she feels fat as well as unloved.

The weather helps, the heat and humidity building into thunderstorms that darken the house and shake the valley—wild and then spent, like her—rinsing everything clean. The road dries in patches, steam lifting off the asphalt. She takes Casey outside to feel the fresh air. She hopes Tommy has a window.

When she pictures him, he's always alone, a silhouette in his cell, though she knows the real danger is when he's with the others. Everywhere he goes, he's surrounded by them—the guards *and* the prisoners.

She doesn't even know if he has his own cell, or if he has to share a toilet with someone. She doesn't think she could do that—

only if she absolutely had to, and then she'd spread a newspaper or something in front of her. But he's not shy like she is; he was always the first to skinny-dip. She used to jag him about just wanting to show off.

She worries about what he's eating, and what his bed's like. She used to bring him his cigarettes; now where's he getting them from?

She could go crazy imagining things. It's better to focus on what she *can* do, and so, Friday, a week after bringing the truck home, she cuts a panel from a cardboard box and neatly magic-markers a FOR SALE sign with Eileen's number and sticks it on the dash of the Dart, wedging it against the rearview mirror. She pulls the car to the edge of the road, angled toward town so people will see it on their way home, then walks back inside and peers through the living room window at it, sure she's just fucked up royally.

Eileen posts a flyer with a fringe of numbers at the laundromat. Now when the phone rings, it could be anyone. Patty's asking fifteen hundred, but she'd take a thousand. She could pay her mother back, pay off the rest of the loan and still have a chunk left over. She's going to start working again, she's got to if she wants to have any kind of life.

Saturday, Eileen and Cy ask if she wants to come to the speedway with them, but she has to be home in case someone calls. When the phone finally rings, it's her mother, confirming that they're still coming for Sunday dinner. Patty doesn't tell her she's selling the Dart—she'll find out tomorrow anyway.

"I don't understand," her mother says when Cy lets it slip over dessert. "I thought you were selling the truck."

"It's paid off," Patty says. "This way we get rid of a bill."

"But it's so big," her mother says. "I can't imagine it gets any kind of gas mileage."

"Twenty-five highway," Patty lies. It's what the Dart gets, or

WITHDRAWN

FOR ALISON AND BEE
AND EVERYONE WHO'S WAITING

was supposed to when it was new. She's memorized the owner's manual, expecting the buyers will have questions.

"That can't be," her mother says, but doesn't call her on it, just as she doesn't ask how Tommy could afford to pay cash for the truck to begin with.

She's only mentioned him once, as she was greeting them at the door. "Have you heard from Tommy yet?" she asked Patty, as if she'd been thinking about him all day—instead of the question being a preemptive strike, getting the bad news out of the way so it wouldn't ruin dinner. It's silly; he's the whole reason they're there—okay, *and* Casey. She can't remember the last non-holiday her mother invited Eileen and Cy to the house.

But Patty has her own motives too. Cleaning up, while Eileen is down in the basement fetching some Tupperware, she tells her mother she's thinking of going back to work.

"This would be to your old job?"

"I'd have to get someone to watch Casey during the day," Patty says.

"Are you asking me?" her mother says.

"I want to hear what you think."

"I think you've got to do something."

Patty agrees.

"If you wanted to do something like that, I think it would be easier on both of us if you moved back here."

Patty acts surprised, though she's already thought of it. After fighting so long to be independent, it's hard to surrender again.

"I've got nothing but room," her mother says.

"That's generous," Patty says, and hears Eileen coming up the stairs. "I'll think about it."

"Do," her mother says, and takes the gravy boat into the dining room, breaking off the conversation, keeping it their secret.

Back at Eileen's, Patty spaces out while they watch TV—*Rhoda* and then *Phyllis*, plucky single women trying to pay the bills. She barely listens, dogged by her mother's offer. She's tired and stoned and wondering if it's too early to go to sleep when the phone rings.

Her first thought is that it's too late for Tommy, but maybe the state's rules are different.

Eileen's closest. She picks up and listens a second. "She's right here."

"I'm calling about the car for sale?" a man says—older, a withered voice.

It's a solid car, she assures him, never been in an accident. The only thing wrong with it is the defroster, and a few small scratches. Patty wants to be honest but feels weird cataloguing its faults, as if she's talking behind its back.

"Why are you selling?" the man asks.

"We bought a new truck, so now it's extra."

She makes sure Cy will be home before scheduling a time for the guy to come over. She hasn't forgotten the voice in the middle of the night telling her how easy it would be.

But, Monday, when he pulls up in his battleship of a station wagon—ladders lashed to the roof, a primered door tied shut with clothesline—she sees he's harmless, a backwoods handyman, someone's grampa. He's come from work and his face is misted with silver paint. He sticks his head under the front end, pops the hood and runs his hands across the engine like a doctor. "Okay if I take her for a spin?" he asks, and they both go with him, Cy leaning between the seats to hear what they're saying. The guy guns it, then lays on the brakes, taking his hands off the wheel to check the alignment. "Drives straight," he says, then, back at the house, has Patty go through the lights and signals while he stands there conducting her.

"You were asking fifteen hundred?" he says, and takes out his checkbook.

"Yes," Patty says, watching him write.

The man rips the check from the book and holds it up like money. "I'll give you a thousand right now."

She was wrong to try to do this without Tommy—or maybe she's greedy. Just yesterday she would have been willing to take a thousand.

"Twelve-fifty," she counters.

The man laughs like this is an insult, and lowers the check. He rubs the side of his jaw, watching her like a gunfighter. "'Leven hundred, take it or leave it."

"It's a deal."

"Man," he says to Cy, as if he's behind all this, "the lady drives a hard bargain."

But later, his check safe in her purse, she thinks he somehow tricked her. She came down four hundred while he only came up one hundred. Tommy would have told him to go blow.

The next day two people call, and two more on Wednesday. "If you don't mind my asking," one man says, "how much did it go for?" Patty decides to lie and then feels even more foolish.

Eileen's taken the flyer down, but the calls don't stop, the stragglers reaching into the weekend, each a reminder that Patty should have held out longer. Whenever she checks the balance of her bank account, she automatically adds the lost four hundred, then subtracts it again.

And still, each time the phone rings, it's him. She dashes in from the other room or from outside, prepared to hear his voice. It's not him. Cy's friend Jeff sounds enough like Tommy that for a minute she thinks it's him, then has to retreat to her room, wounded.

As the days go by, her imagination spins terrible, logical scenarios. The reason he hasn't called is that he's been killed. He's in a coma in the prison infirmary after his cellmate attacked him. He's in solitary for defending himself.

He'll call. It's just a matter of time. She has to stop staring at the phone because, after five straight days in the house with Casey, she's literally going crazy. The TV is full of idiots. She wants to go out and do something normal like see a movie, but she can't. She needs to be here when he calls.

And then, when it actually happens, she's not the one who answers. When Tommy calls, she's in her room, feeding Casey, her shirt hiked up. The phone rings in the living room, where Eileen is drinking beer and painting her toenails. Patty turns her head, waiting for someone to pick up, hoping, this once, that it isn't him.

The ring that should be there isn't, and now she listens, hearing the murmur of Eileen's voice, and then Eileen's moving, getting up, coming toward the door. "Patty, it's Tommy!"

Patty doesn't take her breast away from Casey, doesn't bother running the cord under the door.

"Pats," he shouts, because it's noisy there—a wall of people jabbering so loudly in the background that she laughs.

"I miss you so much," she shouts back, holding the phone close.

"I know, I miss you too. Listen, I've only got three minutes."

But she has so many questions.

"Where are you?" she starts, almost hollering. "Are you okay?"

NEW

∎

AUBURN IS SEVENTY MILES NORTH, AN OLD CANAL TOWN AT THE
top of Owasco Lake. Patty starts off early so she'll be there when
the gates open. There's no fast way, just the square grid of county
roads; she has to go up and then across in steps. It's Saturday so
there's no traffic except fishermen, and still it takes her two hours,
cutting through Ithaca, curving along the shore of Cayuga Lake,
past the leafy summer camps sloping down to docks holding white
motorboats, families still asleep inside their cottages.

Beside her, Casey sleeps in his carrier, his head cushioned by
folded diapers. Her mother bugged her about taking him, but
Tommy said he wanted to see him. The three of them need to get
through this together.

The counselor she talked to on the phone mailed her a sheet
of instructions, and Patty's studied it hard. The first line says:
INAPPROPRIATE BEHAVIOR MAY RESULT IN TERMINATION OF THE
VISIT. It goes on to list conduct that won't be tolerated, including
"foul language," "outbursts of temper," "prolonged embracing,"
and "straddling-type contact." The dress code is all about sex.
There are no tank or tube tops allowed, no plunging necklines, no
tops that expose more than half of the back, nothing made of
sheer material. No miniskirts, no short-shorts or hot pants (not
that Patty would ever wear something like that, and definitely
nowhere near a prison). And right after that, as if the one leads to

the other, it says: CHILDREN MUST BE KEPT UNDER CONTROL AT
ALL TIMES.

She's dressed special for him, a summery sky-blue skirt and
sleeveless top from Shannon that shows off her neck and arms,
well inside the code. She's brought a little ditty bag with makeup
and some Jean Naté to spruce up in the parking lot before she goes
in. She's got Casey in her favorite hand-me-down from Randy, a
sailor suit complete with a terrycloth hat like Popeye's. They could
be going to Sears for their family portrait.

Above the lake, eye-high corn lines both sides of the road;
cows dot the hilly meadows. The instruction sheet doesn't include
directions, so she's following a county map she bought at a gas mart.
The country's easy, just spotting route numbers at junctions, but
when she gets into Auburn the streets are all one way, looping her
around like a bypass. Before she's completely lost she pulls over to
check the map. Only then does she see the prison's not on it.

The instructions don't have a street address, just Auburn Cor-
rectional Facility, Auburn, New York, and the zip code—like she
should know where it is (she should, she thinks; she should have
checked before leaving, she should have asked the counselor over
the phone). The sheet says the parking lot's accessible from Garden
Street. Patty searches the map with a finger. There's an East Garden
Street and a West Garden Street. Beside her, Casey's waking up as
if they're there. The thought of asking someone on the sidewalk
occurs to her—"Could you tell me how to get to the prison?"—
and vanishes just as quickly.

East Garden Street is a major road. She goes right because it's
easier and looks for signs. After a half mile its name changes to Grant
Street and she turns around in the parking lot of a closed Burger
Chef. She heads west, past where she first turned on, until she's driving alongside a pair of train tracks. Beyond them stands an old red-

brick factory, and beyond that, between the factory and a big smoke-stack, a long unbroken wall topped with glassed-in guard towers.

The factory blocks her view and there's traffic behind her so she can't stop. The road angles off, following the tracks, taking her away from the prison. For a while there's nowhere to turn. Finally she catches a right over the tracks and hits a dead-end, a fence with razor wire protecting a black canal that separates the wall from the sooty backs of factories. She has to lean forward and peer up through the windshield to see the nearest tower, a guard inside wearing a cop's pointy hat looking down at her like she's come to break some-one out. She turns around and gooses it back over the tracks—too fast, the truck seesawing on its shocks—and tells herself to slow down. It's not even time yet. She's got a whole half hour.

She ends up circling the prison and coming around the other side on Wall Street, the towers looming right over her shoulder. NO PHOTOGRAPHY PERMITTED, the same yellow stencil says again and again. There are houses directly across the street with neat yards and garages.

Finally, a sign: VISITOR PARKING. She's surprised the lot's so big, and at the number of cars; it's like a dealership, a field of windshields. There are no people, no mothers, no other wives shouldering babies. She snakes her way to the very farthest corner before creating her own spot, squeezing the truck in beside a dumpster, the bumper nosing an overgrown border of daisies and weeds. She puts her face on in the rearview mirror, sprays the Jean Naté strategically. Her hips are stiff from driving, her lower back; she stretches before dealing with Casey, and then is careful to lock up. Walking between the motionless rows, Patty has the dreamlike feeling that she's late. It's a long way, and Casey's heavy in his carrier. She has to stop and switch arms.

Across the tar-seamed street, the prison rises square and stone like her old high school, shut up for the summer. There's no one hanging around outside, and she's afraid it's the wrong day. The front entrance is like a castle, two imposing stone turrets like chess pieces flanking a solid double door. Inside the spiked fence the flag hangs limp, the blue state flag just under it. Patty thinks her eyes are playing tricks, but no, standing on the very top of the main building with his arms at his sides like a diver is a statue of a Revolutionary War soldier. She looks both ways and crosses.

The riveted steel door's unlocked but heavy. She has to wedge a shoulder in and then swing Casey through. As she does, a tall black woman looms close and reaches an arm across her.

"I got you," she says, smelling of fruity perfume. Patty's startled—she doesn't see many black people in Owego—but thanks her and ducks into the dull fluorescent light.

This is where everyone is, a smoky, windowless waiting room like a bus station, rows of orange seats bolted to the floor, an aqua and white checkerboard wall of lockers. A majority of the women are black or brown, and she quickly picks out the few men— standing along the wall so others can sit. The squawling of babies and the babble of conversation wake up Casey. There's nowhere to sit, so Patty stands there, just inside the door, trying to hush him.

"You must be new," the woman says, and Patty nods, a refugee who doesn't speak the language. "You need to go to the desk and fill out a slip."

They must be from the city, she thinks, making her way through the crowd, careful of people's feet. She can feel them watching her as she passes, but in a different way than the guard in his blue uniform—checking out her figure, then hard-eyed, memorizing her, like she might try to pull something. There are too many little kids here for Casey to work on him. He shoves a form across the fake wood counter and turns his back to her, busy with a TV monitor. There's a pen on a chain that doesn't work. "Excuse me," she says, and without a word he spins on his stool and clacks a pen down on the counter. She sets Casey's carrier at her feet and elbows the diaper bag around to her side, digging in her purse for Tommy's inmate number.

The guard looks over the form like she might have left a box empty, then tears the carbon apart and pushes the pink piece at her. "Hold on to your slip. You'll be called in the order you're registered"—meaning she's behind everyone here.

A brown woman older than her mother shoos a boy in his church clothes to make room for her.

"Thank you," Patty says, resting Casey's carrier across her knees.

As they wait, Patty plays with Casey and furtively takes in the room, noting the elaborate hairdos and fancy nails and loud dresses on some of the women, the spaghetti straps and sheaths and cleavage she thought were against the rules. They're so young, she thinks; they could be all done up for the prom. It's got to be at least five hours from the city. When did they have to get up to make themselves beautiful?

It's time, and they let the guard know it. Everyone gradually stops talking. Mothers rein in their children as the whole room concentrates on the front desk. The guard checks his watch and then does nothing, setting off a round of muttering. Patty stays silent, too new to join in. The instruction sheet leaps to mind. She doesn't want to do anything that might jeopardize the visit.

The guard checks his watch again and looks back at his monitor. The grumbling runs around. It's like he's taunting them.

And then he slides off his stool, stands at the desk and calls the first three visitors—by number, fast, rattling them off like a drill sergeant. One woman who doesn't speak English is confused, thinking he might have called her. "Is this your number?" the guard asks, flashing the slip at her. "Then sit down."

The door to the next room locks and unlocks with a buzz. Between the groups of three stretch long lulls. As each goes through, the room slowly clears out, doughnut boxes and coffee cups littering the floor. The old lady beside her gets in around ten-thirty, smiling goodbye to Patty. Casey's cranky, and she's already missed an hour and a half. Tommy's probably wondering where she is. Next time she'll get up earlier. There's no reason she shouldn't be first, living so close.

It's almost noon when the guard calls the number she's memorized. She grabs the diaper bag and lugs Casey's carrier up front, keeping her purse handy to show their ID. The guard isn't interested; he just needs to see her slip. Directly ahead of her is the tall woman who helped her earlier; she's given herself a booster shot of perfume, and Patty thinks her Jean Naté's probably evaporated by now.

There are four more guards in the next room, and a metal detector. Patty follows the tall woman, copying everything she does. She has to show her ID to get her hand stamped, but then the stamp's invisible. The tall woman explains: it only shows up under ultraviolet light.

"No talking," a guard says.

They take her change for the vending machines and count it.

"Please remove your shoes," another guard orders. "Place any objects you have in your pockets in the basket. Remove all jewelry."

She pulls off her wedding ring.

"You're going to have to take the baby out of the car seat."

The tall woman's already passed through the machine. Patty's the last one left. She's surprised when the metal detector goes off with a staticky wowing sound.

A guard waves a black plastic wand over her, stopping in the middle of her back. It's the hook and eye of her bra. It's humiliating, yet Patty thinks they could have just as easily made her take it off.

No one helps her put the baby carrier back together when they finish taking it apart. They stand there watching her repack the diaper bag, then stop her from adding the last two bottles. "You can only bring in one bottle, ma'am."

"Fine," Patty says, and leaves them to go bad in a locker.

At the next counter she's checked against the official visitor sheet. An older man with steel-rimmed bifocals who calls her Mrs. Dickerson carefully unfolds Casey's birth certificate. There's a problem with the hospital bill; it's not considered a legal ID. She needs to apply for a Social Security card for him, but the guy lets her slide this time. While he calls up to have them send Tommy down, he makes faces at Casey, popping his eyes, making a clownish O of his mouth. He assigns Patty a table, telling her she can go right in.

The visiting room is like a cafeteria, rows of neatly spaced tables, a bank of vending machines to one side. The light's brighter in here, as if they're onstage, and there are cameras watching from all four corners. A letter designating each table hangs from the drop-panel ceiling. Hers is T. She sees faces from the waiting room, but also the men they've come to see, prisoners dressed in the same faded dark green workshirts and pants like a legion of janitors. Most are young and muscled, biceps straining their short sleeves, and she can't help it, she wonders if they're dangerous, if right here a fight won't break out. Patty feels their eyes on her and tries not to stare at the dark tattoos on their arms. She follows the farthest row past S, where the tall woman and a man who's large all over are lost in prayer, eyes closed, hands clasped atop an open Bible. Not five feet away another couple are practically having sex, the guy's whole arm up her dress.

The table Patty finally sits at is scratched with graffiti—linked initials and pierced hearts, lightning bolts and skulls. She sets Casey on the tabletop. He's grabby, clawing the air, so she breaks out his bottle. He holds both sides with splayed starfish hands, kicking his feet as he drinks, and she worries, though it's impossible, that someday he'll remember this and hold it against them.

She needs to be upbeat for Tommy, and tries on a smile, but it feels false. Shannon's always been the actress in the family. Across the room, lines of kids feed the vending machines, a constant clatter of change dropping through slots, the clunk of treats falling. It's almost one; no wonder Casey's hungry.

Visiting hours end at three-thirty. They've already wasted half the day.

And still she waits. She takes the bottle from Casey, saving it for later, then burps him on her shoulder, glad to have something to do. She feels stupid, the only one alone in the whole room. She couldn't have been more than five minutes behind the tall woman, now sharing a vending-machine hamburger with her man. Patty wants to go back and ask the nice guard if something's happened, but the door's closed and she doesn't dare approach anyone in here. Even if she's allowed, she doesn't want to stand up and call attention to herself.

He'll come. It's not like he could go anywhere.

As the minutes tick by, her imagination adds to her fears. She can't help it, she sees him being beaten, sees him bandaged and unconscious in the infirmary. She squeezes Casey tighter to make it go away.

And then, perversely, she thinks that if he doesn't come, she won't have to tell him about selling the car. She won't have to admit that she's broke and has to move in with her mother. She won't have to confess that when she called Mr. Mallon, he said they'd had to cut back, so no, he was sorry, but in all fairness they couldn't hold a spot open for her.

In the far corner by the door, a family's singing "Happy Birthday to You." Other voices join in, but softly, as if afraid they might wake someone. Patty listens for the name, and then can't pick it out. Tommy's birthday's in October, she doesn't know what day of the week it is this year.

"Come on," she says.

Every time she's tempted to blame him, she realizes the slowness is deliberate on the part of the guards and not his fault—that they hassle her not because of anything he's done but just because they can.

She rubs her face—her nose is oily, her hair's a wreck, but it's too late to fix it. She licks her lips, thinking of kissing him (no prolonged embracing), and before they're dry again she sees the door closest to her open and there he is in the same green outfit as everyone else, a guard dogging him.

He waves, and she has to stop herself from rising and running to him. She's still not used to the short hair, a reminder of the trial. All week she's promised herself she wouldn't cry, afraid it would make him feel bad, and now she sneaks a shallow breath to quell the tears she feels coming. He shows his ID to a guard at a desk and walks up the aisle to where she stands.

She kisses him, takes him in her arms and squeezes him as hard as she can, as if to leave her imprint on his body. She holds him, feeling his back as if to make sure nothing's missing. They break and take their separate chairs, never letting go of each other's hands. She turns Casey toward Tommy to show him how big he's gotten. Tommy smiles, wagging a finger at him.

"How are you doing?" he asks.

She laughs—it's such a huge question.

"I'm all right," Patty says. "Just tell me you're okay."

"I'm okay."

"You mean it?"

"It's boring. It's like the army. You have to do whatever they tell you."

"But you're okay."

"Hey," he says, "would I lie?"

"Do you have a reason to?"

"Not anymore," he says.

"Did you have lunch yet?" she asks. "I brought change."

The rule is that prisoners can't put money in the machines, so she leaves him with Casey and braves the lines for a pair of fish sandwiches and two Cokes in flimsy cups. When she gets back, Casey is burbling at him, the two of them having their own conversation.

"I wish you didn't look so good," he says.

"No, I'm fat," Patty insists, pinching her hip.

"You look great to me."

"That's just 'cause you're not getting any."

The sandwiches are cardboard, but they laugh at it. As they chew through the dry bites, sipping their melting Cokes, he lists all the dishes of hers he misses. She wouldn't believe how bad the food is here, the same crap over and over—oatmeal and cabbage soup and liver, cherry Kool-Aid. Patty listens intently, watching his face, soaking him in. He seems all right, though she knows he's putting up a front. They're both trying. If he can survive in here, she can find a way to get by on the outside. All week she's waited for this, and now she lets herself fall into him, the lost morning, like her normal worries, forgotten. Around them the guards are watching, but she no longer sees them. Even Casey fades a little, she's concentrating so hard on Tommy. She knows it's a trick, but, leaning forward and holding hands across the table as if this is a candlelit dinner, Patty can almost pretend they're the only two people in the world.

BACKROADS

THOSE FIRST MONTHS, THE DRIVE HOME MAKES HER SICK, A HEAD-ache clamped down like a helmet, her bowels backing up into her stomach. The gold and green countryside doesn't care, the cows and fields shimmering in the heat, the families picnicking at rest areas. Slipping invisible between the other cars, she feels conspicuous, singled out, when there's no reason. For all they know she could be coming from anywhere.

She has the schedule down now. She gets up early to beat the crowd, her mother waving them away from the porch. She's done experimenting and sticks to the quickest route up and back, passing through the same one-stoplight towns and shadowed valleys until she knows every church and farm stand and convenience mart. If she lived down one of these dusty roads, things would be different, she thinks, but it's not a real wish, just a what-if. She shouldn't be dreaming, and keeps her speed up, watching for cops. She needs to get home and get ready for the coming week. Between work and visiting him, she barely has time to do her food shopping.

And then Monday she's up at six and has to say goodbye to Casey—the hardest part of her new job. Russ has gotten her onto his truck (Russ has done everything for them, he's the only one of Tommy's friends who's stuck by them; the rumor is that Gary and Donna are gone, their emptied apartment for rent). She used to bust Tommy's chops about how easy he had it—long coffee breaks and catnaps, knocking off early; now, standing for hours in the sun in her hardhat and reflective vest with a heavy lollipop sign while the guys patch asphalt, she thinks she's earning her paycheck. Hell, summer's easy, they tell her. Wait'll they do the leaves. And winter, forget it. Part of it's just them giving her shit, she understands, being new, but every night she's tired and every morning wakes up aching. Some days she doesn't think she can go on, but shows up and punches in with the rest of them anyway. She makes sure she never shirks, never complains, and still, she knows some of them will never give her respect just because she's a woman. She doesn't care, as long as they don't hit on her.

Being outside is good, and working with her body, sweating her skin clean. In no time she's lost the baby weight and grown muscles, and she's tan. Sometimes she can feel drivers scoping her out as the line files by. It's a feeling she doesn't know what to do with, just as she doesn't know what to do with the heat she feels after seeing Tommy. It's been five months since she had Casey, and her dreams have turned animal.

She gets paid on Friday. The guys hit the Iroquois and bug her to come along. Russ will be there, but still, it doesn't feel right. Her mother's waiting with Casey, and tomorrow she has to be up at five to be first in line.

The weeks fly by like this, her bank balance inching above a thousand, a figure she's secretly proud of, admiring the blue and red punched numbers in her passbook as if they have some magic power.

Her mother's been incredible, watching Casey all day, doing laundry. After dinner, they sit in the cool backyard as the fireflies rise out of the tall grass. When the mosquitoes get too bad, they leave the lawn chairs there and go inside. Her mother reads by the radio while Patty has a glass of beer. Her father watches her watching TV. After Eileen's, it seems quiet, but Patty doesn't mind. The bathroom smells of Comet, and she feels welcome in her old bed, as if it remembers her. In the basement, piled high, the musty contents of the self-storage lurk in a corner, Tommy's recliner buried under boxes.

Friday nights, Patty goes to bed early so she can wake up with the sun; in the morning her mother slips her robe on and starts a pot of coffee. They don't discuss how he's doing, and Patty would never ask if she wants to come along. Her mother can't acknowledge that after everything Tommy is still at the center of her life.

"I can't tell you what to do," she says. "If you want me to tell you how I feel about the whole situation, I'll tell you, but you're probably not going to like what I have to say."

"I already know how you feel."

"Then you know why I feel that way, or you should."

"I do," Patty says.

"There's nothing I can do for him. I know that sounds cruel, but it's true. I'm worried about *you* now. You're the one who has to pick up the pieces, and I know from experience how hard that can be, so I'm going to do everything I can to help you. But I'm not going to lie and say I'm happy about it."

"You don't have to *lie*," Patty says, twisting the word. "Just don't pretend like he doesn't exist."

It *is* cruel of her mother, writing Tommy off and then saying she's doing it for her sake. It wouldn't bother Patty so much if she didn't find herself drifting through the weeks, catching herself making a sandwich for her lunch pail or mindlessly waiting in line at the bank as if everything's fine, as if she's succeeded in forgetting that side of her life.

Because as much as she needs to see him, she's come to dread the drive to Auburn. She feels sick now even before she leaves, sometimes the night before, her stomach gnawing on itself. Tommy's losing weight; his gums bleed. The visit's always too short, ruined by their shared knowledge that it can't last. Unfairly, she antici- pates the hours of letdown after she passes her stamped hand un- der the black light, and the guilt she'll feel for leaving him there. Later, in the truck, she doesn't speak, as if a careless word might break the delicate spell that holds them together. It's only when she clears the southern tip of the lake—twenty miles, a suitable period of mourning—that she turns on the radio and discovers, once again, that the rest of the world is still there.

PRECIOUS MEMORIES

ONE PRETTY DAY IN SEPTEMBER WHEN THEY'RE REPLACING A stretch of guardrail down along the river on 17C, Casey rolls over on his own. "You should have seen him," her mother gushes. He babbles now, yammering at them, and she's afraid she'll miss his first word.

Telling Tommy is hard. She wants him to care but not be hurt.

"Wow," he says, proud. "He'll be walking pretty soon."

Patty doesn't say it, but thinks of all the things he'll miss, the Christmases and birthdays. The appeal process hasn't even started yet. She remembers the days she missed her father most—her graduation, her wedding—times she felt abandoned, even though she knew it wasn't his fault.

At home she takes pictures of Casey asleep in his crib, Casey in his high chair, Casey shaking his key ring. She has her mother take shots of them together in the backyard and picks the best to show Tommy, and then the guards won't let her bring them in unless they're wrapped like a package. What's the difference, she wants to say, but swallows it and comes back the next weekend and fills out the forms. The guards X-ray the package before tearing it apart. They're sorry, but inmates are only allowed a total of ten photographs in their cell at any time, those are the rules. What she needs to do is find out how many her husband already has, then wrap a couple from this stack and resubmit them next week, because, as the sign behind them says, visitors can only leave one package per visit and she's already had hers. And while she knows it's pointless to argue, that it's exactly the reaction they want from her, something they'll joke about later in the break room, Patty launches a volley of curses at them that would make his hockey buddies proud (all the while patting Casey and swaying)—and loses the visit.

"I'm sorry but they were being assholes," she tells Tommy during their regular call, and he agrees. She shouldn't have to take their shit.

He does, and she wonders if he'll get in trouble just for saying this (because they're always listening). She worries that he'll end up paying for her big mouth. The guards have all the power, and they're like cops, they stick together.

The week creeps by. It seems like she hasn't seen him in months. She has the picture of him from last summer on her old bureau facing Casey's crib, and says good night to him before bed, but that's the only reminder of Tommy in the whole house. At work, the guys who know him occasionally mention his name, but mostly they steer clear. Russ is the only one who asks how he's doing, and after a while even that feels more polite than anything. Perry and Shawn haven't bothered to call in months. It's as if he died, as if he never existed.

Sunday she brings him six pictures and prepays to do the click-click, a concession the prison runs. For twenty bucks, another prisoner supervised by a guard takes ten Polaroids of the three of them together, a sort of family portrait. They stand in front of a mural celebrating Auburn history, smiling like pioneers.

The first one turns out the best. It's not very big, and the flash makes his face look pasty, but Patty finds a nice frame for it at the Craft Barn. With the edges covered up, you can barely tell it's a Polaroid. She has to ask her mother if she can set it on top of the TV with her father. For an instant her mother hesitates, as if she has to think, and Patty wants to take the question back.

"Of course," her mother says, and arranges them so they're as far apart as possible.

It's only a couple of days later, stoned and watching Johnny Carson with the sound down low so she doesn't wake anyone up, that Patty realizes how depressing it must be for her mother to have to constantly see the two biggest things that went wrong in her life. And then Patty laughs. She's so stupid. It's not just her mother. It's true for her too.

GHOSTS

∎

AS HALLOWEEN PASSES (POWERWASHING YOLK OFF THE MIDDLE school windows) and the election (rolling the voting machines through town hall) and the last big leaf pickup and the crew starts marking fire hydrants and guardrails for the snowplows, Patty senses the date looming ahead, lying in wait.

She can't believe it's only been a year. She has no reason to go by their old place, but sometimes when the crew's bombing along Frost Hollow Road she'll watch the sign for Spaulding Hill float by and wonder what the house looks like. Probably the same, Mr. McChesney's so cheap. Patty just wants to confirm that it's still there. Their years in that house seem like a kind of paradise; at the time it just felt normal, regular everyday life, no better or worse than anyone else's. She wishes she could go back and enjoy it for what it was, but that could apply to so many things now. And what was it, really? When did he start lying to her about everything?

A week before Thanksgiving the crew is stopped at the Citgo for their morning smokes and coffees when Patty's Dart pulls up to the light. She's never seen the older woman who's driving. She must be the handyman's wife, because it's hers, Patty recognizes the Firestone redlines Tommy bought for her. Standing there, caught for a moment in the open, she has the strange sensation that she and the woman have magically changed places, that she's been lifted out of her life, transported from behind the wheel into someone else's watching body, and then the light turns and the Dart accelerates away. It's Wednesday and they have to stake rolls of snow fence around the softball fields.

Tommy calls that night. When she tries to explain how she felt, he tells her she should have sold the truck.

"That's not what I'm talking about!" she says, and then feels bad. It's hard to argue with him when she's responsible for his happiness. He needs money for cigarettes, and she promises she'll bring a money order on Sunday. And though he must know—really, shouldn't he?—neither of them mentions that it will be a year come Friday.

After her mother goes to bed and she gets Casey down, Patty goes out on the back porch to get high before Johnny comes on and stands there holding herself in the starry cold and thinks of Elsie Wagner teaching her to swim—the chlorine smell and the little, different-colored tiles at her feet like a crossword puzzle, the lanes roped off with blue and white floats like strung beads. Elsie will remember, Patty thinks. Elsie will know exactly what day it is.

BICENTENNIAL MINUTES

THE FIRST YEAR HAS TO BE THE WORST—AT LEAST SHE HOPES SO. She hasn't heard from Albany in a long time, but now she expects the system to take forever. Having Casey helps. When she gets frustrated or depressed, he lets her concentrate on things like creamed turkey and strained peas.

She survives Thanksgiving by keeping busy, helping her mother in the kitchen. Christmas, the two of them drive down to Shannon's together, silent for miles like two old widow ladies, Casey asleep in the backseat. New Year's Eve she watches Dick Clark by herself, clicking it off right after the ball drops, then wakes up early and works twelve hours of double time.

The holidays with Tommy feel like regular visits, just more crowded, whole families coming up from the city, the parking lot overflowing into the side streets. Like last year, Tommy asks her what she wants, and Christmas morning she's not surprised to find a present waiting with the paper on the welcome mat. She thanks Russ the next day, not mentioning how expensive the stroller must have been. They owe him so much already.

January the snows come, knee deep, followed by frostbite windchills, and she realizes the guys weren't kidding about the job. Every day they're digging out fire hydrants and breaking ice that's formed over storm drains, sweating inside the hoods of their heavy jackets. Russ blasts the truck's heater to warm their feet but only melts the snow stuck to their pants, soaking the cuffs. Patty keeps a tin of bag balm in a pocket, rubbing it into her fingers between jobs so her skin won't crack. She offers it to the rest of the crew, telling them it's an old farmer's trick. They're all too macho to borrow it until Russ says he'll give it a try; then they all dig in.

The Steelers are in the Super Bowl again. It pisses Tommy off—with O. J. hurt, the Bills didn't even make the playoffs. Every other commercial is a bicentennial minute, famous actors backed by heroic music telling her how much freedom and equality Americans have. Worse, at halftime Up With People does a fruity tribute: Two Hundred Years and Still a Baby. For the finale they recite the Pledge of Allegiance, hands on hearts. "With liberty and justice for all," the corny voice echoes, and the Orange Bowl blooms with flags, balloons, fireworks. At least the Steelers are losing, but then they come back late and Patty turns it off so she doesn't have to watch another celebration.

CURRENT EVENTS

■

THAT SPRING EILEEN BREAKS HER ARM—NOT PLAYING SOFTBALL BUT the first day of trout season, slipping on a rock, Cy driving her to the hospital in his waders. It's her right arm. After work, Patty delivers casseroles her mother has put together, taking the previous day's dish back with her on the passenger seat. Casey says "Ga-ga" for Grandma. He stands and walks early, before his birthday. Patty witnesses his first step through her viewfinder, and his fistfuls of cake, clicking away so Tommy can be there. Casey falls hard against the coffee table and gives himself a black eye she feels terrible about. Soon he's tooling around the house and they have to put up gates. Easter it snows, covering the plastic eggs dotting the backyard. The snow turns to rain and the river rises. For a week Russ has them sandbagging the levee below the speedway. When the weather turns, her mother finally gives in and has a new roof put on the garage, fretting the whole time over the cost. The crew cuts and rakes all the different Little League fields around town; at night Patty finds grass in her pockets. Her class has its tenth reunion, which she skips, watching TV all evening, trying not to imagine the gossip. In Arizona three inmates are killed in a riot; the pictures on the news of smashed windows and overturned desks make it look like the prisoners went wild, making their demands for better conditions look ridiculous. As June approaches, and her memories of the trial, she reads in the paper that Mr. Ayres has died. Unexpectedly, at home. Patty has nothing against him, so why does she feel guilty? She visits, she writes, she accepts Tommy's collect calls. She pays her ridiculous phone bills and refills his account when it gets down. She teaches Casey to say "Da-da" into the receiver. After Randy and Kyra both get disappointing report cards, Shannon and Marshall decide this is their last year in public school. A gray cat her mother's never seen before prowls the yard for a week and then vanishes. There's a bad accident on the Southern Tier: a trucker has a seizure at the wheel and takes out a family from New Jersey in a van. The bicentennial falls on a Sunday, and Eileen and Cy convince Patty to go with them to the demolition derby at the county fair. She sits there in the stands, afraid to go down and get something at the snack bar in case someone recognizes her. It's stupid, but she imagines Elsie Wagner in her fancy clothes pointing her out in line and screaming things. The winner is a guy Cy knows from a band he used to be in. They meet him in gasoline alley and end up at the Iroquois, Eileen daring anyone to armwrestle her now that she has the cast off. Patty wants to go home but they've got the only car. The guy's name is Trace. He's from Candor, where Cy grew up, and introduces himself like he has no idea who she is. She's wearing her ring, but just by the way he holds on to her eyes and then listens with his head tipped to hear better, she knows he's interested. It's been so long that Patty's flustered—as if she's interested too—and after two beers she tells Eileen she has to go. Later, alone, she's mad at herself for even having those thoughts, and snips them out cleanly. When Eileen asks if she wants to go out again the next Friday, she says she's got to get up early to visit Tommy, and Eileen doesn't push it. For her birthday, Russ drops off a boombox from Tommy and a tape of the Stones' latest album with her new favorite song, "Angie," which she plays late at night, smoking on the back porch. The rest of the summer is patching potholes and oiling backroads, shoveling up skunks. It's bad hot; they go through two coolers a day, refilling it at lunch, plunking in thick disks of ice. She takes cold showers and shakes on baby powder. She plays pat-a-cake with Casey and keeps an eye on her savings and forgets the way Trace looked at her. She gets her hair cut, then doesn't like it, and when she tries to fix it herself she just messes it up worse. Casey's teething and doesn't want to sleep in his crib; he throws his blanky out and stands there wailing, rattling the bars. "Let him cry," her mother says, because she thinks Patty spoils him. Every night it's like this, and she's tired, she needs her sleep. He spits out his whipped beets in a pink mound, tosses his gnawed zwieback on the floor. When she turns off his cartoons because it's his bedtime, he pulls away from her, falls to the carpet and wails, kicking. She describes his tantrums to Tommy, but by then it's too late; she needs the help right when it's happening. August the softball leagues finish their seasons. Eileen knocks in six runs in a playoff game and her name's in the paper, making Patty wonder—for an instant—if she should change hers back. The days are hazy, thunderstorms rolling in after dinner. Her mother's big window fan finally dies, and they make a trip to Sears to replace it, her mother upset that they no longer carry the same model. One lunchtime while Patty's waiting in the truck, she sees Trace come out of the Dandy Mart wearing his Hilltop Collision uniform, but she's across the street and he doesn't see her. Another groundhog takes up residence under the shed in the garden, feasting on her mother's beans and summer squash, chewing holes in her tomatoes so they go black and soft and rotten. Russ lends Patty a trap from animal control, a spring-loaded cage that's supposed to be painless, but every day when she checks it, it's empty. The more Patty looks at the cage, the more she sees Tommy in his cell. She knows it's silly, but she hopes the groundhog gets away. One warm night after supper she goes out to check on the trap and before she's off the porch she smells the freshest skunk she's ever smelled. It's in the trap instead of the groundhog, hissing and lifting its tail. She can't get close enough to do anything, and ends up calling animal control. "What's going to happen to it?" she asks—a dumb question. She shouldn't care; for all she knows it has rabies. Casey builds towers of soft blocks and knocks them down. "Ka!" he says, clapping. Late one night, after Johnny signs off and they play the Star-Spangled Banner, her boombox eats Tommy's birthday tape. Mick's voice wavers in her headphones, drops an octave, warbles, then gives way to a cellophane crackling before she can reach over from her bed and find the stop button. The tape is wound around the rollers and she has to rip it free. She performs surgery with a razor blade, scotch taping the ends together, but knows from experience it won't last. She has Eileen dub her a copy, but it comes out muddy, so she just buys another one, a belated birthday present to herself. And what does *he* want for his birthday? It's not that far off. "French-fried mushrooms," he tells her. "Like we used to get at Dairy Queen." And what would it cost her, to have them herself—ninety-nine cents? She can't even promise him that. Summer's almost over, the Southern Tier a parade of Winnebagos and boat trailers. The crew repaints the school crosswalks and sand-blasts the graffiti off the walls. Patty's hands tingle from the wand; hours later she still feels pins and needles and is clumsy answering the phone. The operator has a collect call from Tommy. It's only Tuesday. Yes, she'll accept, she says, afraid something's happened. It has, Tommy explains. He's gotten a letter from the appellate court in Albany. They'll appoint a lawyer to the case soon. "That's great," she says, because it's the best they could ask for, but for some reason Patty isn't as happy as she should be. "What is soon?" she asks.

THE HAND

IT TAKES THE COURT NINE MONTHS TO APPOINT A LAWYER. BY THEN Casey is riding a tricycle and filling pages with crayoned tornadoes. Everything official goes through Tommy, so she doesn't know until he reads her the letter over the phone. The lawyer wants to review the complete transcript before he sits down with him. The state charges a dollar a copy, and it's 1,600 pages long.

Whenever she calls the new lawyer she gets a machine, and then when she does catch him in, he talks to her like she's an idiot. To Patty, the appeal seems simple: go through the evidence again, bring up the money and the missing guns, then put Gary on the stand and show that he's lying.

"There are two problems with that," the lawyer says. "First, is there anything that connects the money to the guns? And second, even if we can establish a connection, what impact does it have on the specific event in question? What *I'd* like to look at is what kind of precedent there is here in terms of your husband's *legal* culpability. Let's say for the sake of argument that he does push her down and she hits her head. How, legally, does that translate into murder in the second degree, and how is it that in a case with minimal physical evidence he receives the maximum sentence?"

"He didn't *do* it," Patty says.

"That very well may be," the lawyer says. "But I can't prove it. I've got to play the hand I've been dealt."

She can pay for an investigator, he says, but they're expensive. How expensive?

The number seems doable, but she's already started paying off the transcript in installments, like a car. When she sits down with her bankbook she sees she can only afford three weeks. The lawyer says they'd need someone working on it full-time for four or five months to turn up anything worthwhile. Immediately Patty thinks of her mother, and the value of the house, an untapped treasure.

At dinner, over tuna noodle casserole, she carefully explains the situation, sticking to the script she's worked on all day.

"How much?" is her mother's first question—asked matter-of-factly, as if she's interested.

"Two-fifty a week, plus expenses."

"So how much is that total?"

Patty can't lie. "Just over five thousand dollars."

"Before expenses."

"Before expenses."

Her mother shakes her head, pushing her noodles around. "It's too much."

Fork in hand, Patty waits for her to say something else, to go beyond her first offer so they can negotiate.

Her mother senses her waiting and looks up. She sighs and glances away as if she's disappointed with Patty, tired of being put in this position again. "I wish you could see what you're doing."

"What am I doing?" Patty comes back, because she's ready to

fight now, to defend Tommy against her one more time—forever, if necessary.

But the face her mother gives her is open and tender, and her voice is soft. "You're breaking my heart."

THE WINNER'S CIRCLE

IN THE MEANTIME, TRACE DOESN'T GO AWAY. SHE SEES HIM DRIVING around town, passing the other way in the Hilltop's flatbed wrecker as they head out to cut brush or weedwhack ditches. Every time they stop in to the Dandy Mart for lunch she scans the lot, then stays in the truck anyway, as if he might ambush her.

That summer he's racing midget cars, little winged bombs that slide sideways through the turns, throwing rooster tails of dirt. He's in the paper every week, winning or coming in second. Once there's even a picture of him kneeling with a tall trophy by his car, a Hoosier baseball cap replacing his helmet. Patty lingers over his bandito mustache, a lot like Tommy's. Number 17, Tracy Van Deusen. Owego's so small, he has to be related to the farm equipment people. She's been going by Van Deusen's New Holland since she was a little girl, impressed with the rows of red tractors and wagons and combines. The connection makes him seem less of a stranger, almost a neighbor, the reckless boy-next-door.

It's just a crush, she thinks, stupid and high schoolish.

But she's nearly thirty. She doesn't need a fantasy. She already has enough of Tommy, wearing his chamois-soft T-shirts to bed and dreaming he's there with her, summoning his hands when she gives in to hers. She has Tommy, she has Casey. She shouldn't be thinking of anyone else.

He's got a girlfriend anyway, and a pretty one—Kristi Coughlan, the second youngest of the six Coughlan girls, each of them a Dairy Princess. She works the drive-thru at the bank downtown, long straight hair, dresses nice. Patty's almost glad. Leaving aside the fact that she's married, she's never been the kind to go after someone else's guy.

It's silly. She's only really talked to him once, in a bar, after a couple of beers. He probably doesn't even remember her name.

And then one hot day while she's out stopping traffic on Lisle Road, she sees the flatbed waiting in line, five cars back. She's been sweating, splashing cups of water from the cooler on her face so it runs down her front. She's hoping it's not him. Her hair's stuffed under her hardhat and she's wearing mirrored shades and the usual resurfacing getup—safety vest over a plain gray T-shirt, cruddy jeans and workboots. Maybe he won't see through the disguise. She pictures pretty Kristi Coughlan counting out crisp twenties behind her air-conditioned window and thinks it doesn't matter.

At the other end, Glenn raises his arm and spins his sign so she can read SLOW, and she turns hers. The first car rolls by, an older guy inside ignoring her, then a woman in a Thunderbird, a family in a wagon. As the flatbed grows closer, Patty can see it's him, wearing the same cap he had in the winner's circle, and mirrored shades like hers. They could pass each other anonymously, face to face, like spies. She's ready for it as the flatbed rumbles up, and pinches her lips together. She keeps the SLOW sign showing, figuring she'll let him go and then a few more for insurance before stopping them.

As he nears, he smiles and waves—a polite thanks she's fielded a million times with a straight face—but this time she can't stop from automatically waving back. Just a hey, an innocent flip of a hand acknowledging his, and the truck rattles past. No one else sees it, so no one rides her. She tells herself it means nothing. So why, that night, does she replay it again and again? Why does she wonder if Eileen and Cy are going to the races on Friday?

HER OWN SHADOW

OF COURSE THEY AREN'T, AND EVEN IF THEY WERE, PATTY WOULD find a way to beg off. Saturday is visiting day.

Sunday is visiting day.

Saturday is visiting day.

They've run out of things to talk about, so they talk about Russ riding his Harley all the way out to Sturgis in the ninety-degree heat. They talk about her mother thinking about putting in central air and how much that would cost. They talk about Shannon going back to school in the fall (and how much that must cost).

She's eaten everything in the machines except the egg salad, leery of bad mayonnaise. By the end of the afternoon they're scavenging the ballooned bag of microwave popcorn, sucking the tough kernels.

After a good visit, she misses him; after a bad visit, she feels him slipping away. She goes down and visits the bulb-lit corner of the basement every once in a while, folding back the dropcloth and rubbing the naugahyde arm of his recliner and the nicked varnish of the coffee table, remembering whole fall weekends spent watching football, the smell of dinner filling the house like lamplight. She has to duck her own shadow to see. It's like looking at old pictures of them; she gets stuck, and yet when she finally covers up the pile again, that time seems further away than ever.

PRESENT

THE NEW LAWYER THINKS THEY HAVE GROUNDS FOR INSUFFICIENT counsel. And honestly, it's the only way he can see. He's combed through the transcript and there's nothing out of order there. With no new evidence to introduce, they have to throw doubt on the process. It's simple negligence. Tommy's lawyer should have advised him to take whatever plea the DA was offering.

"He did," Patty says.

"He should have been more forceful. No offense, but you had no clue what you were walking into. He's a professional. He should have made you listen to reason."

Patty agrees but doesn't see why that would overturn the verdict. She still wants Gary to tell the truth.

Tommy's not happy either, but it took so long to get this guy that he doesn't want to go back and start all over again. Patty's not sure. If this one doesn't work, can they appeal again?

In a naked effort to cheer her up, her mother makes her favorite, lemon meringue pie. The jellied sweetness and lard-puffed crust only make Patty focus harder on the reason they're having it, but she forks hers up, nodding at how good it is. For a week the pie sits in the fridge, stiffening. Her mother's not wild about lemon, so Patty has to get rid of it piece by piece, sneaking them down the disposal while Johnny's on.

At work she doesn't mention anything. If Russ wants to talk about Tommy, they do it in his office, not in the truck, and even there she keeps things on the surface. Turnover's been high this fall—Glenn's moved to Elmira—and half the crew is new. After Russ, she's got the most seniority (not that it makes a difference in her paycheck). She doesn't tell the new guys on her truck about her husband, lets them think he's waiting for her at home. They're younger, best friends right out of high school, jokers who don't look beyond the next weekend. The ring and her new crow's-feet are enough to keep them at bay.

As her birthday nears, she feels like giving up. Part of it is turning thirty, a number she never worried about before. She can't stay at this job and live in her mother's house forever. She's jealous of Shannon, going back to college to finish up her degree, and pictures herself walking across campus with an armful of textbooks. Where would she get the money? Anyway she hasn't been in class for twelve years, and wasn't very good at it then. Every morning she pores through the classifieds, inching a fingertip down the columns, but the only jobs she's qualified for are waitress and maybe line cook, and they pay less than she's making now.

During her birthday call, Tommy says that if the appeal doesn't go through he'd understand if she wanted to leave him and start over, an accusation that makes her cover her face and shake her head. She's never said anything about that to him or to anyone. She's barely allowed herself the idea, immediately vetoing it as a cowardly way out, Nixon flashing his victory signs and flying off in his helicopter. Does this mean *he's* quitting? She thinks it must be her fault, her negative attitude rubbing off on him. She tells him not to write off the appeal. Anything can happen. They're due for some good luck. But afterward, alone, she knows it's a lie.

A KIND OF HOLIDAY

RACING SEASON IS OVER, BUT SHE SEES TRACE EVERYWHERE—OWEGO'S not that big. Only briefly, from a distance, a greedy surveillance. He always seems to be in a hurry, as if he can't slow down. He's familiar to her now, his Hilltop uniform, his tight stride across the Dandy Mart lot, the way he swings the cardboard box of subs and sodas up into the cab of the flatbed and climbs in after it. She waits to see him, wakes up wondering if today they'll finally meet.

"I think I'm getting a crush on you," she might say, like it's a problem they could work out together. Because it can't be love. She doesn't know him at all, only that she gets excited when she spies on him, that he makes her nervous and unsure and dreamy as a teenager. How does love start? Was it like this at the beginning with Tommy, a sudden, dumb attraction?

The best they could hope for would be secret meetings at his place, the pain of coming together and then being apart, the illogical jealousy, the complicated lies (her mother watching Casey while Patty's in Trace's bed, resting slit-eyed with pleasure), yet when she looks at Trace the rest of the world disappears and she's herself again, a woman with the usual desires.

Maybe all she wants is the intrigue. She has to be so responsible in everything else, maybe she feels she deserves this fling as a reward, a kind of holiday from her other life. That it's all in her mind makes it safe. If she never acts on her feelings, she never has to give up her fantasy. It's the best explanation, because otherwise none of it makes sense. She doesn't want to hurt Tommy or have people around town talk about her that way. She's practical, despite what her mother might say. She likes to think she'd never sacrifice what she has for something as undependable as romance. There are so many other things she really needs.

TIN MAN

LIKE EVERY YEAR, THE SUNDAY AFTER THANKSGIVING CHANNEL 5 shows *The Wizard of Oz.* Casey watches for about ten seconds before he totters off to play with his gas station. Her mother's seen it too many times to be interested and takes her magazine into the living room, leaving Patty to follow the four misfits as they make their way to Emerald City.

She wonders if Tommy's watching, if the other guys voted for it over *The Six Million Dollar Man.* From what he's told her, they like ragging on shows, laughing and talking back to the actors. She can't see them sitting still for a fairy tale.

Dorothy tosses the bucket of water and the Wicked Witch of the West melts into a puddle, guaranteeing their reward, but the Wizard turns out to be a fake. It must be her worry about the future, because this time Patty sees herself not just as Dorothy, as she has since she was a little girl, but as all of them. She already knows there's no place like home; that's not enough. She wishes she was smarter for Tommy about the legal stuff, and braver dealing with the system. She wishes her heart were pure.

BUTTERFINGERS

THE MESSAGE IS WAITING FOR HER WHEN SHE GETS HOME FROM hanging the bristly tinsel bells and reindeer and candy canes on the light poles downtown. Her mother took the call, jotting down the time and the number for Patty on the pad in the kitchen.

"What did he say?" Patty asks.

"He didn't say anything. He wants you to call him."

It's five-thirty. He's probably gone already, but she calls anyway, on the off chance he's working late. It could be good news. Usually she has to call him.

It barely rings twice.

"Mrs. Dickerson," he says. "I'm glad you caught me. Have you talked with your husband?"

"No."

"I was hoping he might have called you. That's all right." He stops and starts again. "Last week we submitted the brief and our supporting materials to the court."

Then why are you just telling me now, Patty wants to say.

"Considering what we had to work with, I think we did everything we could."

Again, she waits.

"Today I received word from the DA's office that someone there *has* been assigned to write an answering brief to ours."

"Okay," she nudges him.

"Mrs. Dickerson," he says, as if she doesn't understand, "the court has agreed to hear your husband's appeal."

He goes on, but, clutching the phone, Patty's remembering the first call that freezing night after the game. She reaches for the counter, rests against it like a tired swimmer using the edge of a pool. Tommy probably wasn't allowed to call her because he wasn't signed up for that time. Her shock turns to gratitude, then caution, the fear that they're only postponing a deeper disappointment.

Her mother's happy for her, and Eileen. Patty lets them know what the lawyer said about getting their hopes up, to show she understands how long the odds are. They already think she's being unrealistic. But that night when Tommy calls he plays down their chances, and she has to be encouraging. "You don't know," she says.

In bed, she allows herself a daydream of how it would be, the three of them together in their own place somewhere outside of town. She sees them in the backyard, a sunny day, Casey digging in his plastic turtle sandbox, her and Tommy watching from a picnic table. She knows it wouldn't be a perfect life, that they'd have the same problems everyone does, but there'd be good times too, times when all three of them would be happy just being together. Simple things like eating dinner or watching TV, waking up and making love, getting ready for work.

Deep down, she knows they won't win. And there's no one to tell, no one to share her secret with.

It's a weird side effect, but over the next couple of days she's clumsy, bumping into doorframes and fumbling away her keys as if she's pregnant. At work they ride her for spilling a coffee in the truck, and while she laughs with them, she's worried it might be more than just nerves. It's the holidays, but she's lost weight, and she hasn't slept well in months. A hit or two before bed seems to help, but makes waking up harder. Her first cigarette gets earlier and earlier. Driving in, she feels spacey, dazed, as if she might drop off behind the wheel and roll it in a ditch. And this is after good news, she thinks. She can't imagine how she'd be feeling if the court had turned them down.

For the rest of the world it's Christmas. The decorations are done, the spotlit crèche outside of town hall, the wreaths on the courthouse doors. The days are short, and driving through town after work she sees dark shapes stopped to peer in the display windows on Front Street. Miles into the countryside, houses rise out of the night like UFOs. One of them is her mother's, a colored string of lights blinking in the dogwood. Rolling up in the truck, Patty feels a nagging blankness instead of pleasure. It's only six and Casey will want to play, her mother will want to talk. She takes off her gloves and rubs her eyes, using the moment alone to recover, to change into the Patty they know.

RAISE PLOW

IT'S LATE FEBRUARY BEFORE THE DA'S BRIEF ARRIVES AND THEIR case is finally scheduled. It's really going to happen, the lawyer warns her. He understands she's been waiting a long time for this.

Patty knows he's getting at something but can't read him over the phone.

The whole thing only takes fifteen minutes, which Patty thinks is a joke, and then they won't hand down their decision for a month or two. He says there's no need for her to come to Albany. It seems wrong to Patty that she won't be there.

"What do you think you're going to do there?" Tommy asks with a shrug, and he's right. Her being at the trial didn't help, and she was pregnant then.

The morning the lawyer is supposed to argue their case, she goes to work like usual. It's supposed to snow, so they bolt on the hoppers, load them up with cinders and hang around the garage, breaking down old road signs and listening to the weather bureau on the scanner, waiting for Russ to make the call. Patty doesn't trust the radio. She keeps going to the sooty window behind the welding screens, as if Tommy might show up and surprise them all.

Everything she sees is charged—the dark sky, the leaning trees. A sparrow perches on the mirror of his truck, then flits away. WRONG WAY, one sign says; PASS WITH CARE, says another. She gouges a knuckle on a stripped screw and has to suck a thick drop of blood from it. Far off, the clock tower chimes. Later, from the hills, comes the crackle of guns; it's still deer season, one of his favorite times of the year, their freezer heaped with meat. She can't help but think of Gary and the rifles and the money, and how the court won't hear the whole story.

The front moves in from the west, following 17 across the Southern Tier. The weather bureau's forecasting three to six inches along the river, more in the hills. It's snowing in Elmira when Russ finally emerges from his office, wearing a scarf along with his Pirates cap and clapping like a coach. "Let's hustle up," he says, and assigns them their trucks. He gives her the north side of town because 17C is his and he doesn't trust the new guys with the railroad underpass. As she heads out, chains ringing, she goes by the Citgo and the darkened pizza places, the falling-down rowhouses, and realizes it's the same road she and Donna took to the county jail so long ago.

She patrols North Avenue back and forth from Depot Street all the way to the town line, doing the slippery bridge over the creek, then raising the plow and turning around in the bare lot of the boarded-up Dairy Queen, the yellow light wheeling out in front of her. Flakes dissolve against the windshield. The snow's wet, bending branches so they scratch at the cab, piling up on the stones of Evergreen Cemetery, icing the wipers, covering up her tracks. She's not surprised when Russ lets them know they're not stopping for lunch. The weather bureau's changed their prediction; now it's six to ten inches, possibly a foot at higher elevations. They're looking at some serious OT—news that brings whoops from the new guys. Patty should be happy—the money will help with Christmas—but now there's no way she'll get home in time to call the lawyer and find out how it went. She gets a sub at Lawler's Market and calls her mother from the pay phone outside to let her know she won't be home till late. She could ask for the lawyer's number, or have her mother call, but it's too early, and part of her doesn't want to ask how it went, not yet. The snow's falling harder, wetting her hair as she stands there. She climbs back in the cab and keeps going, scraping back and forth through town as the day darkens and the streetlights pop on, trying to fight the sky to a draw.

CONTINUING THROUGH

DAYBREAK

HER MOTHER'S STAYED UP FOR HER, WRAPPED IN AN AFGHAN, AS IF Patty's back in high school, sneaking in from a date. The lawyer called twice, she says, impressed. The second time he left a message: everything went fine; all they can do is wait.

"How did he sound?" Patty asks.

"I don't know. Normal."

Patty thinks of calling in sick tomorrow so she can talk to him, but knows it won't make a bit of difference. It's up to the judges now.

Casey's asleep, his blanky clutched to his cheek. Outside, the snow falls steadily, brushing like sand against the windows. Patty uses the bathroom and slips under the covers, her lower back clenched from driving all day. She's exhausted but can't sleep.

Lying there alone, the snow sifting down outside, Patty multiplies today and tonight by twenty years.

She closes her eyes, listening to the snow. She'll sleep, she thinks. The night will pass, if only because it has to.

THE LAST

THE COURT MAKES ITS DECISIONS AVAILABLE ON THURSDAYS, SO every Wednesday she goes to bed thinking tomorrow might be the day. When she visits Tommy, they talk about anything else. He walks Casey to the vending machines and holds him up so he can put the change in, and again Patty wonders how much of this Casey will remember. Maybe if Tommy gets out, these hours will fade away, be replaced by Saturdays fishing Owego Creek, or Sunday dinner at Grandma's. But Casey loves his cupcakes from the machine, he loves trying to slap Tommy's hands on the table before he pulls them away.

Patty still looks forward to holding Tommy's hands across the table. She still needs to look into his eyes to know he's all right. But since the lawyer told her the court was going to hear their appeal, Patty hasn't been able to stop thinking of what will happen if they get turned down. She sees herself driving back and forth to Auburn for the next twenty years, both of them growing old as Casey grows up and learns how fucked-up his parents' lives are. Tommy was being honest when he said he'd understand if she left him. Now she wonders if she could, if she had to for Casey's sake.

She goes to Eileen, stopping by after work. Eileen makes instant and listens without judging or giving advice. Patty knows she won't discuss it with their mother—maybe Cy, but he's safe, Eileen would never forgive him if he told anyone. As if to make things even, Eileen offers her a secret: they're getting married.

In June. Nothing fancy, just a small ceremony at their old church and a reception for friends at the Moose Lodge. Eileen's news makes her own problems seem worse. She's instantly jealous, wanting Eileen's life—unfair, after everything Eileen's been through, and just as quickly Patty's sorry for being so selfish.

"I want you to be my maid of honor."

"Matron of honor," Patty corrects her. "Of course I will. Let's see the ring."

Eileen holds her hand up to model a thin gold band. "We're saving for a diamond."

"When did all of this happen?"

"We've been living together for five years."

Patty wonders if she's pregnant.

"When are you going to tell Mom?"

"Soon."

"Can I be there? Please?"

"You're going to: Easter."

"Oh shit, that is going to be classic."

"Thanks."

They have to throw a shower for her and have a last girls' night out. Already Patty's trying to figure out who she has to call and how she'll fit this into her schedule. Shannon's not going to plan anything.

At home, Patty's surprised at how easy it is to keep her secret. She's gotten used to hiding her life inside, smuggling it through the day past Russ and her mother and Casey—past Tommy and Eileen, if Patty's being honest.

Thursday, nothing happens. And the next Thursday. And the next.

Easter comes early. In the backyard, the plastic eggs glow against the snow. Bending down to grab one, Casey spills his basket, and Patty gets a cute picture of him. He gobbles chocolate and then won't touch his ham. Cy's dressed up and uncomfortable, but holds Eileen's hand as she tells her mother over dessert. For proof, Eileen flashes the ring.

First thing, her mother looks to Patty.

"I knew the day would come," her mother says to the room at large, ever the actress. "The last of my girls." She gets up and hugs Eileen, and for the first time Patty can remember, her mother actually kisses Cy.

The shower turns out to be a pleasant distraction. There are only a couple of awkward pauses when Patty introduces herself over the phone. When she explains she's arranging a surprise party for Eileen, everyone forgets about her and wants to know what to bring. It's a relief to decide what kind of cake to have, to choose the lilac pattern for the paper plates.

Tommy's sorry he won't be there for the wedding. Patty doesn't say you never know, he might be able to make it after all. She wants to think it's a good sign the court is taking so long, but by now she's so turned around that she thinks it doesn't matter.

And then, when her mother calls the garage after lunch one Thursday to tell her the lawyer just called, Patty's not ready. After the years and months and weeks, after the long days and nights, the endless hours of waiting, she stalls before the phone in Russ's office, stealing a last few seconds of quiet before she dials the number and learns what she knew all along.

MAID OF HONOR

∎

SPRING, THE BUSY TIME, IS OVER. THEY'RE DONE WASHING THE sand from the roads with the sweepers and lumbering water trucks. They're done getting the ballfields in shape and painting the gazebo on the courthouse square, done spreading bark mulch on the traffic islands and turning on the water fountains in the town parks. It's June, and while school isn't out yet, it feels like the middle of August. Like every summer, they patch the roads, shoveling hot asphalt into the potholes. Patty drives the mini-steamroller, wearing an old golf hat of her father's to keep off the sun. The sweatband is leather, blackened and cracked over the years; it smells like the inside of Eileen's softball glove and leaves a gritty streak across her forehead. The steamroller vibrates under her, an oversized motorcycle. When she climbs down at the end of the day, her body's still shaking inside her skin. But better than flagging traffic. She'd go crazy if she had to stand there all day again, nothing to concentrate on but her own thoughts.

It's racing season, and every day on the way home she drives by a black and blaze-orange billboard advertising that fact. Sometimes she hates Trace for being so close. They've seen each other in passing—once twice in one day. He smiled, said "Got you again." The young guys on the truck gave her shit, but not Russ. When she imagines spending time with Trace she wonders if Russ would tell Tommy anything.

There's a reason for her worry. Trace is going to be an usher. As the matron of honor, Patty's going to be matched up with the best man, but she won't be able to avoid him at the reception. They'll be drinking and dancing, and everyone will be watching. If they disappeared—say they went to the bathroom at the same time, just by coincidence—she knows people would talk.

And still, she thinks of sneaking out with him, using the noise and confusion as a screen. Her mother's shelled out for the Parkview instead of the Moose. At first Patty minded because it's a block from the courthouse, but she's fine with it now. She imagines her and Trace slipping across Front Street and disappearing into the shadows of the trees, finding their way by moonlight down to the river, just walking and talking, their glasses empty. They wouldn't have to do anything special, they could just watch the cars going over the bridge. Maybe if it was cool out he'd drape his jacket over her shoulders, the satin slippery on her skin.

It's silly. He'll be with Kristi Coughlan, and—guaranteed—she'll be wearing something sexier than her robin's egg bridesmaid's dress.

Shannon's offered Kyra as a babysitter; she's thirteen, just old enough. Tommy says to have a good time and sleep late Sunday and not worry about him. She protests, promising she'll come Sunday afternoon. He's been down since the court denied their appeal, they both have, but Patty doesn't know what else she can do. It's not like she's missing the visit on purpose; it's just bad timing.

She's checked with Prisoners' Legal Services. They can ask the lawyer to go even higher and ask the court of appeals if it will hear the case. The lawyer's not sure it's worthwhile. "If there was something of constitutional interest, I'd say let's go for it," he says, "but they're not going to want to mess around with an insufficient counsel claim."

"What's it going to hurt to try," Patty asks, and feels—as she always feels, dealing with the state—that she's being made to beg. By the time she's done with him, he agrees to do it, except now he's convinced her it won't work.

It's hard, in the middle of all this, to feel as happy for Eileen as she really is. She finds the perfect gift at the mall—a big new microwave with a carousel like Eileen's always talking about—and splurges. She buys too much beer for the shower and then has to encourage Eileen's friends to drink it up. Most of her softball team is there, so they do, toasting her with dirty jokes and then solemnly promising to always keep a spot in the lineup for her. Patty's saving her big speech for the reception, but stands at the dining room table and raises a bottle to Eileen, saying what she can't say tomorrow when Shannon's there: that she's always been her favorite sister. Everyone laughs and claps as Eileen staggers over and throws her arms around her and the flashbulbs pop. But then, when all the cars out front are gone and Eileen's helping her clean up, Patty's not sure if she's relieved or insulted that no one asked after Tommy.

It's worse at the wedding, surrounded by so many couples. She's matched up with the best man, Woody, Cy's buddy from the nursery, a total Deadhead. He wears Blues Brothers shades to hide his pink eyes and giggles in the middle of the vows. In the receiving line outside, friends of her mother's from church kiss Patty's cheek and congratulate her, comment on her road crew tan (has she been on vacation?), then have nothing to say. "And Shannon's just graduated from college," her mother says over and over. To Patty, it sounds like bragging. Isn't this supposed to be Eileen's day?

Trace is there with Kristi, like she figured. He looks good in his tuxedo, clean-shaven, his long hair combed back like a rock star's mane. When they met on the lawn before the ceremony, he shook her hand and asked how she's been, but since they've been outside,

Kristi's attached herself, hanging on to one hand like she's afraid he'll run away. The two of them stand with the other ushers and bridesmaids on the sidewalk, passing a bag of rice, waiting for Eileen and Cy to run for the limo. Patty keeps an eye on him between greeting people, as if they're there together, Kristi the intruder.

The line dwindles to a last few old couples who didn't feel like standing, and then the photographer has the family pose before the doors (Shannon conspicuously not part of the bridal party with her grasshopper-green sundress and matching bag), and then just the bride and groom. Patty has her own camera out as the photographer finishes and ducks for cover as everyone lets loose, a hail of rice bouncing off Cy and Eileen and the side of the limo as they pull away.

There's a noticeable letdown after they're gone, a momentary confusion, people trying to find their rides. Trace is driving a shiny black Firebird with a gold phoenix on the hood. He opens the door for Kristi, dips to tuck in the train of her dress before closing it, as if they've been doing this forever. Woody's disappointed when Patty tells him to go ahead without her, as if he had plans for them. She finds Kyra and Randy entertaining Casey in a playground behind the church (she remembers the shiny, dented slide) and they all pile into her mother's ugly LeSabre.

Her mother drives dangerously slow, hunched over the wheel, giving way to other cars at stop signs. Patty's impatient with her for no reason and turns to the backseat. Kyra's trying to amuse Casey with a pop-up book. She's almost as tall as Patty now. Randy's a teenager, his forehead bumpy with zits. Even Casey seems huge to her, pudgy legs sticking out of his car seat; pretty soon he won't need it. It's just the wedding—a kind of milestone—but Patty feels like she's been standing still while time's passed her by.

"Didn't she look beautiful?" her mother says.

"She did," Patty agrees. She can't remember her mother ever talking this way about Eileen. It's just the emotion of the day. Patty doesn't remind her of all the names she's called Cy over the years ("a ne'er-do-well," "a no-goodnik," "Mr. Hippie Dippy"). God knows what she's called Tommy.

By the time they get there, the lot of the Parkview's full and they end up walking along the shady block, the river off to their right, glinting through the trees. It's pretty, the last afternoon light soft on the grass, and Patty resolves to forget everything for one night and have a good time.

It seems that everyone's beat them there. The bar's mobbed, the wedding party at the raised head table already eating their salad. There's an open spot between Woody and Trace. She locates Shannon and Marshall and tells Kyra to come get her if Casey gives her any trouble. He's clingy after being with Kyra all day. "It's okay," Patty says, pointing, "Mama be right here."

Up on the dais, Woody stands to help push her chair in. "You've got to be careful not to lean back too far," he says, because the edge is right there. She lays her napkin in her lap and nods "hey" to Trace, who glances up from his conversation with Eileen's shortstop Carol, then turns away again.

"Can I get you something from the bar?" Woody asks.

"A margarita. If they have them."

"If not?"

"Jack and Coke?"

He leaves her alone with Trace, still talking with Carol. He's halfway through a tallneck Rolling Rock and hasn't touched his salad. He's still wearing his jacket but has ditched his bow tie and unbuttoned the top stud of his shirt, his Adam's apple filling the notch. She notices his hands are dirty, grease worn into his fingertips. She's so close she could sneak her hand under the table and touch him. She scans the room for Kristi to see if she's watching them but can't find her. Woody's caught in the crowd at the bar.

Carol gets up and pushes her chair back carefully, and Trace swivels around to face Patty, as if they've been talking all along. She's about to ask if he isn't racing tonight when he reaches back between them and hands a waiter his empty and orders another.

"And a margarita," he adds.

"Salt?" the waiter asks, and Trace deflects the question to her.

"Please," she says, sending him off. "Thanks."

"You're welcome. It's nice." He motions to the dance floor and the tables with tall lilies for centerpieces, the whole place draped in twists of white and silver crepe paper.

"It was my mom's idea. Eileen was going to have it at the Moose."

"This is better."

And Patty hasn't been mistaken all these months; she feels the same way she did that night in the Iroquois. He makes her sit up a little straighter, aware of her bare shoulders. All she wants to do, she thinks, is keep talking like this.

"You're not racing tonight?"

"I'm letting my little brother drive. I haven't been running so hot anyway."

"No, I see you in the paper all the time."

"Not lately."

"I didn't know your brother drove."

"Yeah," he says, and as he explains, Patty watches his face and loses her grip on the words. They're not important, only that the two of them are finally here together, the way she and Tommy are after a long week apart.

It's so like her to think of him now, to ruin this. She's not even flirting with him, but she can see how Tommy would take it, as if he's watching over her. Where is he right now, in line for dinner, watching TV? Who's *he* talking to?

"What about you?" Trace is saying. "What are you up to?"

"Just working," she says.

"I see you driving a steamroller the other day?"

The news thrills and terrifies Patty. She tries not to let it show. Eileen and Cy are crossing the dance floor toward them. A clinking starts up, grows loud, whole tables chiming their knives against their water glasses. To silence them, Eileen and Cy kiss. Patty and Trace clap like everyone else. Woody's headed toward them with their drinks. She still hasn't seen Kristi and wonders if they had a fight. The Coughlan girls seem so prim and proper. His family probably approves, thinking she'll steady him.

Woody hands the drinks up from the front, then comes around. Eileen and Cy have taken their places in the middle. The busboys in their black vests are clearing the salad plates, the servers bringing in trays of stacked silver covers. Carol hustles back from across the room, lifting her hem to climb the three steps at the end. With everyone there, there's no chance of talking, and Patty licks the salty rim of her glass and takes a long, chilly sip.

"That looks good," Trace says.

"Have a sip."

"That's all right," he says, craning around for the waiter. "I've got a beer coming here somewhere."

"You can have that other margarita if you want. I can order another one."

"No," he says, and she doesn't press him, not with everyone around. She busies herself with her clasp purse, pinching out her cigarettes and lighter and the folded yellow paper with her speech.

When the chicken cordon bleu arrives the waiter lifts the cover in front of Patty, releasing lukewarm steam that wilts her bangs. She drinks too fast because she's nervous, then just picks at her food.

"How do *you* rate?" Carol jokes when her second one arrives.

Patty tries to take her time with it. She has to make her speech soon. After that she can have as many as she wants.

Ding ding ding ding, and they kiss again, Cy dipping Eileen deep to hoots and whistles. It's only been seven years since that was her, Patty thinks. But like any drunken thought, it never connects, just fizzles away, replaced by a sneeze, by the next bite of chicken, by a sip from her sweating water goblet.

Champagne arrives in skinny glasses, the bubbles making straight lines. For the toasts, Patty realizes in time.

The other tables are just getting dinner as theirs is being taken away. Patty glances over at Kyra to make sure Casey's eating. He seems fine, Mama forgotten. Kristi's behind them, at a table by the bandstand with some of Eileen's teammates. She thinks it's a good sign that Trace hasn't said a word about her—as if they've agreed to keep things just between them.

The waiter automatically brings another round. Patty finishes hers for courage during Woody's speech. The applause fades as he sits down, and it's her turn.

She stands and crosses behind Woody's chair, the speech in her hand, holding on to his shoulders like a railing so she doesn't pitch off the back. She can feel the whole room watching, their faces moving with her. Eileen's smiling, and Cy, dressed so nice, and she recalls how good they were to her when it first happened, how they took her in. She bends down to hug Eileen and then Cy, and she's crying. She didn't mean to, but she is, and she has to borrow a tissue from her mother.

Once she's recovered, Cy hands her the mike.

"I knew I'd cry." The room laughs. "I'll probably do it again, so just bear with me."

The paper scuffs the head of the mike as she unfolds it, a sudden blast of wind. "Sorry."

"'Eileen,'" she reads, the words echoing from the PA, "'you were always the wild sister of the three of us. I remember growing up, how if one of us broke something we'd blame it on you, like the lamp in the sewing room. Sorry, Mom.'" She nods to her in apology, the way they practiced. "'You used to jump off the back porch like us even though you were half our size, and whenever there was a bug we needed killed, you picked it up and took it outside in your bare hands. I don't know why you're so fearless, you just are. Through the years I think we all worried about you because of that, but now that we're older I wish I was more like you.'"

Awwww, everyone says.

"'Cy,'" she says, putting a hand on his shoulder, "'*you're* fearless for marrying her.'" Big laugh. "'Seriously, I can't think of a better combination than you two. I remember when Eileen broke her arm, how you dressed her every morning. I won't mention how you *un*dressed her every night. You guys are always there to help and support each other. You've really helped me too, and I'll never forget it. I love you both so much.'"

She's left her champagne at her place, so she borrows Woody's, raising it as cameras flash and chatter, then hugs them both to polite applause.

Back at her chair, Trace is waiting. "You did great."

"I need a drink," she says, and drains her champagne. It's not a line; she concentrated so hard reading her speech that she's given herself a headache, a trapped air bubble seeping through her brain.

She tries her water but the ice just makes it worse, leaving a thin, sour aftertaste.

Woody's going on a bar run. "You want anything?" he asks Trace.

"That was nice of him," she says when he's gone.

"Wood's a good guy."

The band's onstage now, strapping on their guitars, fingering the electric keyboards, thumping the bass drum. Again, she's aware of how close Trace is, their legs almost touching. Once the dancing starts, she'll lose him to Kristi. Patty wants to make a date with him, nothing romantic, just a promise that they'll see each other again.

"You racing next weekend?"

"If it doesn't rain."

"What number are you?" she asks, like she doesn't know.

He tells her, and that's enough, that's all she wanted.

The band tunes up, and then the girl singer's at the microphone, calling Eileen and Cy out for their first dance—"Wild Horses." After the first chorus, Cy offers her mother his hand and draws her onto the floor. Eileen has to make do with a distant uncle of his.

And, shit, here comes Kristi, just like Patty figured, skirting the sidelines, heading directly for them. With her long hair and heels, she looks too big to Patty, big all over—her height, her smile— like some kind of farmgirl movie star. What chance does Patty have against a Dairy Princess?

"I hope you don't mind if I steal him," Kristi asks her and Carol, and Patty feels herself smile out of reflex.

When he's gone, Carol scoots over one seat to talk. "I always thought this was a breakup song," she confesses.

They watch them dance, Patty stabbing her dead lime wedge with her plastic sword. Kristi's taller than he is.

"There's your date," Carol says, spotting Woody passing the cake table with his hands full of drinks.

"He's trying a little too hard," Patty says.

"Nothing wrong with that."

"No, you're right."

They clam up as he nears.

"I got salt like you like," he says, reaching Patty's margarita up to her, and she thanks him. The cold sweetness goes good with her cigarette. The next song's a fast one, and Woody asks if anyone wants to dance.

"Sure," Carol says, letting her off the hook. They leave her alone with their beers. Patty feels exposed, the only one left at the table, and when she drains her glass she takes the opportunity to hit the bathroom. In the locked stall, she hangs her head and closes her eyes, listening to the chatter of the girls brushing their hair at the mirror, the door opening and closing, letting in bursts of music. She's not drunk, she just needs to slow down, have a glass of water, maybe eat a piece of cake or something.

When's the last time she was completely shit-faced? She can't even remember.

It's not going to be tonight. People will talk.

It's not like they don't already.

"Fuck 'em," she says softly, floating in the dark, the voices loud around her.

But she's good. She has a Tab and then a glass of water with her cake, eating it with Casey and her mother and Kyra and Randy. Shannon and Marshall are out on the floor, flaunting their dance lessons. Eileen and Cy are taking off soon, and she corrals Woody and Carol and Trace and Kristi and the rest of the bridal party to decorate Cy's truck with shaving cream and balloons and empty beer cans, clapping as Carol rolls a glow-in-the-dark rubber over the antenna.

She feels better outside, calmed by the darkness, the music a muffled pumping trapped inside the walls of the Parkview. The night is cool but humid, the moon bright above the telephone wires. From across the park, she can hear the low, constant passing of the river, like far-off traffic. When she was a teenager, her crew used to hang out here after dark, down by the water, drinking beer and talking about how far you could go if you followed it downstream—through Binghamton and into Pennsylvania, past Harrisburg and into Maryland, through the Chesapeake Bay, all the way to the ocean. You could go anywhere. Now here she is, twice as old as that girl and still stuck in the same place. But seriously, where would she go? She doesn't want to move to Auburn and live with the guards.

"Here you go," Woody says, handing her a joint. She takes a hit and passes it to Carol. The weed takes hold of her instantly, lifts her above her worries. She's not here to mope around; she's here to party for her sister. By the time the truck's done, they're all stoned and goofing, Trace chasing Woody down to the next streetlight with a shaken-up beer. "It's rented!" Woody hollers, and for some reason it's the funniest thing. All night long they say it to each other, about anything.

Once Eileen and Cy take off, the old people leave and the party starts. Her mother says she's had enough fun; she's going to take Casey and Kyra and Randy home. Shannon and Marshall have already split for their motel ("Hubba hubba," her mother says). Patty says she'll get a ride with Carol or one of the other girls from the shower. "Don't be too late," her mother warns. Patty says she won't, she has to get up and see Tommy.

She goes back to margaritas until the bar runs out of mix, then switches to Jack and Coke. The bathroom reeks of weed, and Carol's got coke. They do lines in her car—her and Woody and

Trace and Kristi all jammed into her Civic, passing the scratched mirror between the seats. The coke is a bitter drip down the back of her throat, and she borrows Woody's beer. They all go back in and dance up a sweat, come back out after the band stops and pool their money for another half gram. There's an after-party forming, a convoy that snakes through the north end of town to Carol's sister's place, where the guy in charge of the stereo wears a Burger King crown and shades and plays nothing but reggae and the living room table is a huge wooden spool from the power company. Everyone's dancing, partying in different rooms upstairs with the doors locked. At one point Patty goes outside to cool down and finds a girl passed out on a chaise longue. Later she watches two guys have a fake fight in the hallway and knock a picture off the wall. They just shrug and walk away. It's late. The fridge is picked clean of beer, all the crisper drawer and door and butter compartment hiding spots empty, the kitchen counter an army of dead soldiers, the sink a nasty ashtray. Trace and Kristi are gone, but Woody's still hanging in there, tagging after Carol. It's three and then four and then a quarter to five and Patty needs to go home. Woody finally drives her, turning the heat up when he sees she's shivering. And he *is* a good guy, Woody. He walks her to the door to make sure she's safe, stepping back at the last minute to let her know he's not fishing for a kiss.

It's open. She thanks him, then waits till he's gone to turn out the porch light.

Inside, she tries to be quiet, carrying her shoes in one hand. Casey's asleep. Her alarm clock says five-thirty, meaning he'll be up in an hour. In the blinding bathroom she shakes her head at herself in the mirror, the black holes of her pupils nearly eclipsing the green, then concentrates on squeezing a line of Gleem on her toothbrush. The taste makes her spit and rinse again. Thinking ahead, she takes three aspirin, gulps down two fast glasses of water and refills it to have by her bed.

As she lies there in the dark, the night comes back to her in flashes, a crazy waste of time and brain cells (not to mention twenty bucks). She doesn't understand why she didn't just come home after the band stopped. She feels cheap and foolish—guilty, even though nothing happened (as if it ever could). That she's lonely is no excuse, or that it's been a long time since she really let herself go. Maybe there isn't a good reason, but she lies there wide awake, her whole head pulsing, trying to forgive herself, knowing, the whole time, that it's not up to her.

A WHOLE NEW WORLD

SHE LIES TO HIM. EVERY TIME SHE TALKS TO HIM, SHE NOTICES things she says. She tells him she doesn't mind the drive, that it's pretty this time of year. She tells him things are going fine at work, that she has enough money, that something might come of the new appeal. She tells him she's always thinking of him. She tells him Casey's doing great at daycare.

More often, she lies by not telling him things. She doesn't tell him how worried she is about the numbness in her mother's fingers or about Casey pushing the little girl off the bleachers at Eileen's softball game. She doesn't tell him that she's tired, that she dreads working another winter on the truck. She can't tell him how she almost went to the speedway by herself Friday night. She can't tell him how the other day when she burned the omelet she was making she dumped the pan in the sink and kept walking, out the back door and into the yard and the rain, where she didn't even scream, just stood there swearing and clenching her hands.

Meanwhile, she's lying to everyone else. There's another new crew at work that has no idea who she's married to. She hasn't told Russ, but every Sunday she's been screening the want ads, looking for a factory job like the one she used to have—indoors, sitting down, making something with women her own age. IBM's too close, even if she could get in. She's hoping for something out of town, out on the highway toward Binghamton or Elmira. On the application, she knows she'll leave the space for her husband's work number blank—if she puts him on there at all. She'll do what she has to to start fresh in one part of her life, but right there, that's a whole new world of lies.

So when they learn that the court of appeals has refused to hear their case—that, for all practical purposes, Tommy will spend the next twenty years in prison—Patty thinks at least that's one thing she won't have to deceive herself about anymore.

ACCIDENTS

ALL FALL SHE SEARCHES FOR A NEW JOB, LIKE THAT MIGHT SAVE HER. The economy's supposed to be in such great shape, but nobody's hiring, and she's not qualified for anything that pays more than she's already making. She goes through the rows of classifieds half-heartedly, crossing off the same ads as the Bills lose week after week. Her birthday's come and gone; frost's wilted the garden. They've started leaf pickup and hooked the tire chains onto the school buses. It's just a matter of watching and waiting for the snow.

After every failed appeal, Tommy tells her she'd be better off forgetting him. This time he thinks they should get a divorce.

"Who's going to send you money for your cigarettes?" she asks. "Who's going to come visit you? You've got a family that loves you very much, sometimes I think you forget that."

Is it a test? It drives her nuts to have to listen to it again and again. And there's that small, secret part of her that agrees with him.

Sometimes Patty thinks he doesn't understand that she has other problems besides missing him. Part of that's her fault for not wanting him to worry about small stuff. When the washing machine breaks and floods the basement, what's he supposed to do about it?

Casey's different. She doesn't know what to do with him. Twice in the last week he's had an accident in his pants at daycare. He's been out of diapers nearly a year, so it doesn't make sense.

"Maybe he wants to stay home with your mom," Tommy says.

"Oh, I know that," she says. "He always gives me a hard time when I drop him off. He says none of the other kids play with him, but when I talk to Florence she says things have gotten a lot better. And he's fine when I pick him up, he's running around with everyone else. The whole reason he's there is to play with other kids his age. He's not learning anything staying home by himself."

"What if you have him wear diapers when he's there?"

"I don't want to do that—that's going backwards. He's *supposed* to be toilet-trained. That's one of the requirements for going there. They shouldn't have to deal with his mess."

"I bet it happens all the time at a place like that."

"That's what I'm telling you," she says. "It *doesn't* happen."

"Did you talk to him?"

"I tried. He was embarrassed, and I didn't want to make him feel worse. I told him to tell someone when he needs to go, but he knows that."

"Do you want me to talk to him?" Tommy says.

"And say what?"

"I don't know, see if I can find out what the problem is."

"When are you going to do that—Sunday, with everyone around? I don't want to do that to him."

The silence on the other end of the line means he's run out of answers.

"I'll take care of it," Patty says. "I just wanted to let you know what's going on."

"Thanks," he says, and the rest of their conversation goes okay, but when she gets off the phone she feels like a bitch. She's not, she thinks. She's just tired of having to do everything herself.

HUNGER

THANKSGIVING ARRIVES, A GRAY ANNIVERSARY. THE SNOW FALLS, the plows roll out. Christmas, Casey breaks one of her mother's favorite ashtrays, chips of emerald glass skittering across the kitchen floor, a shocked second of surprise, then tears. Dick Clark welcomes another year.

Patty lives weekend to weekend and tries not to notice time passing, the calendar pictures flipping. It's impossible: at work she cleans up after the seasons. At home she struggles to stay ahead of Casey, who's outgrown his summer clothes.

He's always been big like Tommy; now he's thickened, turned husky, waistless. They have to watch what he eats. Like any kid, he loves junk food—doughnuts and sugary cereals, cookies and chips. Keeping sweets out of the house is easy; they just don't buy them. Her mother moves her butterscotch drops and peppermint twists from the junk drawer to the middle shelf of the cupboard, and still he grows.

He's hungry all the time. It's the way he attacks his plate that worries her—doglike, as if he's starving. She's hardly started hers and he's ready for seconds. Patty makes new rules to slow him down: finish chewing before taking another bite, only two glasses of milk per meal. If he wants a snack he can have an apple. When they go to Shannon's for Easter, Patty stands her ground, confiscating his basket, and Casey pouts the whole way home.

It's a problem at Auburn, all the crap in the machines. Patty has to warn Tommy; she needs them to be on the same page. He doesn't agree with her. It's been a ritual of theirs, a special family treat, and he doesn't want to give it up.

"I was fat till I was thirteen," he says. "Then I grew six inches and got teased for being a stringbean."

"Did you like being fat?" Patty asks. "Do you think it's healthy? I don't. And you weren't that fat. You were solid. You used to run around and do things with your friends. All he does is watch TV.

Look at him next time and tell me if you think he's healthy. Then you can buy him whatever you want."

"Okay, okay," he says. "I didn't know it was such a big deal."

Has he been listening to her at all? He's always asking her what she's up to, like he's keeping tabs on her, but the next time she talks to him he's forgotten everything she said. Sometimes she thinks he's not really interested, that he's just making conversation, passing time with her until he has to go back to that other world he lives in. But this isn't like her mother having the driveway resealed or Eileen and Cy going to Watkins Glen for the races. This is his son.

"It's important," she says gently, and he relents.

Visiting is already hard. Casey hates going. In the morning he's deadweight; it's a chore getting him out of bed and dressed. He complains that he's missing his cartoons, but Patty notes the way he sticks close to her in the waiting room. The other kids run around, laughing and tripping over people's feet; they pester their mothers and draw with crayons and play cards on the floor. There aren't enough seats, and the etiquette is that only adults get chairs. Casey stands facing her, hands on her knees like she's home base in a game. He'd climb onto her lap if he could still fit. Patty tries to make things easier by reading to him from picture books, but today the guards are being slow, and there are long dead spots.

"You like football?" a heavy, gap-toothed woman sitting next to her asks Casey, and he curls away from her. "You gonna be a football player, I bet."

"He's a Bills fan," Patty says, though so far he's shown no interest.

"They can use a good player. I like the Redskins 'cause I used to live in Washington."

This is all aimed at Casey, who keeps his head tucked into his shoulder.

"He's shy," Patty says.

"That's all right. He came to see his daddy, not me. Ain't that right?"

"Casey, answer the lady."

"That's right," the woman says, then turns to Patty. "It's hard on them, the way they do it here. I hear they're getting them trailers in though, like they have downstate? Now that's the way to go."

The trailers are for overnight visits. It's a new program for prisoners who've done good time. The whole family spends the weekend together inside the fence, in a trailer set up like a mobile home. You bring your own food and do your own cooking. Every couple of hours they check on you, but basically they lock you in for the night and leave you alone. They've had it at Wallkill for a couple of years.

It sounds like a visiting room rumor, too good to be true. To be with Tommy again, alone. She wonders if the trailers have surveillance cameras in them, if somewhere they'd be on closed-circuit TV, people listening in, like their phone calls.

Would she really care?

When they finally get inside, it seems everyone around them is eating. The man at the next table's lips are dusted bright orange from a bag of cheese curls, one of Casey's favorites. Patty sees Casey looking at them and pats his arm to break the spell.

Tommy's heard of trailers at other places, but doesn't think they're supposed to get them here. And like that he shoots down her idea, like it could never happen.

"You don't know that," she says. "They could be putting them in right now and not be telling us. That's how they do everything else."

"I'll ask around."

"*I'll* find out," she says. "If they're coming, we're going to be first on that list, I don't care what we have to do."

He adds nothing, as if to say she can try if she likes. She wants more of a reaction than that, but she's gotten her point across.

"How's your money?" she asks.

Casey's quiet like always, sitting still like he's being punished. He's good though, he doesn't tug on her arm and bug her for a treat, while across the room the vending machines ring like a casino. When he looks that way, Tommy cuts his eyes toward him and makes a sad mask of a face, and she softens. They compromise. She springs for popcorn, an old standby.

"Easy there," Tommy says as Casey stuffs his face. "It's not a race."

A couple minutes later he has to tell him a second time.

"I'm sorry," Casey says.

"Don't be sorry, bud," Tommy says, "just cool your jewels."

See? Patty wants to say, but holds off. She takes a handful. It's light and fake-buttery, but she's not hungry. She only eats her share so Casey won't.

BUTTERFLIES

MAY, THUNDERSTORMS POUND THE VALLEY, SENDING THEM OUT TO clean up downed limbs, feeding the woodchipper in the leafy humidity. They can't even move some of the bigger ones. Earphones muffling the high motorbike whine of the engine, Patty strips the smaller branches with a chainsaw, then cuts them into easily digestible lengths.

It's warm, steam rising from the asphalt, and her goggles keep fogging. She has to take them off and clean them with the tail of her shirt. One of the young guys isn't wearing his, and she feels like a mother, yelling at him to put them on. The chipper whirs empty, then shears, drowning her out, sending a spray clattering against the metal bed of the truck. Another guy's running up and tossing branches into the chipper like he's hurling a javelin.

"Hey," she has to say, "let's quit messing around before someone gets hurt," and even after that she sees them grinning and joking behind her back.

It seems she's got a new crew every year, meaning she has to prove herself to yet another set of overgrown, macho kids. It's not that hard—she knows the job inside out by now—but it does make her life rougher than it really needs to be. She's been stressing safety since day one with these guys. She shouldn't have to tell them simple stuff like this.

That's what she's thinking as she revs the engine with her trigger finger and lowers the bar into the gnarled bark of an oak. It's like holding on to something alive. She locks her elbows, the vibration buzzing up her forearms, her clenched fingers tingling. She doesn't lean on the saw, just lets the chain chew through the wet wood. The cut parts, gravity widening the gap as the limb sags, the last couple of inches pinching the bar, almost stopping it. Patty backs off and gives it more throttle and goes in again, but she must hit a knot or a spike, an old braid of wire eaten by the tree— she doesn't bury the tip like Russ warned, she's careful about that—

because the saw jumps in her hands, the bar kicking back at her. She sees it coming up and jerks her face away.

She doesn't have time to think of the chain brake. It's disengaged because she's squeezing back the front handguard; all she'd have to do is let go. Instead, she squeezes harder and tries to dodge the bar. It's faster than her, catching her in the side of the face.

It's like a punch. Patty goes down, dropping the saw and grabbing for the hurt. On the ground, she realizes what happened and feels torn skin, a burn like a brand. She can't see from the eye she's covering with both hands. She's afraid to take them away.

She lifts one. She's wearing gloves, so the blood on her fingers looks black as oil. The other glove's worse. Her eye stings, but she can see.

"Aw shit," one of the guys is saying, leaning in and then turning away.

"You're all right," another says—Brian, his name is. "It just looks bad. Can you walk?"

Patty hadn't even thought of trying. She just wants to sit here for a minute. She's having trouble getting her gloves off. Her earphones are gone because she can hear. What happened to the saw?

"The saw's okay," Brian says. "Don't worry about the saw."

The blood's red and slippery on her hand, filling a fingerprint.

"Keep pressure on it," Brian says, and covers her eye with her palm again, and then they're lifting her under the arms and helping her to the truck. Her legs work fine; she can see. It's just a cut. She feels stupid, like she's screwed up. What will Russ say?

They put her in the middle of the front seat and give her a wet wad of napkins from lunch to hold against her eye like a poultice, and she remembers the game she and Shannon used to play, taking turns standing at the bottom of the basement stairs while the other dropped the basketball at the top and how once it came off a step too fast and hit her in the forehead before she could get her hands up. She fell so hard she smacked the back of her head against the stone wall, but they weren't supposed to be playing that game anymore, and when her mother came down to find out what the sound was, Shannon said the door and Patty just went along with her.

Brian's driving, taking over the situation, and she's grateful, even if she hates being saved.

"I think I'm okay," she says, and dabs at her face with the mass of napkins—sopping now, bright red against the white.

The nearest hospital's Robert Packer in Sayre, where she had Casey, where her father died. By the time they get there the napkins are dripping down her wrist and arm, and a nurse guides her straight through the emergency room to a stretcher-bed in the back. The guys have to wait outside.

The young doctor with the scruffy beard holds Patty's head in both hands, tilting the wound to the light and leaning in like he's going to kiss it. It's shallow. He says they can get away with some butterflies instead of stitches and let it mesh naturally, especially where it is. He cleans the cut and swabs it with some ointment, then sticks the strips on to hold the skin together, and writes her a prescription for some antibiotics. They've got her insurance, they'll mail her the bill.

Russ is in the waiting room; he's sent Brian and the guys back to work. He inspects the butterflies like he's a doctor.

"I guess I must have hit a knot or something."

"It happens."

He's brought the best of the town pickups. They slide down the ramp onto 17 and head east. The sun's shining, the road's dry except the edges. There's a good two hours till quitting time, and Patty wants to go back and finish the day.

"I don't think that's such a hot idea," Russ says.

"If you were me and you had to work with these guys, what would you do?"

The crew's surprised when they pull up and Patty gets out. They stop the chipper to look at her butterflies.

"I'm lucky it hit me in the head," she jokes, but no one laughs.

She thanks them and they shrug it off. Cars are passing, heads turning.

"Okay," Russ says, "break's over. These people already think we don't do anything."

Her goggles are in the truck, and she's freaked to find a white gouge in one cup of her earphones. She gets a new pair of gloves, Brian surrenders the saw to her, and they set to work again, seriously this time, no grab-assing.

Patty primes the engine, pushes in the choke and yanks the cord, and the saw buzzes. She doesn't check to see if they're watching her. She steps up to the limb and starts in on it, lopping off the green branches as she goes, careful of the tip, her head just that much out of line with the bar so if it kicks it will hit her in the shoulder instead.

Punching out back at the garage, they all say good night to her, see you tomorrow.

Even in the truck, driving home, she doesn't give in, or when her mother acts horrified, telling her she's been worried all along that Patty might get hurt, the job's just too dangerous. She tells Casey she's fine, that the butterflies are like having a band-aid. It's only in the locked bathroom, turning her face to inspect the damage, that she feels sorry for herself and angry at Tommy, though she knows it's not his fault.

The next morning, she goes to the mirror hoping her head will look better, only to find she has a black eye on that side, the pooled blood under her skin the color of raspberry jam.

"You look like you've been in a fight," her mother says at breakfast.

Casey stares until she tells him he's being rude.

There's no way to hide it.

"Husband do that to you?" jokes the lady at the drive-thru at Dunkin' Donuts. It amazes Patty how many people say this like it's funny. It's almost a relief to get to work, where the guys know what happened.

As the week passes, the eye softens and darkens like a bad pear, brown surrounded by yellow. Saturday, while she's out shopping with Eileen at the mall, a saleslady kids them, "Little sibling rivalry there?"

"It doesn't look that bad," Tommy says, but it's been five days and she's prepared him for it. His first reaction is to touch it, but of course he's not allowed.

The rumor about the trailers is true, he says. They're starting a program this fall, but it's only for guys who've done five full years. He's still got a whole year to go before they can sign up.

Patty's careful not to pick at the cut, once the doctor peels off the butterflies. Every night before bed she uses the tube of ointment he's prescribed to keep the new skin flexible. As June passes, the seam's barely noticeable, a faint scratch in her tan. She glops on sunblock to protect it when they're patching asphalt, and soon she's her usual overall bronze, her eyes a raccoon mask from her sunglasses. By the end of July she has to search her temple for the telltale line. In the mornings, before work, she turns on the light above the sink and leans in close, ignoring the deepening creases beside her eye, the stray gray hairs. The scar only shows if she turns her head a certain way, and even then it fools her sometimes, flashes, there and not there, a visible badge of her toughness one minute and then gone the next, as if nothing ever happened.

A FRESH START

THE FIRST DAY OF KINDERGARTEN, SHE TAKES PICTURES OF CASEY
on the front porch with his lunchbox. He stands at the top of the
stairs and hangs his head, condemned. Last night he cried. She
doesn't remember being terrified like this. To her, getting to ride
the bus with Shannon was a big deal. Eileen was the one that cried
because she was stuck at home. Maybe he thinks they're sending
him away.

"Come on," Patty says, "smile."

"I don't want to," Casey mumbles.

"Come on, the bus is going to be here soon."

"I don't care."

"Well I do," she says. "I want to be able to show your father
a nice picture of you, so quit with the whining. Look up."

He looks at her, miserable. "I don't feel good."

"You felt good enough to eat your breakfast. Now smile."

Just getting him to look at the camera is a victory. She's taken
a half day to see him off because she knew he'd be like this. She
reels off some shots, then has her mother take some of them together. Patty lays an arm over his shoulders. He submits to it, and
she imagines how sour he'll look beside her smile, the mismatch
funny to someone who doesn't know them. But it's true too—
she's glad to have him in school, finally; daycare was expensive and
he hated it there.

"I don't feel good," he says.

"You said that already."

"Really, Mom," he says, "my stomach hurts," and he clutches it with one hand.

"You're just nervous, it's natural. Let's go wait by the mailbox."

She takes his limp hand in hers and swings it between them as they walk down the driveway. It's still summer, the sun through the trees a bright lemon-lime. In the distance, she can hear a diesel gearing down to climb the hill, and thinks it's perfect timing.

"It'll be fun," she says, and turns toward the noise of the bus. Beside her, Casey makes a strangling sound, his throat hitching like he's going to throw up—a tactic he uses at the dinner table when he doesn't want to eat his beans.

"Don't you dare, mister," she threatens him, sticking a finger in his face.

He hitches again, his neck stretching forward, his mouth opening, loosing a yellow gush of vomit that splashes over her sneakers. She keeps ahold of his arm as he bends at the waist and retches again, a blurt of Apple Jacks and milk and orange juice.

"Is everything all right?" her mother calls from the porch.

"Does everything look all right?" Patty shouts back.

The bus clears the crest of the hill and flashes its amber caution lights and then the reds, the hinged stop sign extending as it slows. Patty catches the driver's attention and waves him past, but he stops anyway.

"Go," Patty tells him. "We're not ready."

He folds the door closed and a strip of faces slides by above them, pointing and laughing.

Casey's sobbing in hiccuping gulps, his face red. Finally he subsides, wiping his eyes with the back of a hand.

"Are you all done?" she asks.

"I think so."

"Feel better now?"

"Yes."

"Good."

She walks him back to the house without a word. "Go brush your teeth. I'll drive you."

He doesn't argue with her, just trudges upstairs, still carrying his lunchbox.

"I don't think he did it on purpose," her mother says.

"I know. He just got himself worked up."

"I can watch him if you want to go to work. It's no problem."

"I don't want him to miss the first day of school."

"I was just offering," her mother says, and turns away, breaking off the conversation. It's not the first time Patty's been outnumbered in her own house. Over the years she's stopped letting it bother her. If she's wrong, she's going to be wrong following her instincts, not someone else's.

When she comes back from getting her keys, Casey's standing in the front hall.

"Are you ready?" Patty asks.

He dips his chin and they head out to the truck.

"Have a good day," her mother calls after them, and Patty has to prompt him to wave back.

At the bottom of the drive, she swerves so the wheels straddle the splotch of vomit, knowing her mother will have it hosed off by the time she gets back.

They ride in sunny silence for a while, the truck holding the hilly curves, the creek off to their right peeking through the guardrail, then crossing underneath them and following on the other side. An open shed of a bus stop passes—the stop where Margie and

Peter Holman got off—and she remembers school being a place to meet her friends and escape the boredom of home, a place she could make herself into someone else. She glances at Casey, slumped and glum.

"So you're not talking, is that it?"

He doesn't take the bait.

"Think you can go the whole day? I bet Mrs. Parrish would love that."

They break out of the woods and onto a long flat between green fields. The bus is up ahead, just turning onto Whitmarsh. They pull into line behind it, waiting as it picks up.

"Mom," he finally says.

"Yeah," she answers.

"Does Mrs. Parrish know Daddy's in jail?"

Patty wants to be able to say no, but it's a matter of public record—and memory, the ability to reach back five years and match their last name to the trial. A month ago, when she got his room assignment, she decided not to have a talk with Mrs. Parrish, thinking it might prejudice her. Now she thinks she was being wishful. Five years is nothing. There have to be thirty teachers there; it only takes one to infect the rest.

"I don't know," she says. "She might. Why?"

It's unfair, turning the question back on him, and when she glances over, he just shrugs and mumbles "I don't know" like he doesn't care.

At daycare he made the mistake of telling the other kids—to impress them, maybe.

"Listen," she says. "You tell Mrs. Parrish if anyone says anything. And you tell me as soon as it happens. You hear me?"

He nods, hunching like he's in trouble. This is exactly what she didn't want to remind him of.

The bus pulls out and they follow it down the broad curves to town, caught in its snaking tail. Patty wants to give him a pep talk, tell him he'll see, this year's going to be different, that it's a whole new bunch of kids. She wants to tell him not to be afraid, but thinks that might frighten him even more.

"I understand that you're nervous," she says, watching the brake lights in front of her. "What you have to remember is that everyone's nervous. It's the first day for everyone."

"I know," he says. She wants to say he'll do fine but doesn't push her luck, and anyway, they're almost there, the bus making a wide right onto Depot Street, the same way her old bus used to come.

The school's only a few blocks. They're not allowed up the turnaround with the buses; there's a side lot where parents wait in line to drop off. As they inch up, she sees he's concentrating like he's getting ready to jump out of a plane.

"You've got your lunch," she says, like they're going over a checklist, and then it's their turn. She pulls up to the marked spot and puts it in neutral. "Kiss," she says, and leans across to squeeze him. "I love you," she says, and then, as he's navigating the door, can't help adding, "Have fun," just like her mother.

She waves as he shoves the door closed with both hands. She should be relieved that he's going at all—it's what she's battled for all morning. She watches him walk away until he's gone, absorbed in the stream of kids headed for the doors. There's nothing more for her to do, and she has cars behind her. Driving away, she feels like she does every weekend, leaving Auburn. Tomorrow, she thinks, he's taking the bus.

MONKEY WARD

▪

THAT FALL THE SOUTHERN TIER HAS A LONG, BRILLIANT INDIAN
summer. The trees keep their leaves well into November, when the
rains come, making cleanup a nightmare. Brian's gone to SUNY-
Binghamton and they're shorthanded. Every night when she gets
home her back aches from shouldering a racketing leafblower all
day. In bed, her hands cramp, keeping her awake.

She has an application in at the Montgomery Ward in Sayre,
where Eileen has a friend whose aunt is assistant manager. They
always hire people on for the holidays, and if they like you, you
can stay. She'll be making less money, but at least she won't be tired
all the time.

Her mother's glad Patty's finally come to her senses. "But,
Montgomery Ward?"

"It's just for now," Patty says.

Her plan is to finish leaf season and give Russ notice, then
take off the week before Thanksgiving. She holds off telling Tommy
till the last minute because she knows he'll try and talk her out of
it, and then when she does, that's exactly what happens.

He doesn't understand why she'd leave a good job where there's
someone looking out for her—and for less money? They end up
arguing over the phone and then again when she visits. Finally,
after she's already handed in her notice, he apologizes, or tries to.

"It's your life," he says. "You want to go work at Monkey Ward, that's your choice."

"It's not my life," she says. "It's just a job. You and Casey are my life." She can't explain to him that a new job in a new town will let her start fresh.

Her last day, Russ has a sheet cake for her with pink icing that says GOOD LUCK. Patty makes a speech, saying she'll miss everyone, but she won't miss digging fire hydrants out of snowdrifts. She won't miss shoveling up roadkill. The guys raise their sodas to her. And that's it; after a rainy afternoon hanging around the garage, she empties her locker and punches out, thanks Russ one more time for making a place for her, and then she's alone, on her way home with her last paycheck. It seems unreal, too easy. She doesn't trust the feeling of lightness, of having money in her pocket and no place to go.

The next week she sleeps in and drinks coffee in her bathrobe, watching specials about the hostages in Iran, nagged by the fact that she could be visiting Tommy. Her mother's in and out, paying bills, running errands. Patty helps her do the Thanksgiving shopping, the two of them braving the chaos of the big Tops in Johnson City. In the crush of carts at the deli counter, she feels out of place, as if she should be at work. Wednesday they spend in the kitchen, like every year, the calm before the storm, but it's different, knowing she starts Saturday, when everyone else is off. She's tired and down, when there's no reason to be. It's just a mood, she thinks, like the gray weather outside.

Thanksgiving is busy. Kyra's grown up over the last year, and while Patty's happy for her, the change makes her feel old. Her mother asks Eileen and Cy when she should expect another grandchild, and Eileen stuns everyone by saying, "Soon, we're hoping." Marshall's been promoted to regional sales manager; Shannon's doing her student teaching at Randy's middle school.

"Patty's got a new job," her mother offers.

Patty has to defuse their congratulations, saying it's just temporary.

"Where?" Shannon asks.

"Indoors," Patty says for a laugh, but they wait and make her say it. The whole room pauses to process the two words.

"That's a switch," Shannon says.

"I think the winters were getting to her," her mother explains, and it's safe for everyone to agree with that.

Later, when they're doing dishes side by side, Shannon leans in and asks how Tommy's doing, as if it's a secret.

"He's all right," Patty answers.

"If there's anything we can do," Shannon says, "just let us know."

"Thank you," Patty says, instead of asking where she was five years ago.

In bed that night, Patty resents the assumption that she needs money. When's the last time Shannon had a real job? Patty would love to have someone else pay for her to go to school, but she's got other responsibilities.

Friday when she visits Tommy there's no crowd, and while processing is quicker, she feels singled out in the waiting room. She misses the noise and the little kids. Casey takes advantage of the emptiness, trying seat after seat until she tells him to stop. Instead of leftovers, she has Polaroids of yesterday for Tommy. He lingers over the turkey and candles, laughs at the shot of Cy and Marshall at opposite ends of the couch. "We watched the game here," he says. "Pretty pitiful."

"Mom told everyone about my new job."

"What'd they say?"

She has to be careful with Casey right there. "They're glad I'm going to be inside. They're not too sure about inside where."

He nods and then shrugs, like, what did she expect?

"You know," she says, "it would be really nice if just once some-one would tell me I'm doing the right thing."

"Look, you're doing great, you both are. I know how hard it must be to keep things together out there, and you're doing it."

"So why'd you give me a hard time about working at 'Monkey Ward'? Did you think I was going to work on the truck for the rest of my life?"

"No," he says, and rolls his head like his neck's stiff. Beside her, Casey's pretending to be interested in the pictures.

"Hey," Patty says, and gets the attention of both of them, though she only wants Tommy's. "I can do a lot of things myself, but I still need your help. You don't have to pretend you're thrilled with every decision I make, just tell me I'm doing all right."

"You're doing all right," he says.

"Thank you. That's all I wanted."

"So when do you have to be in?"

Seven, but the drive over to Sayre takes half an hour, and she wants to look nice, so she needs to be up at five, five-thirty at the latest.

"It's going to be very different," she says.

"You'll do great," Tommy says, and later, as she's leaving, wishes her good luck, but on the way home her mood changes like it always does, and she thinks she bullied him into it.

She tries to get to bed early, making a turkey and cranberry sandwich to take tomorrow. She's gotten used to staying up till midnight, and lies awake, afraid she won't sleep, but soon she's dozing, dreaming, and when she surfaces again the clock says it's half past three. She manages to drop off again, only to be ambushed by the beep of the alarm. The sun isn't up yet, and the house is cold. She gets dressed and spends time on her hair, worried that the blow-dryer might wake up Casey. It doesn't, but her mother comes down in her robe to make coffee and see her off, talking about her plans to make soup, breaking Patty's concentration so that only when she's halfway to Sayre, flying along the deserted highway, the tall weeds frosted in the ditches, does she remember her sandwich.

The store bookends a plaza with a giant Wegmans and little shops in between. She's supposed to park around the side even though the lot's empty, the carts locked away. She's a good twenty minutes early and thinks she might be the first one in, but as she passes the front doors she sees people moving inside. Around the corner, a dozen cars are nosed in against the wall. She takes the first open spot, aware that the white Monte Carlo next to her might be her boss's. She backs up so the truck is straight with the lines, as if that will magically make everything perfect.

A tall guy with glasses lets her in, leaving the keys in the door for the next person. She's supposed to meet Jill. Patty's only talked to the aunt of Eileen's friend over the phone, so she's surprised to find that the young black-haired woman at the back of the store is wearing the right nametag.

Jill takes her farther back, into a cinder-block storeroom where she outfits Patty with a sleeveless vest like the one she's wearing, tan with a chocolate collar. She already has a nametag made up for her, except this one says TRAINEE.

Newcomers start on the floor stocking and straightening, keeping the aisles clean and anything else the department managers or cashiers need. The first thing Patty has to learn is the layout of the store. Jill gives her a map and a cart piled with cast-off merchandise to go back on the shelves. "Come find me when you're done," she says, and walks away.

As Patty works, she thinks how weird it is being in a store before it opens—almost fun, as if she's trespassing. The muzak that usually comes from the ceiling is turned off; except for the steady clash of the cart as it rolls over the floor, it's quiet as a library. The lighting is flat and weak, overhead fluorescents that leave dim patches in the air. Patty roams the aisles from Toys to Housewares on a reverse scavenger hunt, turning in circles, backtracking. She hurries as if she's being timed, trying to memorize as she goes. It makes sense that Sporting Goods is beside Hardware, and Hardware next to Garden, but why is Health and Beauty after that? The hardest part is remembering what's on special in the displays dotting the main aisles. She passes a column of Danish butter cookies three times before realizing they match the tin she's got in her cart.

By the time she gets to the bottom, it's almost nine. A clump of customers loiters outside, ready to storm the doors. She tracks Jill down in Layaway and shows her the empty cart.

"Great," Jill says, busy with the guy behind the counter. "Grab yourself a flyer so you know where the specials are, then ask Helen in Stationery what she needs."

The customers are all lost, and while some of them are impatient, most are willing to let Patty lead, following her through the aisles like children. No one recognizes her. They thank her and wish her Merry Christmas, the old ladies calling her "dear." People chatter at her, thinking out loud, asking her advice like she's been there for years. When she runs a price check, she hustles, and the cashiers seem to appreciate it. Jill swings by to see how she's doing and takes her to the break room where there's free coffee and someone's brought in a tray of homemade cookies. She gets thirty minutes for lunch, just enough to slip over to the Chinese takeout with some of the cashiers. This is nothing, they say, just wait. That last weekend before Christmas, it gets really hairy. Otherwise it's pretty easy, they agree. It can get boring; you don't want it too quiet.

Patty can't imagine that. The place is packed all afternoon. The cashiers keep her hopping, the speakers in the ceiling calling her name. By the end of the day she doesn't need the map, but takes it home anyway.

Sunday's the same, except she's with Janine in Pets. On a price check, she passes a wall of TVs in Electronics and misses having football on all day, but she likes watching the fish and listening to the parakeets, the squeaking wheels of the hamsters, and wonders if Casey might be interested in something like that for Christmas. It's a calm department, a backwater tucked into a corner, and that week as she rotates through Music and Boys and Baby and Photo, she decides she likes Pets best.

"If I can get you there, I'll get you there," Jill says. "No promises. Can you work tomorrow?"

Friday's her only day off, and she has no way of telling Tommy.

"If you can't, just say so."

"I've got an appointment in the morning," Patty says. "I can come in after lunch."

"And work till close?"

"Sure," Patty says.

The next morning she cuts her visit with Tommy short and drives straight from Auburn to work in a freezing rain. He said he understood, but all the way down she feels bad. When the truck slips, she thinks she doesn't want to die with things this way between them. She gets in late and has a horrible day in Garden, Molly the department manager talking her ear off about soil and fertilizers and the right-size pot. Friday's payday, but Patty didn't start till last Saturday, so she doesn't get an envelope like everyone else. When she finally does, the next week, she's shocked at how small it is for all the hours she's putting in.

She doesn't complain. The key is making it through the first ninety days and moving up to cashier. Like the other girls said, this is the hardest part. She needs to see this as an investment, a step up to something better. The constant loop of Christmas music is driving her crazy, and the fake smile she has to wear even when she's tired, but she's saving money on presents with her employee discount, and now that the weather's turned, she's glad she's not out on the truck. It's just a job, she thinks. She doesn't have to love it.

ADDITIONAL COMMENTS

THEY DON'T GIVE GRADES IN KINDERGARTEN, JUST CHECK MARKS for behavior. Casey's are all good or outstanding (better than Patty ever got, her mother notes). Beneath the filled-in grid, Mrs. Parrish has written: *Conscientious student. Could talk more.* Patty congratulates him, and they celebrate with his favorite dinner, fish sticks and french fries, but when she goes to open house and meets with his teacher, it's the one negative she zeroes in on.

"It's nothing to worry about," Mrs. Parrish says. "Some kids are naturally shy. Sometimes it has to do with the jump from preschool to kindergarten and takes care of itself after the first term. I just thought I should let you know."

"Thank you."

"Otherwise he's a real pleasure to have in class. He's one of our best readers."

"He's getting along with everyone?" Patty asks.

"I'd say so. He's in a nice group of boys."

Patty wants further proof, but that's all the time they have. When she gets home, she tells Casey the good things Mrs. Parrish said and suggests it wouldn't hurt to speak up more, but doesn't push it. He's always been quiet; even when he was a baby, he barely cried.

She should be happy he's doing so well at his new school, but now she's sensitive about how little he actually says. He's polite, answering a direct question with a word or two, and occasionally he'll ask her something simple, like what's for dinner, but they go days without having a real conversation. He doesn't tell jokes or stories for attention, and during their Wednesday night phone call she has to prompt him to speak with Tommy. Even when he's watching cartoons, he doesn't laugh out loud.

"You were quiet," her mother reminds her.

Not like this, Patty thinks, but agrees with her. It's easier, and since she's never around now, there's nothing she can do about it. She feels bad for working so much, missing weekends with him. He hasn't seen Tommy since she started. It's just till the Christmas rush is over; by then she should be back on some kind of normal schedule.

In the meantime, she pays Casey special attention, playing Chutes and Ladders with him, watching TV under the comforter. Part of it, she's convinced, is that he's an only child. He spends too much time alone. She tries not to be obvious, but she seizes every opportunity to be with him. At the dinner table, she asks him what was the best thing that happened to him today. And the worst? At bedtime she reads to him, and has him read to her. When they're done, she runs through their plans for tomorrow, messing up on purpose to coax a reaction out of him.

"He's so serious," she tells her mother, the two of them going over their Christmas lists, ignoring the claymation special on TV.

"Like someone else I know."

"Even at his age?"

"*Especially* at his age."

At work she has imaginary conversations with him, tries out openings, dreams up topics they might discuss when she gets home.

He lies on the carpet, his stocking feet pointed toward the radiator, and draws pictures Patty wants to find meaning in—portholed planes flying over mountains, boxy cars driving down highways.

"How was school?" she asks.

"Okay," he answers, without looking at her.

"Play with anyone special at recess?"

"Adam and John."

He's not interested, and she's tired. She knows better than to make this into some big test.

As she reads the paper, the silence builds. Finally, dinner's ready, and she sends him into the kitchen to help her mother set the table. Out of habit, she's cruising the classifieds, stopping at jobs she's qualified for but not really reading them. She's concentrating on the soft racket coming from the kitchen, the hum of the overhead stove fan, the ding of a pot lid against the cutting board, the clash of the silverware drawer, listening for the sound of his voice. So why, when it comes—the run and rise of a question followed by her mother's indulgent laugh—does she feel hurt?

OFFICIAL NOTICE

∎

MONKEY WARD IS BORING, CHASING THE SAME PRICE CHECKS EVERY shift. The only new skill she's learned is how to refill the soap dispensers in the bathrooms. It's past Valentine's, and Jill's still bugging her to work weekends. Patty hasn't finished her ninety-day probation, so she can't say no. She can't explain that she needs to take her son to see his father in Auburn.

Tommy's lying when he says it's all right. It's been so long that Casey asks when they're going to see Daddy.

"Soon," Patty promises, and makes good on it, but then the next weekend she ends up working, and the next. For the money she's making, it's just not worth it.

That Thursday, when Jill corners her in the break room and asks if she can come in on Saturday, Patty says she has a family commitment.

"I really need someone," Jill says.

Patty doesn't remind her that she's worked six of the last seven weekends. She just shrugs like it's out of her hands. "I wish I could help."

"What about Sunday?"

It's this kind of crap, more than the boredom and the measly paycheck, that convinces Patty she has to quit. She wrestles with the idea all weekend, running it by Tommy, because she's not sure. She thinks she should wait until she has something else lined up.

Tommy thinks she should go in and do as little as possible until they fire her. But it doesn't matter if she's fired or quits by herself, since she hasn't worked there long enough to collect unemployment, and besides, she doesn't want to be like that.

She keeps looking, keeps working. As the end of her probation nears, she thinks everything will change when she makes cashier; when it doesn't, she decides to find out when she'll become eligible for unemployment. She thinks of calling Russ and trying to get on a truck for the summer, then remembers how hot and dirty patching asphalt is. There just aren't a lot of jobs out there. She could find something in Binghamton or Elmira, but she's already doing a half-hour commute.

Being a cashier is strange, the way people look through her, like she's a machine. And then there are the ones who want to be her friend. The weekends are the hardest, fighting a line all afternoon. By the end of the day all Patty wants to do is make a boxed dinner and watch TV with her eyes closed. And then she has to get up early and drive to Auburn.

She's making enough to pay the bills, but it feels like she's wasting her time. Eileen and Cy are trying to get pregnant and saving for their own place. Shannon's teaching. Even her mother's started volunteering at church. Though it's only been five months, Patty feels like she's going nowhere. She has to remind herself that she originally saw the job as temporary. She can give it up anytime she wants.

And she's eligible for unemployment now. She could quit and take a paid vacation. If she waited till the summer, she could spend a whole month with Casey.

June comes, and the end of school. The days are easier, the store empty all week long. Even the weekends are dead, unless it rains. Patty doesn't see how they stay in business.

She's still weighing quitting when Jill gathers them at the end of another slow Friday and tells them she has some bad news. Headquarters has decided to close the store. If they want, they can have personnel forward their applications to the store in Johnson City, but she can't guarantee there will be any openings.

The decision's easy for Patty. It's no decision, really. Right then and there, by doing nothing, she quits.

ELIGIBILITY

THAT JULY, ON THE DAY TOMMY'S BEEN IN AUBURN EXACTLY FIVE years, they sign up for the Family Reunion Program. They've waited so long that handing in the form feels like an accomplishment.

The coordinator who looks it over cautions Patty that there's limited space; she won't even estimate how long it will be before they're contacted. In the meantime, she has a stapled handout of rules they need to familiarize themselves with. Patty reads them that night, as if they'll be doing it this weekend. Already she's putting together a menu, and a shopping list. She's got to bring in everything, down to the salt and pepper. They'll have pots and pans there, dishes and silverware (meaning she'll have to wash them all twice—before and after). It doesn't say anything about knives.

She's enjoying not working, taking Casey for rambles over the old Indian trails in the woods beyond the end of the yard, cutting through jungly patches of ferns, lying down on the mossy bank of the creek to show him water bugs and schools of minnows in the same sandy pools that fascinated her and Eileen when they were his age. She tells him about her father hunting wild turkey back here, how the big birds sleep in the trees. Every day they go farther in, exploring half-remembered spurs that wind up the hillside. They choose a rise that has a vantage of the main trail and build a lean-to, a secret hideout for Casey. She packs lunches so they can stay out all day and eat them sitting in his fort, watching the wandering flights of bugs. Back here where they can barely hear the road, the afternoons are endless and brilliant, made for daydreaming, but what she dreams of isn't Tommy sitting in the sun with them, finally free, but their first real night as a family, locked inside a dark trailer behind razor wire.

It will be months, at the most a year—at least that's what she thinks, the closeness with Casey making her optimistic. He seems happier. He has a friend, Adam, who comes over to play. On hot days, Adam's mother Beth drives them to the town pool and Patty lies out on a towel in the backyard like she's at the beach, drinking a beer and listening to her father's old leather-cased transistor. It's like a vacation, except she doesn't have a job to go back to. She tries not to let it ruin things. She's fine as long as she's getting paid. Eventually the checks have to stop, summer has to end. Patty doesn't need her mother to tell her that.

One blinding afternoon she's lying on the towel, sweat glazing her skin, when her mother comes running outside with the envelope with the Family Reunion Program logo in the corner. Her mother hands it to her and then stands there as Patty tears it open.

It's just an acknowledgment, a carbon of their application. It takes her a few days but Patty comes to see it as a good sign. It's the fastest the system's ever gotten back to her.

She's not surprised that she hears nothing for the rest of the summer, or in September, when she starts at the Fotomat, or October, when she quits to fill in at the daycare run by Eileen's friend Katie. She doesn't freak out when Thanksgiving and then Christmas come, another solitary New Year's. The hostages are released the day of Reagan's inauguration, and while she's annoyed at the yellow ribbons and tickertape parades, she can't watch the reunion scenes without imagining Tommy in her arms, the promise of a new start. The anticipation actually makes time move faster, each passing day bringing her that much closer to him. She keeps the carbon of their application in a folder like a receipt, visiting it from time to time to prove to herself it's real.

Katie doesn't need her for the summer, so she takes a waitressing job—the first and last she'll ever have—at the Ruby Tuesday's in the mall. It's like Monkey Ward, they're always bugging her to fill in weekends. She resents the customers with their bags of expensive crap, how impatient they are, as if their time is worth more than hers. "Do you think we can get some ketchup?" they ask.

It's been a year since they signed up for the program and they're no closer than they were last August. Back then, she made a point of sitting down and bracing Casey, since he gets weird about visiting. Now when she reminds him, he mumbles and shrugs like he's ducking an unpleasant chore. She doesn't blame him for being afraid. At some point they're going to shut the door and he's going to be alone.

The thought gnaws at her as she serves the shoppers' kids their buffalo wings and mozzarella sticks. When he's with Adam or John, he seems like any other boy his age, silly and intent on whatever game they're playing; it's when he's alone that he goes silent, closing himself off with the TV or a library book, retreating to his lean-to in the woods. She worries that he's growing up too serious, and that the visit will only make things worse. She thinks of going without him the first time, just to check it out. Tommy will understand.

And still she catches herself falling into fantasies of how it will be: how he'll play with Casey, how she'll make his favorite dishes, how they'll hold each other all night long. She knows it won't be perfect—they'll be in a trailer—but compared to the visiting room it'll be heaven.

She begins to expect the letter. Every day the mail lets her down yet she comes back the next day just as hopeful, sustaining a kind of cheerful insanity, a manic belief she realizes she can't afford to lose.

She faces Ruby Tuesday's the same way, zipping her tips into a long wallet and ignoring the bullshit. She works when she wants to, and if they don't like it they can let her go. She'll be thirty-five next July. She's had too many crappy jobs to sacrifice her real life for another one.

And so she works, she waits, leafing through the mail each day, watching Casey watch TV the same way her mother hovers over her later.

"It's going to happen," Patty tells her. "They don't just let you sign up and then forget about you."

"I wouldn't think so," her mother says.

"They don't," Patty says.

But as the days go by, she wavers. She comes to expect nothing, and proves it to herself by not rushing out to the mailbox when she hears the jeep. Instead she sends Casey, who dawdles up the drive, spilling flyers and magazines.

"Thank you," she says, taking the pile from him with both hands, and one day late in August, as if to reward her, the letter is there. She doesn't call for her mother, doesn't stop Casey from wandering off. She's hedging her bets, ready for bad news, or no news at all. In the kitchen, alone, she sits down to open it—slowly, as if it might change her life.

THE EMPIRE STRIKES BACK

ALL WEEK SHE BUYS THINGS AND SETS THEM ASIDE SO PACKING THE night before will go easier: a red Nerf football with the Bills' logo on it; mini cardboard salt and pepper shakers like you take to a picnic; a new shortie nightgown still in its nest of tissue paper. She follows the long list of dos and don'ts in the packet the coordinator sent. No glass bottles, no aerosol cans, no alcohol (and that includes mouthwash and perfume), no candles, no rope. Not all of it's common sense: no newspapers from that day, no photo albums. She needs to be careful; she knows they'll confiscate anything iffy. She calls to make sure she can bring a homemade lasagna.

The open bags distract her—all of them labeled with his name and ID number on masking tape. She can't remember the last time she and Tommy took a trip, probably when they went camping and it rained. She sees them playing cards in the truck with the heater whirring, then stops herself with a quick shake of her head like she's chasing a fly.

She's sure she's forgetting something. Brand-new underwear, two new bras, two pairs of shorts, her best pair of jeans, two tops, flip-flops . . .

Casey's taking his own pillow and a box of his favorite cinnamon Pop-Tarts—a bribe she wishes she resisted. She's bringing a deck of cards and some books for them to read. She's still not sure it's a good idea, bringing him. When she asks him what's the first thing he wants to do with Daddy, he doesn't have an answer.

"The first thing I'm going to do is give him a big kiss and a hug," she says.

Her mother's offered to watch Casey, but they're already signed up as a family. And they *are* a family. Patty's not about to give that up now, when they're almost together again.

Eileen kids Patty that she'd better double up on her pills, and while Patty goes along with the joke, she's embarrassed—and feels bad for Eileen, since she and Cy have stopped trying. It makes Patty think how hard it is to keep anything secret. She and Tommy will find a way to be intimate again, she's not worried, but that time should be theirs alone, not shared with the rest of the world. In a way, it's already spoiled.

The crack about her pills opens an even deeper chasm. Because they've never had a chance to be together, she just expected that Casey would grow up an only child. Now they have to make a decision. Six years between siblings isn't that much, or seven, considering. Patty's always wanted a girl—three girls, ideally, a rerun of her childhood. That's not going to happen, but one is a possibility. It's another reason she envies Shannon, her bond with Kyra. It seems just more of Shannon's luck, having one of each (and more of Eileen's, having none). Patty thinks she's too young to give up that part of her life. It feels wrong, like she's closing off a whole future, one richer, more intricate than the one she can see.

She's so close now, a day, then less. She can't stop watching the clock, turning her wrist over to check, like she might miss it. At the P&C in Waverly she makes a ceremony of buying the fresh fruit Tommy requested. She doesn't mind standing in line while the old lady in front of her fumbles with her coupons. Everything's arranged: she's off this weekend, there's gas in the truck, she's got traveling money. At home, after dinner, she packs Casey's bag, leaving his toothbrush holder on the sink for the morning. Once he's down, she puts together a box in the kitchen, her mother offering to help and then watching from the table. Patty knows she's going to say something, so why all the suspense?

"What time are you leaving?" she finally begins.

"I don't know," Patty says, "ten?" like she hasn't planned it to the minute.

"It's going to be lonely around here," her mother says.

"Next time you can come with us."

"No thanks," her mother says, like it's a joke.

"I'm serious."

"I know you are."

Patty wonders why they do this to each other. She doesn't want her mother to come, even if by some miracle she'd consider it; she only said it to get her going, which is dumb.

In the morning, her mother comes outside to see them off, and Patty wants to apologize. It's only as they're hugging goodbye that Patty thanks her for everything, as if they're moving, setting off for a new life.

"Well," her mother says, "say hello for me."

Casey's waiting in the truck. Patty takes an extra minute to make sure the lasagna's secure, then glides down the drive, one arm out the window, waving backwards.

The drive up is drenched in a clear summer light. The lake camps are busy, their turnarounds crammed with station wagons. She sees a family out water-skiing, glimpses their white wake between the speeding trees. She points them out to Casey, too late, but just laughs. Usually she has to put on an act for him; not today. For the first time since she's made this drive—and she's done it hundreds of times, she knows the names on the mailboxes, knows the gardens and lawn ornaments, the junked cars outside the body shops—she's not going to have to see it all again tonight.

She hangs on to the mood through downtown Auburn, across the tracks and along Wall Street, where there's special Family Reunion parking along the wall. She's left enough time to find the entrance so they don't have to go wandering around with all their stuff.

Processing takes two hours (for no reason; there's six of them and they've all been cleared in advance), and the cell of a waiting room is so air-conditioned it's cold. It's also non-smoking and doesn't have any vending machines. Casey's the only child. Of the other visitors, only one's a regular, a short, Spanish-speaking woman who takes the bus from Albany; the others must be from downstate. Since it's their first time, Patty has to show her marriage license. She and Casey have their pictures taken. Patty thinks it's for an ID, but after she signs hers, the officer slides it into a file and she sits down empty-handed.

They're all moved together, like a team. "Ladies," the officer at the desk says, taking a key ring from a locked drawer, "please follow me, and for your own safety, stick close."

She takes Casey's hand and looks down at him to show it's okay, this is just like a regular visit, and sees from his eyes that he doesn't believe her. She bends to him, letting the others go ahead. "This is the worst part, right here," she promises. "All we have to do is get through this, okay?"

"Okay," he says, but unsure.

The guard has to call inside to have the door buzzed before he can open it with the key. He closes it after them, calls using a wall phone with no dial, and the bolts clack home. One at a time, they pass through a metal detector while a pair of guards root through their bags, stirring and jabbing their clothes with a steel rod. As the guards are working over Patty's red bag, one of them stops the other, reaches in and pulls out her brand-new nightgown and kneads the package with both hands. They handle Casey's PJs the same way, squeezing them as if they might be hiding a gun.

She knows Tommy's going through much worse, that before he can see them he's strip-searched, told to open his mouth, to bend over.

For Patty, that's the mystery at the heart of visitation. The way the system's set up, it's like a price they're supposed to pay over and over until they give up and stop loving the people they've come to see, and stop coming. That's why she has to submit, why, even as she hates everything about this place, she needs to be here. Maybe next time she'll leave Casey at home.

Now that their bags are cleared, the guards look through their food. It's crazy—Patty dropped her box off at the front desk when she first signed in and no one's inspected it yet. The same two that searched her bags lift out her coffee and her new shampoo and set them aside, and then her deodorant.

"Alcohol," the guard in charge explains, and when Patty protests, shows her where it's listed in the ingredients. "When you boil it down it's the same as Sterno."

"There's no alcohol in my coffee."

"It's a glass container."

"It's plastic," Patty argues, because any idiot can see it's plastic meant to *look like* glass. It makes no sense: the lasagna's in a Pyrex dish and it's fine.

"I'm sorry, ma'am."

"What kind you drink?" the woman from Albany asks. "I'll lend you some."

"Thank you," Patty says, still pissed off. The coffee's the least of it. She doesn't know what she's going to do with no shampoo and no deodorant. Casey's got a small bottle of baby shampoo. At least they didn't take her lotion.

She commiserates when one of the women from downstate loses a can of cherry pie filling. They all lose something; it's like the guards can't let them get away clean. They get receipts for everything they have to leave behind. When they're done, none of the guards helps them lug their stuff down the long gray tunnel of a concrete block hall. She has to use both hands, leaving Casey to tag along at her elbow. No one talks. At the end they stop for a closed door. There's only a small window in it, the kind with chicken wire, but Patty can see it leads outside, a mesh of fence catching the sunlight. Her bag is slipping lower on her shoulder, and she has to shift, kneeing the box higher to get a better grip. The head guard calls on his walkie-talkie, and the lock rattles. When he opens the door, the heat pours in, muggy and suffocating. A couple steps and they're outside, inside the prison, a high concrete wall rising to the sky like a castle.

The trailers are straight ahead, regular two-tone mobile homes like anywhere, and there are their men, Tommy the tallest of them, waving from behind a gate in a high cyclone fence that another guard is opening. The gate swings free and there's nothing between them but a patch of crabgrass. Suddenly they're all running, the guards forgotten, no longer in charge. Patty's hands are full, but she's running, and he's running to meet her, to hold her and take the box and the bag from her. As he kneels to say hello to Casey, she keeps a hand on his shoulder, as if the two of them are magnetized. Casey's slow to hug him and won't give up his bag. She smiles at Tommy as if to say it's okay, give him time, this is all new to him.

It's new to her too, and a shock, after all of her daydreams, to have the guards lock the gate behind them and retreat into the tunnel, leaving them in a scrubby yard with a jungle gym and a slide, a few weathered picnic tables and a single drooping basket-ball hoop. Like the other couples, they ignore this equipment and head for their designated trailer, but before Patty steps up and into it, she sees Casey looking out at the second fence, maybe a hundred feet away, that separates them from the rest of the prison.

Inside, it's dim and musty, orange-and-brown-flowered curtains pulled over the windows. With every step Tommy takes, the whole thing sways. The ceiling's too low, and he has to walk hunched over. When she was a kid, a couple of her friends lived in trailers, and this one looks about the same—the oven door opening into the hallway like an ironing board, the kitchen table like a booth in a diner—except this one's deserted, blank as a motel room. Tommy sets the box down and turns on the light. "You're down this way, pardner," he tells Casey, and before he sets off after him, gives her a deep, breathtaking kiss.

"No fair," she says, and starts setting up house.

The tap sputters, hissing air. The fridge isn't cold. She checks that it's plugged in and turns it up, lifts out the racks and ice trays and dumps them in the sink. She has to wipe down the counters and stovetop, give the table a good going-over. The formica's a bright orange, the whole trailer done in a horrible sixties decor like a coffee shop, including a striped bathroom.

"Where'd they find this thing?" she asks Tommy. "It's like no one else would buy it."

She's at the sink, rinsing the silverware. He comes up from behind and holds her, kisses her neck, a hand slipping under her shirt.

"Where's Casey?" she asks, leaning back into him.

"In his room."

"What's he doing?"

"I don't know," he says. "Unpacking."

"Does he need help?"

A footstep and they both turn. She twists out of his arms as Casey clumps up the hall, a hand on the wall like they're in a submarine.

"It's hot in here," she says. "Why don't you two go see if you can open some windows."

Casey slides across the booth and pulls back the curtains. The windows are louvered slats of glass that crank up and out. Their view is of the trailer next door, and beyond it, the basketball hoop and the wall, straight lines wavering in the heat. The problem, Patty thinks, is that there aren't any trees.

Tommy goes through the groceries like he's opening presents. He holds up the lasagna like a prize, peels a banana, takes a bite and groans to show how good it is.

She makes them sandwiches and lemonade, letting the cold tap run. At home she eats her lunch out on the back porch, but she wants them to forget they're in prison, so they stay inside, pretending they're all alone. There's barely a hint of a breeze. They sit at the booth, Tommy squeezing her thigh under the table. Casey takes advantage, pouring himself a second glass of lemonade, digging deep into the bag of Fritos. Patty wants Tommy to step in, but he doesn't seem to notice. "Okay," she finally says, "let's save some for tomorrow."

There's only room for one person to clean up. Tommy volunteers so she can get herself settled. Casey tags after her, stopping in the paneled living room, where there's a TV with a cable box on top like at Eileen's. Casey appeals to her, hopeful.

"Okay, but it goes off when I say," Patty says.

On the far wall hangs the phone the coordinator warned her about—black and old-fashioned, a prop from the Cold War. When it rings, Tommy has to stop whatever he's doing and go outside to be counted. The coordinator said it will ring around ten times during the visit, at predetermined intervals. For some reason she expected it would be in the master bedroom, but why should anything be designed for their convenience?

The bay window in the bedroom faces the bay window of the next trailer, maybe twenty feet away. She supposes it's better that they hear the neighbors than have Casey hear them. The bed is two unmade beds pushed together, a stack of sheets reeking of bleach, and for a moment, standing there with her bag, the cheapness—the ugliness of it—is too much for her. This is supposed to be their special time together, but the place feels like a cheap motel. Tommy hasn't said anything about it yet, and she decides she won't either.

Once she gets the bed made, the room's slightly more inviting. She's still paranoid, checking the ceiling fixture for a camera. As she lays her clothes next to Tommy's prison greens in the sheet metal dresser (mingling them, as if it's forbidden), she imagines someone in a tower watching her on a flickering monitor. It seems impossible that they'd leave them alone.

"Hey," Tommy says, poking his head in, "you okay?"

"Yeah," she says, and it's not a lie, because she can open her arms and hold him against her, close her eyes and rest her head against his neck like they're slow-dancing, and for a moment everything's fine. The problem is letting him go.

"Let's just stay like this," she says.

"Okay."

"I mean forever."

"Okay."

From the other room come the synthesized blasts of intergalactic battle.

"*Star Wars*," Tommy says. "They're showing both of them back to back."

"I don't think Casey's ever seen them."

"I have," Tommy says, and reaches behind him to close the door.

"No," Patty says, stopping his arm. "We'll have time tonight."

"What's another six hours."

"Four. Come on, don't make me feel bad about this."

They break with a kiss and join Casey on the couch, Patty sitting on Tommy's lap, her arms wrapped around his.

"You know what I could go for?" Tommy says.

"What?" she asks, afraid she might have forgotten to bring whatever it is.

"An ice-cold beer."

"I know."

On screen, Han Solo and Chewbacca are flying the Millennium Falcon through a slowly closing pair of hangar doors as lasers ricochet everywhere. They escape out into starry space where there's just the soft rumble of their engines.

"This is weird," Tommy says, "watching TV without everyone shouting."

"It's nice," Patty says. Beside them, Casey's intent on the set. She wants him and Tommy to spend time together, just the two of them; it's one reason she brought the football. She should send them outside—it's past four, the day's almost gone—but when the first movie ends, Casey wants to watch the second, already coming on.

"Please?" he lobbies.

"Ask your father," she says.

Tommy checks with her first, like she's the final authority.

"Don't look at me," she says, and just then, as he's about to say yes, the phone rings.

"Sure," Tommy says, as Patty climbs off to let him get it.

"I'll be back," he tells her.

"You better be."

The whole trailer lifts an inch when he steps down. She can hear the chained gate clinking over Yoda's lines. She explained the count to Casey ahead of time so he wouldn't be surprised; now she wishes he was more upset about it, instead of caught up in a galaxy far far away. At least he's consistent, she thinks. It's his way of dealing at home. Why should it be any different here?

Tommy returns, apologizing. A minute later, someone knocks on the door, and he has to get up again.

She tries not to eavesdrop, afraid something's wrong. If the prison goes on lockdown, the visit's over.

"Pats!" he calls from the kitchen. "It's for you."

It's the woman from Albany with a cupful of freeze-dried crystals. Patty thinks she should invite her in, but the woman says she doesn't want to interrupt. Patty makes her take some strawberries.

"You didn't tell me you got busted," Tommy says.

"They took my shampoo too. I hope I don't gross you out."

"I'll have to give you a bath."

She shushes him, with Casey right down the hall, but lets him feel her up. "Okay, that's enough." It's like high school, wanting to give in but having to push him away. It's crazy, and selfishly—not seriously—she thinks maybe she should have left Casey at home.

"Just you wait," she warns Tommy.

"That's what I've been doing."

They pinch and poke and push each other like little kids. It feels natural, the way they've always talked at home, clinching in the kitchen, roughhousing on the couch. They can be silly in a way they can't in the visiting room; half the things they're doing now would get them thrown out.

Patty tries to provoke Casey with a finger in the ribs.

"Mom," he says, "quit it," warding her off with one arm, his eyes never leaving the screen. Again, she feels like they're wasting time, like they should be doing something together. They can watch TV at home—except they can't, not like this.

She needs to relax. As hard as it is for her to believe after waiting five years, there will be other visits. They're here, that should be enough.

Casey moves to the floor so he won't be distracted. He sits cross-legged, hunched forward, as if the set is drawing him in.

She and Tommy take over the couch, cuddling, sharing a sweating cup of lemonade and an ashtray. They stretch out the conversation of a regular visit, Tommy asking after her mother and Eileen and Cy, how Ruby Tuesday's is going. They both know the answers—there's nothing new, nothing urgent she needs to say to him. Tonight, maybe, she'll tell him she's been thinking about another baby—just thinking; she doesn't want to alarm him.

The station has padded the movie with commercials, but Casey never loses interest. Patty brought popcorn, but it's too hot, and she'd planned on having it tomorrow night anyway—that was supposed to be movie night. As *The Empire Strikes Back* drags on, Tommy raids the refrigerator, sneaking folded-over pieces of salami until she has to cut him off, saying she's going to start dinner pretty soon. By request they're having curried chicken salad, and for dessert, no-bake cheesecake with a graham cracker crust. She's been waiting for the day to cool down, but it's getting late. When the phone rings for another count, Patty takes it as a sign.

The burners are electric, and the galley heats up fast; she blots the sweat at her hairline with her wrist and worries that she'll stink of boiled chicken. She'll have to take a shower later. She knows Tommy will want in, but if they lock the bathroom door, will they still be able to hear Casey?

Dinner turns out all right, considering how little she has to work with. There are no pickles because they come in real glass jars,

no ice cream because it would have melted while they were waiting to be processed, no ice-cold beer. The cheesecake is still soupy
in the middle because the fridge isn't cold enough, so they wait
on it, doing the dishes and then going outside to play three-way
war at the picnic table.

It's cooler out now, and the wall's dark. Another couple's bar-
becuing at a built-in grill, something Patty didn't know was allowed.
The sun's almost down, a bank of clouds above them tinted the pink
of old postcards. Tommy searches the deepening sky like he's
expecting something.

"We never get to see this," he says.

Patty wants to see the stars come out, but the spotlights pop
on, bathing everything a harsh silver, throwing the net of the fence
over them, and they retreat inside. By lamplight the trailer's not as
ugly. The cheesecake's ready, or close enough. Casey doesn't like it,
and Tommy has to help him with his. After, Tommy does card
tricks for them, making Casey laugh, and then it's Casey's bedtime, even though it's not completely dark.

Patty's plan is to make the evening just like one at home, and
runs a bath for him. The tub's short, the rubber flower decals
bleached white. She scrubs it with dish soap and scalding water
before letting him get in, sits sweating on the closed toilet lid while
Tommy stands in the doorway, as if he's not allowed in—or is he
embarrassed, because when it's time for Casey to get out, Tommy's
gone, reappearing only when Casey's got his PJs on.

"Where'd you go?" she asks.

"I put water on for coffee."

Like every night, Casey leans back into his pillow propped
longways and reads his bedtime story aloud. By now he's memorized all of his books. He flips the pages with confidence, but he
seems to be going slower than usual, focusing, trying to get every

word right. Tommy's properly impressed, nodding at how good he is, but what's even better is seeing Tommy kiss him good night for the very first time.

There's no night-light, so Patty promises they'll leave the hall light on.

"Go to sleep," she orders, pulling the door halfway.

In the kitchen, as Tommy's pouring coffee, she asks what time everyone wakes up around here. Before he can answer, the phone rings.

"Seven," he says, and searches for his shoes.

She uses the time alone to open her new nightgown and lay it out on the bed. Next door the curtains are drawn, only a seam of light sneaking through. She closes their own curtains, then notices a mosquito bouncing against the ceiling fixture. There's nothing to swat it with except the cardboard from her nightgown. The mosquito's out of reach so she has to climb up on the bed and then duck down so she doesn't bang her head on the ceiling. She can picture Tommy finding her like this; it's enough incentive for her to nail the mosquito on her first try, leaving a bloody smear by the light. She rubs at it with the cardboard but it doesn't come off and she gives up, hopping down and smoothing the covers before he can return.

When she heads back to the kitchen, Casey's coming up the hallway.

"I heard a noise."

"That was just me," she says, turning him around. She tells him about the mosquito as she guides him back to bed. "Everything's fine," she says, as Tommy returns, shaking the whole trailer. "We're both right here and we're not going anywhere, okay?"

He says, "Okay," but timidly, and she leaves the door three-quarters open for more light.

"What's up?" Tommy whispers.

"He heard a noise."

"Does that happen a lot?"

"Depends," she says.

"He's getting big."

"Like his father."

They take their coffees into the living room and end up making out on the couch like teenagers, eyes closed, teeth clicking. She slips underneath him, he moves on top of her, and she feels the whole trailer shift. She struggles to the surface and holds him off with one hand, swallowing, shaking her head. "You know he's going to be out here any second."

They leave their coffees.

"Lock the door," she tells him.

She'd wanted to take a shower and model her nightgown for him to make their first time special, like a second honeymoon, but that plan seems silly now. She pulls his shirt over his head, then raises her arms so he can do the same to her. He's put on muscle from lifting weights and has a dark farmer's tan, a white stripe at each bicep. Chest to chest, they clutch at each other. She grips his shoulders, and he lets her inch him back toward the bed and push him over so she can work at the button of his jeans. She's tugging them down when she hears the doorknob rattle behind her, and stops.

A knock.

"Mom," Casey calls.

"Yeah, babe."

"I heard another noise."

"It was probably just us."

He tries the knob again.

"What do you need, hon?"

"I can't sleep," Casey says. "Can I come in with you?"

Tommy sinks back, his arms limp above his head. Patty bends and lays a palm on his cheek, turns his face to her and kisses him.

"Hey," she whispers, "at least we weren't on the couch."

She backs off the bed and tells Casey to go get his pillow, opens the dresser drawer and pulls on her regular nightshirt—one of Tommy's old T-shirts, worn thin.

The bed's a double, barely big enough for the three of them. She's squished in the middle, Tommy's arm thrown over her. Even with just the sheet on it's hot, and Casey's wide awake.

"Close your eyes," she says.

In the dark, the edges of the curtains glow. The room slowly fills with shadows.

They wait for him to doze off, listening to the hum of an industrial blower somewhere, the climax of a TV soundtrack from their neighbors', a lone plane crossing high above them and then fading to nothing. She lies still, aware of the silence, of Tommy's hand warm on her stomach. Casey's breathing turns ragged, long drawn sighs, and finally subsides, a soft inrushing whistle, his lips parted. Patty prays the phone won't ring.

The problem now is getting out of bed without waking him up. She gives him a few more minutes to go completely under before she taps Tommy's arm and points to the door. They won't be gone long. If he wakes up, she'll say Daddy was sick and they had to go to the bathroom.

They tiptoe the length of the hallway, following the walls. It seems wrong, using Casey's bed, but it's the only place. In the morning she'll switch the sheets.

They close the door because she wants the light on. She wants to see his body as she remembers it, to go over it inch by inch. He has bruises on both knees—"the bunk always gets you," he says— but otherwise no scars, no new tattoos. She knows she's changed after having Casey and working on the truck and waitressing; it's been five years. If he sees the difference, he doesn't mention anything. His hands seek out the same places, his kisses feel the same. She wants him now, and tells him so, but when she reaches for him, he's not ready.

She tries the spidery touch of her nails, the ridged friction of her fingertips—old standbys. And she understands. He could be nervous, after so long, or paranoid (because she is, imagining cameras everywhere). She coaxes him, nipping at his chest, scooting lower on the bed so she can get at him.

From far off comes the hooting of a train approaching a grade crossing, the thrum of a diesel burrowing through the night.

"Shit," Tommy says, sitting up.

She doesn't quit until he stops her, gripping her shoulder, and she realizes the drumming has grown louder, the mournful double note of the horn that much closer.

"It's coming here," Tommy explains, and she remembers the tracks along the wall.

It gives them a way out, and they take it, finding their clothes, creeping through the kitchen again and getting back in bed with Casey before the freight roars by. He stirs but doesn't wake up. It's funny but Patty doesn't dare laugh. Tommy lies on his back, staring at the ceiling.

She taps him and points to the door.

He just shakes his head.

She gets up anyway, rolling over him, taking him by the hand, and he can't protest without disturbing Casey.

"Come on," she says in the living room, "I'll make you something to eat."

"I'm not hungry," he says, but a minute later he's looking in the fridge. It's almost midnight.

She cuts them each a piece of cheesecake—firm now, perfect. They sit on the same side of the booth, hip to hip, eating. The cheesecake is too rich, gluing their mouths shut, keeping them from speaking. She runs them a glass of ice water, the cubes cracking.

"Sorry," he finally says, and starts to say something else.

"Shhh." She puts a finger to his lips and kisses him. "Just be with me."

That should be enough, and it is. It has to be. And then, when the phone rings and he has to leave again, she doesn't even have that. Even here, she waits for him.

GRATITUDE

SHE'D NEVER TELL TOMMY, BUT BEING ON TRAILERS MAKES REGULAR visiting that much harder. There's not enough time, and not being able to touch him the way she wants to is unsatisfying. The room is crowded and loud, with the machines and all the little kids. There's nothing for Casey to do, and then on top of that they have the long drive back.

Talking with the other wives, Patty finds out that at some places they get FRPs five or six times a year. Here, because of the demand, they're scheduled once every four months.

They do get better at it, after that first disaster. She doesn't expect as much, so there's less pressure on everyone. She under-

stands that he's as uncomfortable as she is, maybe even more paranoid, having to live with people watching him all the time. It's not
until their fourth visit that he's able to make love to her, and even
after that there are times when all she can do is hold him and tell
him it doesn't matter. And it doesn't. For forty-four hours, they're
a family.

Like any family, they settle into a routine. Gin rummy, Fritos,
TV. Through these early years, the menu stays the same. One
night of the two, they have lasagna, and always, tons of fresh fruit.
In summer they barbecue steaks and make flavored ice cubes with
Kool-Aid; in winter they tear up crusts for the birds. Christmas
comes whenever they're together, and their birthdays, their tenth
anniversary. Sometimes they get lucky and they're scheduled right
on the day, but it really doesn't matter.

The count still interrupts them, but no longer has the power
to devastate her, only the final eight o'clock call that says they've
got an hour left, and by then she's happy, filled with new memories.
One time she has her period and it rains all weekend, and they
have a great visit. The stove's broken, the toilet backs up, Tommy's
got the flu, Casey falls off the monkey bars—that's just life. Later,
she knows, these little disasters will help them place the time they
spent together, will become—like Eileen hooking their father's ear
with her very first cast—their most cherished memories.

NEAR-SIGHTED

IN FOURTH GRADE CASEY HITS A ROUGH PATCH. EVERYTHING UP through open house goes okay, but a couple of months in, his math teacher sends home an interim report warning Patty that he's in danger of failing. There must be some mistake, but there are his grades, broken down into logical columns. She knows his homeworks and test scores are A's because she's seen them. She doesn't understand why his class participation is a D and his quizzes are F's, and, more important, why she hasn't heard about it until now.

When she asks Casey, he says Mrs. Muller doesn't like him. He sits all the way in back and can't see the board, and she won't let him move up.

"Did you tell her you can't see?" Patty asks.

His yes is defensive.

When she asks how long he hasn't been able to see the board, he shrugs.

"He's got your father's eyes," her mother suggests.

Patty tests him by having him stand across the room from the TV showing the local news. Every photo over the anchorman's shoulder has a caption. "What's it say?" she quizzes him.

Casey cranes forward, squinting, then just shakes his head.

The cost of it panics her. She's working off the books for a friend of Eileen's, painting interiors, so the trip to the eye doctor and then the glasses from Lenscrafters come out of her pocket.

She tries not to ride Casey about how expensive they are, but when he leaves them in the plastic tray at the metal detector, before she can catch herself she reminds him sharply in front of the guards and the other women and then has to apologize in private.

She doesn't apologize for yelling at him that spring, when he loses them in the river while fishing with Cy and Eileen. By then she's between jobs again, and instead of a day's pay, she sees a chunk of their savings being swept downstream.

It turns into a daily battle between them. Casey hates his glasses, hates the way they look, hates taking care of them. The pair he lost were scratched and smeared, and while she lectures him about his new pair (even more expensive), within a month they're beat to shit.

"He's nine years old," Tommy says in a letter. "I'd worry about him if he took good care of them."

They write more now, trying to pinch pennies. Patty takes maybe the most boring job of her life, cashiering at a big discount liquor store in Vestal. It's steady, and she only has to work nights twice a week, but it's depressing, between the older regulars cashing their pension checks and the college kids stocking up for the weekend. Patty remembers how she and Tommy used to party, all the risks they used to take. She hasn't gotten stoned in years, and that lifestyle seems childish now. He was drunk that night, and while that's no excuse, she's sure it had something to do with what happened. It makes the job harder. When she sells a couple gallons of grain alcohol to a bunch of students or a five-dollar bottle of scotch to an old-timer, she can see all the possible consequences, none of them good. She wonders if she's getting old.

Early one morning while she's driving to work, flying along in the left-hand lane of the Southern Tier, the truck suddenly loses power, slows down, sputtering like she's run out of gas. The needle's past halfway. She's awake enough to signal right and coast onto the loose shoulder. By then it's completely dead, it just clicks once when she turns the key.

She props the hood open to take a look. Everything seems to be in place, the battery cables are solid, the belts and hoses are all connected. The Apalachin exit is just around the bend; she leaves the hood up and starts walking. She's nearly to the ramp when a state trooper pulls in behind her, his tires crunching.

"Nice timing," she says before turning around.

She accepts a ride to the truck plaza, where there's a pay phone. She thanks the guy, making it clear that it's okay to leave, but he curls around the pumps and idles near the far entrance of the lot like he's keeping an eye on her.

She calls the liquor store to say she'll be late. The truck she has towed to a garage in Apalachin she finds in the Yellow Pages, with instructions to call her before they do anything. Cy and Eileen are already at work, so she asks her mother to come pick her up, then drives her mother home and takes her old LeSabre to work. All day she broods on how much the truck's going to cost. It's got 140,000 miles on it, but most of that's highway, driving back and forth to Auburn. Shelving margarita mix, she takes a minute to figure out how many times she's made the drive—something like five hundred. But the truck's never given her problems before, and it's a part of her and Tommy.

At the end of the day she calls the garage, but they haven't had a chance to look at it. When she gets home, she asks Eileen what she thinks. It sounds like something electrical, Eileen guesses; it could be as simple as a cracked distributor cap or it could be more involved, like a bad alternator, she'll just have to wait and see.

What Patty wants isn't a diagnosis as much as some guidance. She's not going to talk to Tommy until she sees him this weekend.

Does Eileen know a local garage that will do an honest job, like the Hilltop? Maybe Cy could talk to Trace.

"You didn't know?" Eileen says. "Trace is in Syracuse. He got a sponsor up there."

"That's great," Patty says, yet she feels stung, like finding out an old boyfriend from high school is getting married.

Eileen goes on, oblivious. Towing the truck on a flatbed from Apalachin would be expensive. It's better to find out what's wrong with it before she does anything.

The next day when she calls the garage the mechanic says she's going to need a whole new wiring harness. They'll have to special-order the part because the truck's so old. He does the math out loud for her. With labor, they're looking somewhere around five hundred.

He waits for her decision. In the old days she would have told him she needed to check with her husband. She's tempted to do it now, just to buy herself some time. Instead, a simple logic kicks in. She was willing to spend three hundred, three-fifty tops, so this is just a hundred and fifty extra. Would she trade the truck for a hundred and fifty dollars?

"Go ahead," she says.

As soon as the words are out of her mouth, she knows she's made a mistake.

The feeling that she screwed up stays with her until she tells Tommy everything. She's relieved when he agrees with her that the truck's got a lot of life left in it. He doesn't seem surprised that the problem was the wiring harness.

"How much?" he asks, because she's pussyfooted up to it.

"Five hundred."

"That's not bad," he says with a shrug.

And then two weeks later, as she's bumping over the railroad crossing north of town, the head gasket blows and the engine spews a geyser of coolant that films the windshield and stops traffic in both directions. She hears what the guy driving the wrecker says, and the guy at the garage, and Eileen and Cy and her mother, even Tommy (who's not mad at her, just bummed), all of them giving her the same advice, and while she finally does let go of the truck, cleaning out the cab before it's hauled off to the junkyard, there's some small part of her that insists it can still be fixed.

LACERATIONS

IT'S APRIL WHEN HER MOTHER FIELDS THE CALL FROM THE CHAP-lain and immediately calls Patty at work. Tommy's in the hospital. He's going to be okay, they said; they just wanted to notify her.

"What happened?" Patty asks from the manager's booth over-looking the rows of booze.

"He didn't say."

"What hospital's he at?"

"I guess the one there."

Patty tries the counselor but it just rings. There's no point go-ing home, but she does anyway, dialing until her ears are sore. She's taking a break when the phone rings.

It's a collect call—Tommy, from the infirmary.

"I figured they'd screw it up," he says. "It's nothing, I just had a little accident in the kitchen. A couple stitches is all. They're not even going to keep me overnight."

Now that she knows he's all right, Patty can break down.

"Whoa, whoa," he says. "It's just a couple of little cuts."

"Where are they?" she asks, thinking of his hands.

"On my lower back."

"How do you cut your back?"

"I wasn't watching where I was going and I kind of backed into the edge of this table. It was just one of those dumb mistakes. Don't worry, they're taking care of me here."

"How many times did you back into it?"

"Hey," Tommy says. "It's all taken care of. Like I said, it was a mistake."

Sometimes on trailers when he's asleep she'll run a finger over the three short scars, but when she asks him to explain he just says that's over and they end up fighting. "You don't want to know," he says, and while it's true, in some way she already does.

SPACE INVADERS

THAT SUMMER MARKS TEN YEARS HE'S BEEN IN AUBURN. THOUGH they don't celebrate the occasion, it's hard not to look back (to look forward, the stretch ahead even longer). Tommy's gotten better at managing his time the last couple of years, setting goals instead of just living for their next FRP. He's earned certificates in construction carpentry and cabinetmaking, machine shop and small-engine repair, and has a regular work assignment stamping license plates. It's boring, and he only makes thirty cents an hour, barely enough to cover his cigarettes at the commissary. Patty knows he's ashamed of having to rely on her money orders, so anything that lets him pay his own way is a help.

In the same way, Patty feels she's taking advantage of her mother. She and Casey have been in her house for too long. At this point she doesn't see how they'll ever leave. The down payment for the used Horizon she drives ate up what little savings she had. She doesn't even like the car—it was all she could afford—and now on the first of every month she has an extra bill she can't let slide. Her mother says she understands if Patty can't give her anything for rent, but Patty thinks she needs to at least help with the food and the utilities.

Some months she can't. She's been bouncing between jobs. At Kentucky Fried Chicken, her shift supervisor's a high school kid, and she lasts only three weeks. She waitresses for the catering service out of the Treadway Inn, but summer's a slow time. They only do functions one or two nights a week, and it's straight hourly, no tips, and the heavy trays are hard on her back.

She's careful with her money, but Casey's growing. When they hit the back-to-school sales, she finds he's gained two sizes. He's going to be bigger than Tommy, except he's not athletic. Like any kid, he loves TV and playing video games, and as Christmas approaches, he lobbies hard for an Atari system like his friend Travis's. She tells him they can't afford it, but he thinks she's just joking with him, that after they open all the presents she'll surprise him with one last box. Her mother offers to lend her the money or to buy it herself, and Patty has to tell her not to. A week before Christmas she sits down with Casey to explain the situation and finds herself apologizing, but angrily, as if it's someone's fault besides hers.

Casey just nods, keeping quiet, as if waiting for the conversation to be over so he can leave.

"I'm hoping next year's going to be better," she says, almost a promise. Does she really believe that?

It's got to be. She has her application in at a bunch of places. The job she really wants is on the canning line at Ann Page Foods in Horseheads. Cy's cousin Mary Beth told him about it, so it hasn't even been advertised. It's a long commute but steady work with union benefits and a shot at overtime. Her fantasy is that she gets the job and then saves enough so they can move into their own place—not in Elmira but right here, on the west side of town. She wants to keep Casey in the same school so he can be with his friends. It's taken a while, but he seems to have found his crowd, and she doesn't want to mess that up.

She never hears back from Ann Page. She takes a job she saw in the paper—dispatcher at a trucking company in Nichols. It's closer and pays almost the same, but instead of being with a dozen other women, she's the only one. The office is a trailer crammed with file cabinets, and her boss chain-smokes little cigars. When she gets home at night she smells like a burning tire. For five months she keeps the job for the lack of anything better, but when one of the truckers makes a blatant pass at her and her boss treats it like a joke, she quits right then and there, grabbing her purse from her bottom drawer and stomping out to her car. Her mother says she did the right thing. Patty doesn't tell Tommy the whole story, and doesn't have to; it wasn't like she ever thought of the job as long-term.

So she's between jobs again when their next FRP approaches. Belatedly, they're going to celebrate Casey's birthday. She'd hoped to have enough for the Atari by now, to show him things ultimately do work out. Instead, she's going to make him a devil's food cake. She doesn't want to ask her mother for anything else, so she has to borrow forty dollars from Eileen to buy groceries. It's not the first time Eileen's helped her out, and driving home from the ShurSave, Patty tries to think of a way to pay her back. Make dinner for them, take them out to the races. Everything depends on her getting another job, getting some money, and as usual when it comes to her money troubles, soon she's imagining Shannon and how easy her life is.

She doesn't want to be old and bitter, but here she is, almost forty, and broke, and they're not even halfway yet.

The only thing that keeps her going is the FRP, and now she's worried about the four months after that. She catches herself looking past their visit, and she can't afford to. She has to appreciate whatever time they have together and not try to hold the whole twenty-five years in her head at once, otherwise the size of it will drive her crazy. It's like the AA bumper sticker she sees everywhere— One Day at a Time.

When she gets home the house is empty. Her mother's got an altar guild meeting and Casey's bus isn't due for another hour. Patty takes advantage of the unexpected privacy to stash the cake makings in the bottom of a box she's started. She just needs to remember the eggs Saturday morning.

She's in the middle of burying the baker's chocolate when the phone rings. She's hoping it might be NYSEG calling about the meter reader job, but it's the coordinator from Auburn. She's calling about their FRP scheduled for the upcoming weekend. She hopes she's caught Patty before she's made too many arrangements because she's afraid it's been cancelled.

"What?" Patty asks, because it doesn't make sense.

"I'm sorry," the woman says.

"Did something happen? Is Tommy all right?" She thinks of the stabbing. It has to be serious to cancel a visit this late. Either Tommy's gotten into trouble or the whole place is on lockdown.

"Your husband's fine as far as I know. The reason for your visit being cancelled is that he's been transferred."

"What?" she says. "That's impossible. He hasn't done anything."

"I don't know what the reason for the transfer is, all I know is that he *has* been transferred."

Her certainty freezes Patty, and she understands that nothing she can say to this woman will get their FRP back. That's minor.

"Where is he?" she asks.

THE MIDDLE OF NOWHERE

HE'S IN CLINTON, ALL THE WAY UPSTATE, ACROSS THE MASSIVE GREEN patch of the Adirondacks, near the Canadian border. Like Auburn, the prison itself isn't on the map—as if it doesn't exist—just the town of Dannemora. She has to prod Casey east to find it in the corner by Lake Champlain, a dot at a crossroads, even smaller than Owego.

At least she can make it there taking all interstates: 88 from Binghamton to the Thruway, then straight north on 87. She uses the weblike guide on the back to add up the mileage. It's over six hours with pit stops. They'll have to leave around two in the morning to beat the bus from the city—except where is she going to get the money to pay for gas? And how is she going to drive twelve hours after waking up at two? What about in winter, when it snows, because it's like being at the top of Vermont, and she can't afford a motel. It's just too far.

They're never given an official reason. When Tommy finally calls, he says the guards pulled him out of the plate shop in the middle of his shift. They'd already broken down his cell. One of them was carrying a cardboard box with his stuff; the other had his paperwork. The three guys in the van with him were all in the middle of long bids and up for good time. He says it like they made a mistake, like there are rules.

It's only later, when she's talking with Prisoners' Legal Services, trying to find out how to reapply for their FRP, that a volunteer explains that inmates sometimes get moved just because they've been in one place too long. They get to know the guards too well. They can get away with stuff that other inmates can't, and the others naturally resent it.

Patty doesn't buy it—Tommy's never mentioned being friendly with any guards, only that some of them are assholes and some aren't—but it makes as much sense as anything else. And really, at this point the reason doesn't matter.

The woman at Legal Services seems to understand. Her husband's a lifer; he's been all over. Because she's been through it, she has answers to questions Patty hasn't even thought of, like how to request the package guidelines for Clinton, since they're different from Auburn. Visiting's going to be different too. "From what I hear it's not as bad as Attica or Greenhaven," she says. "Just cold."

They talk a long time, almost like friends. Patty admits that lately it's been hard on her financially; the transfer couldn't have come at a worse time. The woman asks if Patty's in touch with any support groups, then gives her the number of an outreach ministry in Elmira that runs a bus every weekend. "They take donations," the lady on the phone says, meaning it's okay if she can't pay.

They can help her find a job; in the meantime, if she's having trouble making ends meet, they can help her apply for welfare.

Patty says she's just interested in the bus for now.

She decides not to make Casey go with her this first time, and she can tell he's relieved. Eileen drops her off in the parking lot at midnight. On the bus a minister wearing an expensive-looking sweater hands her a pamphlet and encourages her to sit anywhere, they're not full tonight. The pamphlet's religious, and for a minute she's afraid they'll have to listen to a sermon as they ride, but once they close the doors and get going, he just sits up front by the driver.

17's empty, the lights whizzing by outside.

She wakes up in a city that turns out to be Albany. The door's open, letting in the cold. It's four in the morning and people are climbing aboard, filing down the aisle. A woman her mother's age shuffles past, clutching the unwanted pamphlet to her purse. Someone up front has a baby that only stops squawling when they get back on the interstate. By then Patty's wide awake, her feet swollen and crampy from sitting for so long. There's no smoking, no scenery but a wavering strip of guardrail in the darkness that hurts her eyes. All she can do is take off her shoes and tuck her legs up on the seat, make a pillow of her bag and try to ignore the clip of the tires galloping over the expansion joints. Eventually she succeeds, dropping into a series of weird dreams she can't remember when they pull into a truck stop outside of Plattsburgh for gas.

Dawn is breaking. In the pink light she can see other buses in the plaza with them—the women from downstate she used to wake up early to beat. She knows it's wrong, but she wants the driver to hurry up so they can be first in line. While they're sitting there, one bus pulls out, then another, and another.

When they finally set off again, the driver leaves the interstate and heads straight into the hills. The two-lane blacktop follows a brown-bottomed trout stream between steep slopes of pines. Everyone's awake now, trying to put themselves together, teasing and spraying their hair. Patty's mouth is sour and her cheeks are hot, as if she has a fever. As they wind through the valley she joins the line for the bathroom, her toothbrush in her makeup bag. When it's her turn she splashes water on her face only to discover they're out of paper towels. She has to pat herself dry with toilet paper, then appraises what she sees in the mirror.

Even in the weak light, the bags and worry lines draw her attention. In two months she'll be forty, an age she never thought she'd be. She rubs in cover-up and takes extra time to fix her eyes, ignoring a knock on the door. Some blush and lipstick for color. It's not perfect, but it'll have to do.

She's back in her seat and ready for action when the bus pulls into Dannemora. The town's even smaller than Auburn, a dozen square blocks dwarfed on all sides by the endless green hills. The prison comes right to the curb of the dinky main street, the long front wall looming over the road like a dam. Thirty feet up, railed catwalks connect glassed-in gun turrets like the tops of lighthouses. On the other side of the street sit white frame homes with garages and yards, a Winnebago, a boat under a tarp. The bus slows to turn into the visitors' lot and the baby up front wails, inconsolable. There are marked spots in the middle for buses. There have to be at least six of them there already.

The prison seems even bigger when she steps down. It's cold for this time of year, and quiet: she can hear the wind in the flags out front. When she stands still, she catches clouds sliding west across the top of the hills. It looks like rain.

Once everyone's off, the minister leads them inside a separate visitors' center like they're a tour group. They're lugging packages, bags, dresses on hangers. The waiting room's bigger here, but louder, more crowded. The other buses must be from the city. A lot of the women look like they're dressed for church, in flashy outfits with matching hats. Patty's aware of her whiteness, and the guards'. Since it's her first time, she has to fill out new paperwork—or the old guard fills it out for her, incredibly slowly—meaning that of all the people on her bus, she's the last to get a number.

The waiting is the same, and the lazy pace of processing, the head guy at the desk calling three numbers and then a few minutes later three more. The guards stand aside, businesslike, trying not to get involved. She reads the paperback of *The Mammoth Hunters* Eileen lent her, checking her watch every so often. When the guy finally calls her, it's ten-thirty.

They walk across the lot to the prison entrance. The scanners here are different—fancier, brand new. If you beep at all, they pull you aside and wave a black wand shaped like a Dustbuster over you, front and back. Patty leaves her bag in a locker, knowing her cosmetics will never make it through.

She passes and moves with the group to the visiting room. There aren't separate tables for them to sit at, but a series of long counters with visitors on one side and prisoners on the other, everyone packed in shoulder to shoulder, kids sitting on laps. When she takes a seat at an empty place, she finds there's a divider underneath. While she waits for Tommy to be brought down, she tries to ignore the private conversations on both sides of her and looks around the room for clues to how much contact is allowed. All over, couples are holding hands, and there, a pair leans across the counter and clinches, then sits down. The guard at the desk notices but doesn't stop them. It must be permitted, Patty thinks. No one would come this far and risk losing a visit. Still, she needs to make sure, and she's relieved when she spots another couple embracing.

It always surprises her how he looks the same no matter how she's feeling. He's still lean and muscled—in better shape than she is. His hair hasn't changed in years, maybe a few white threads in his sideburns, and he's wearing the same dingy state greens she'll never get used to. She stands and squeezes him, the stubble of his jaw brushing her cheek, a feeling she's forgotten she missed until now. Every time, seeing him in person reminds her of how weak her memory is.

They break because they have to, pull their chairs close and take each other's hands.

"How was the bus?"

"Easy," she says. "I should have brought Casey."

"How's he doing?"

"Good. He's ready for school to be over, that's for sure."

"I thought he was getting straight A's."

"His trouble's getting up in the morning. He keeps missing his bus. I swear, one of these days I'm going to make him walk."

Patty knows at some point she'll have to tiptoe around her money troubles and how it's going to make visiting him that much harder, but their problems can wait. They talk about the coming summer and what she wants for her birthday (nothing, just their FRP). They talk about her mother's garden and laugh at how Patty trapped that skunk one year. Tommy says she won't believe it, there are gardens here called courts, a whole hillside of them out back where different cliques hang out.

"That's weird," she says, trying to picture it, and the conversation stalls, letting in the clunk of the microwave's door, the electric hum of something cooking. It's not awkward anymore; after so many years they've gotten used to the silences.

"You hungry?" Tommy asks, and they hit the vending machines—picked clean, only some coconut yogurts and soggy meatball subs left, a few rusty cans of tomato juice. She brought all this change and there's nothing to spend it on.

She knows she shouldn't let it get to her, but she's tired. She's kept things together for so long that she doesn't know what to do now that they're falling apart. She wants to confess everything to Tommy, to melt down right here so he'll comfort her, except she'd never do that to him, especially not now, in a new place.

"Hell," she says, "let's live dangerously," and punches the button for a meatball sub.

They talk about getting back their FRP. Patty tells him about Prison Families and how they hooked her up with the holy roller bus. She doesn't mention what the lady said about applying for welfare.

"So how is it?" she asks.

"It's not bad." He thinks, tipping his coffee cup to see it's empty. "It's different. You get used to having the same people around so you know what to expect. I don't have a work assignment, that's the worst thing."

"It's going to be cold," she says.

"Yeah, I was going to ask you to order me some long johns. A lot of my stuff didn't make it."

"I'll send a money order," she says, as if it's no problem.

She misses the privacy of their FRP, the luxury of whispering in bed, cooking for him. Soon they're at the part where Tommy asks after her mother and Patty dismisses him: "You know her, she never changes." It's nearly three. Around the room, people are watching the clock to make sure they get every minute. Even before the guard calls over the PA that visiting hours are over, Patty feels flat and disappointed.

And there's no reason to be. He seems healthy and in decent

spirits, considering, and whatever was going on at Auburn is over, she hopes. She mulls it over on the bus, green scenery sweeping by the window. The rain's gone and the sky's rosy. Around her everyone's changed back into their street clothes. They're chatting and laughing, riding the high of seeing their men. Usually Patty's happy after a visit, still full of him, already looking forward to the next one, but today she feels strange and out of it, as if she's getting sick. Part of it's how far away he is, because as much as she wants to believe the distance doesn't matter, it does make a difference, but part of it's also that her life is such a mess right now that she feels she can't help him.

The first thing she needs to do is get a job and hang on to it, it doesn't matter what. Tomorrow she'll hit the classifieds; Monday she'll call Prison Families. Visiting won't be easy, but she'll find a way, even if it means taking the bus every other week. Eventually they'll get back their FRP. Things can only get better.

LAST NAME FIRST

THE WOMAN AT PRISON FAMILIES WALKS HER THROUGH THE GUIDElines over the phone. What surprises Patty the most is how they're eligible for welfare. Their family income is well below the maximum, and has been for years, meaning they could have been getting checks all along. Patty thinks she was stupid not to do this before. After how much the state has taken from them, she's not ashamed to ask for something back.

She doesn't tell anyone she's applying. She drives down to the state office one morning and submits last year's tax forms and signs the papers for a woman who doesn't ask her any questions, then drives back home and tries to forget about it. If she's approved, the first check should arrive in thirty days. In that time, with Cy's help, she lands a job as a health aide at Riverview Manor and does what she swore she'd never do: goes back to Ruby Tuesday's.

She gets up at six and makes Casey breakfast, then leaves her mother in charge of getting him on the bus. The job at Riverview is half dealing with patients and half housekeeping—mopping up bathrooms, peeling wet sheets off beds. Her shift starts at 7:30 and ends at 4, which gives her just enough time to get home and feed Casey before the dinner shift. She works lunch Saturday and Sunday for the tips, but because of visiting she sets up her schedule so she has every other weekend off.

When she gets her first welfare check, she can't believe how small it is. She crumples the envelope and buries it in the kitchen trash, deposits the check at an ATM. She uses the money to pay back her mother for the phone bill, since Tommy's calls cost more now. At first her mother says she can't accept it, but Patty convinces her.

She's tired all the time, like when she was on the town truck, but that was a long time ago. She sleeps so deeply, drops off so easily that she worries she's too old for this.

The biggest drawback is not seeing Casey, but he's at the age where he doesn't want her hanging around anyway. He's got a small core of friends, including Adam, who he's known since kindergarten. They hang out after school and take the late bus home. Their latest kick is skateboarding. Casey's always complaining that he has to borrow his friends' boards. Patty's not sure how serious he is, but when she goes to pick him up one day, she catches him practicing tricks on the handicapped ramp with everyone else watching, and though he makes her laugh—this huge kid on a tiny board—he's actually pretty good. She still feels bad that his birthday got pushed to the side; now that she's got some money, she asks him which he'd rather have, the Atari or a skateboard. He gives her a look like she must be kidding him. The only catch is that he has to wear a helmet. He can pick it out himself, but he's definitely getting one.

She knows sooner or later he'll take a bad spill and her mother will go I-told-you-so, but Patty has so few chances to spoil him, and he is getting straight A's. At the bike store, paying for the board feels extravagant and reckless—it's half a Saturday's tips—and when they're in the car again and Casey thanks her, she says, "Just don't break anything."

Otherwise she's careful with her money, writing up a budget and sticking to it. She's not crazy about taking the bus, but it's cheaper than driving, and she's not sure the Horizon could stand the wear and tear. She donates twenty dollars per trip, thirty when Casey's with her. He hates going, and she understands. She doesn't like seeing Tommy like this either.

She's still waiting to hear about their FRP when she turns forty. It's a Wednesday, and she's scheduled to work her regular shifts. Her mother has a cake for her after dinner, and gives her the handmade card Tommy sent. That's not all: there's a present from him, though the wrapping paper is familiar, straight from the basement.

"I helped a little," her mother admits.

As Patty tears the paper away, she sees she has the present upside down. It's a picture frame with a foldout fin in the back, and she flips it over. He's drawn a pencil sketch of the two of them from an old photo, a kind of valentine. The frame is made of dozens of red and white Marlboro softpacks woven together in an intricate two-tone pattern, like a tile floor. Casey and her mother are impressed by the frame, but Patty's more interested in the young couple in the drawing, knowing, as she does, what happens to them. It seems like the wrong thing to give someone turning forty, reminding her of the carefree people they used to be.

Her mother and Casey have teamed up to get her a backpack just the right size for the lockers, with lots of pockets, proof that they do listen to her. When she picks it up, it's heavy, something plastic rattling inside—tapes, and a Walkman with those lightweight headphones she's seen other women wearing on the bus. Casey's dubbed her favorite albums. He says there are enough tapes to last all the way up there and back.

The cake's homemade, and she's happy with her gifts. It's a milestone, she supposes, forty, but she really wasn't expecting anything. So it's a good birthday. She doesn't mind working her shift at Ruby Tuesday's. When there's a birthday on the other side of the room, she joins the crowd around the table and sings along with the rest of the waitstaff like she does every night.

The weeks pass so fast. Casey's bored, and bugs her mother to drive him to friends' places. He pitches a tent in the backyard and invites Adam to sleep over. When that's too tame, they want to camp in the woods, but Patty vetoes the plan. The tent already smells of cigarettes, an allegation Casey denies. It makes no sense—he's on his own all day long—but she wants them where she can keep an eye on them.

As July turns to August she expects she'll hear about their FRP. When she doesn't, she doesn't freak out. There's no time to mope. Fridays there's barely enough time to get to the bank and deposit her checks.

She's going along fine, and then in the middle of August, between the wilting heat and the freezing restaurant, she comes down with a cold and has to take time off so she doesn't infect any of the patients. She only misses three days, but they seem endless. She sees why Casey says he's bored. The TV's crap. She never understood why Eileen shelled out for cable until now, and gives in.

She's glad to get back to work, at least at Riverview. She's gotten to know some of the patients and likes delivering their meal trays and making sure they're taken care of. She wheels them to the sunny common room overlooking the river and helps them play bingo. She finds their hearing aids and rewinds their books-on-tape. A lot of them just want to talk, and Patty can sympathize. The nurses give her grief because patients ask for her by name. For once she feels needed, part of the place.

It makes Ruby Tuesday's that much worse. After dinner, she's tempted to call in sick and just lie on the couch and watch the new cable. She hates changing into the uniform and pinning on her nametag, hates the twilight drive and all the mall traffic. By the time she punches in she's dull and clumsy. Busy nights she can't keep up; slow nights she doesn't make any money. She tries to remind herself that a second job is necessary, but by now she's dug herself out of the hole. Driving home one night, she falls asleep at the wheel and only wakes up when her tires rumble over the shoulder, and that's it, she quits.

She's doing all right with just the one job and welfare, and after her first three months she gets benefits. Now when Casey complains about a sore throat she can take him in and get him checked out. There's even a pharmacy card, the first she's ever had. She keeps it in her purse like a secret weapon.

Labor Day weekend she works her regular shift for the double time. The next day, school starts, so Casey's out of her mother's hair. They should be hearing from the FRP coordinator any day now. Patty knows she'll come home late one afternoon and the letter will be there on the kitchen table. Like everything in her life, it's just a matter of time.

BIENVENUE À NEW YORK

IT DOES COME, BUT NOT UNTIL OCTOBER, AND THEN THEY'RE scheduled for the week before Thanksgiving—not the weekend, like she's used to, but Thursday and Friday. She doesn't think she should pull Casey out of school, so she goes alone, driving the Horizon, since there's no bus during the week. The trailers there are the same, only colder, the water out of the faucet freezing her front teeth when she brushes. They spend a lot of time under the covers. She fixes him an early Thanksgiving dinner, and then, Saturday morning, the call comes and she has to leave.

The drive's not so bad split up. The next time she makes it, it's spring and Casey's with her. When they leave Owego it's sixty degrees; five hours later they're crawling along the Northway in a blizzard, following the blinking lights of a tractor trailer. In the summer, half the cars heading south have Quebec plates; in the fall they return, a reverse migration.

That winter he'll have served exactly half of his minimum sentence, meaning he's halfway to his first crack at parole. Neither of them mentions it as they miss another Christmas together, another New Year's, but Patty can't help but run the numbers. It's impossible to imagine another twelve and a half years like this. It already seems like forever.

WE ARE THE CHAMPIONS

THESE ARE SOME OF THE HARDEST YEARS, THE LONG MIDDLE OF HIS sentence, when they're so far apart. He's applied for a transfer to Elmira, but, according to Prisoners' Legal Services, his chances are slim. She's thought of moving to Plattsburgh, but what if they transfer him again? She doesn't want to take Casey away from his friends. Tommy agrees. They write more now, they visit when they can, they have their FRP every three or four months. Now that Casey's a teenager, he's busy with his friends, and moody like Eileen used to be. He can be sweet, helping her mother with dinner, and then he can turn around and be completely thoughtless. Patty has to badger him to come with her.

"Don't you want to see your father?" she asks.

"Yes," he says defensively, as if there's no right answer.

"He doesn't have to come see me," Tommy says, "but he shouldn't be giving you a hard time."

"He's not," Patty says, because it's true but also because she's the peacemaker. He and Casey haven't grown close the way she hoped, and now she needs to protect them from each other.

It's hard, because as Casey goes through high school, she becomes more and more frustrated with him. He still gets straight A's and hangs around with the same slacker friends, he even gets a job washing dishes at the Parkview, but what little time he spends at home he's shut up in his room like a bear. At night when she's ready to go to bed, she sees a line of light under his door. She knows he stays up till two or three reading and listening to his headphones, and then he has to get up and catch the bus at seven. In the morning he's sullen and touchy, banging out of the house with red eyes and wet hair, wearing the same black jeans he had on the day before. When Adam drops him off after work she's in bed already and hears him come up the stairs and take a half-hour-long shower, then close his door. When they do have to talk, to go over their schedules or arrange for him to be picked up, he listens as if he needs to be somewhere else and she's taking up his time.

She knows he's smoking and worries that he's drinking.

"Now you know how *I* felt," her mother says, and while Patty sees the double standard, she lets Casey know he's not fooling her. She sits him down and makes it clear that she's not going to have him sneaking around behind her back. She knows from experience that people his age are going to party, that's just natural; the important thing is to know how much is too much.

New Year's Eve, or New Year's, since it's two in the morning, his so-called friends dump him on the frozen lawn at the bottom of the driveway, passed out and jacketless, reeking of vomit. When he wakes up around dinnertime, she explains that he's grounded for the next month—and he's paying for the lost coat, a harsher penalty, since he's been saving to buy a car once he gets his license. She says she'll have to talk to his father; they might have to re-think that decision too.

By the time she talks to Tommy, Casey's apologized (he's as embarrassed as he is sorry) and she's calmed down. Tommy asks her to put him on, and Casey stands there listening to the lecture, saying nothing but a glum "Yes, sir," then retreats to his room.

"What did you say to him?" Patty asks Tommy.

"I told him what I always tell him. I told him he needs to be thinking about helping out instead of making more problems for you."

"He didn't do it on purpose."

"What, get drunk?"

"Get sick."

He thinks she's being too easy on him. "Christ, you'd think a kid who weighs that much could hold his liquor."

It's a shame, because it ruins what should be a good time for them. The Bills are cruising through the playoffs, beating Dan Marino and the Dolphins and then, in the AFC championship, the hated Raiders. They're going to the Super Bowl.

It's like a holiday, the anticipation. While the rest of the country is tying yellow ribbons around their coachlights and watching the flak float up from Baghdad, the Southern Tier is gearing up for a party. Even her mother asks Patty if she thinks they stand a chance, as if admitting the possibility. The seasonal aisle at the ShurSave is done up like a used car lot in twists of red and blue crepe paper. Patty can't resist a package of paper plates and napkins with the Super Bowl logo. "Let's go Bills!" her cashier cheers, setting off the whole checkout, and Patty feels weird. For so many years she's been out of step with Owego; now all of a sudden she's part of the crowd.

Casey seems to be the only one immune to the craziness, disdaining the big game and the war, as if they're both rigged. His skateboard sports a NO BLOOD FOR OIL sticker that upsets her mother. As if to make a point, he goes snowboarding with Adam the day of the game. Cy and Eileen bring two sixes of beer, and Patty makes her hot wings. All afternoon she feels dizzy. Most of the guys in Clinton are from the city; if the Giants win, Tommy will never hear the end of it. She's told him not to bet anyone but knows he probably has. At halftime it's 12–10 Bills. "This is exciting," her mother gushes, but Patty doesn't like it. She wants a slaughter like the Raider game.

The Giants take the lead halfway through the fourth quarter, 20–19. The Bills get the ball back but have to punt. There's barely two minutes left when their defense stops the Giants.

She can't watch as Jim Kelly leads them downfield. Every play she bows her head and covers her face, waits for Cy and Eileen and her mother to shout or groan with the outcome. The Bills are moving. "They're doing it," her mother keeps saying, driving Patty insane because she knows nothing about football and how quickly things can fall apart.

With eight seconds left they have the ball on the Giants' 30.

"This is it," Cy says as they line up to kick.

This, Patty watches, standing, holding hands with Eileen, who's holding hands with Cy, who's holding hands with her mother, the four of them linked like dancers at a Greek wedding.

Here's the snap, and the hold. The kick is up. It's long enough, the ball turning over and over, and then, incredibly, it crosses in front of the right upright, passes between the camera and the goalpost, breaking the white line and continuing to slice right, no good.

"Oh shit," her mother says, and lowers her arms as the Giants' sideline erupts.

There are no flags. The game's over.

Patty drops back onto the couch. She feels sorry for Tommy, and for herself, and promises she'll never let herself get worked up like this again over something so dumb. But then, the next year, when the Bills lose their second straight Super Bowl, she feels exactly the same way. And the year after that. And the year after that.

THE CLASS OF '94

THE GUIDANCE COUNSELOR LIKES CASEY'S GRADES. SHE WISHES HE had a sport or at least some extracurricular activities to round out his application, but his academics are so strong that she's not worried. She knows Casey's decided on computer science as a major, but has he thought about what *kind* of a school he's interested in? Because, really, with his SATs and a transcript like this, he can go anywhere he wants.

It's midmorning and Patty's in her work uniform. That might be the reason the woman goes over the financial aid form so thoroughly. At first Patty's insulted, and then grateful, since she has no idea how they're going to pay for this. Casey's going to have to apply for student loans and hold down a part-time job, but even that's not going to cover some of the places the counselor's talking about.

One name that comes up over and over is Cal Poly. Patty jokes that it's too far away, she'll never see him again. At heart she's partly serious. Why does he have to move two thousand miles away to type on a computer? Cornell's forty minutes from their front door, and very good, according to the counselor. SUNY-Binghamton's another possibility, or Elmira as a fallback.

After the meeting, Patty wants to talk but he has to go back to class. The bell rings, and the halls fill with teenagers, making her feel ancient, a fake, her jacket not quite disguising her uniform and white shoes, and she flees. The drive back to work gives her too much time to think about him leaving. Even if he's only at Binghamton, he'll be out of the house. She can't believe it's really going to happen.

She's always known he was smart, and while she's celebrated his report cards over the years (and kept them, an envelopeful in the top drawer of Shannon's dresser), she's just expected good grades from him, because they both know he's capable. Patty only realized how much she'd taken that for granted when the counselor showed her his transcript—a solid wall of A's. She was proud, but also a little intimidated. The last couple of years she hasn't pushed him; he's done it all by himself. And she knows how hard it is. She's been going to night school for her supervisor's certificate, and even though she's motivated and the professors are lenient, she still gets B's. Like her father reading while the three of them battled over the TV, Casey has the ability to block out the rest of the world and focus on one thing. Her worry is that he's *too* good at it, like her father, never letting anyone get close. She thinks he'll be happy to get away and be out on his own, the way she was, breaking free of her mother's house. She can see why California would seem ideal.

It's his decision, she tells him. Wherever he chooses, somehow they'll find a way. Patty expects him to be more excited about the whole process. Every day he gets a stack of form letters and catalogues from all kinds of colleges, but she never sees him reading them.

Tommy's more excited than he is. When they talk on the phone, he tells Casey about a show on computer graphics he saw on the Discovery Channel. He thinks they should visit MIT, it's supposed to be the best for that.

"Are you interested in MIT?" he asks, because Casey hasn't said anything.

"I don't know," Casey says.

"Where *are* you thinking of, then?"

"I've got to look at my stuff first."

After Casey's safely off, Tommy says he doesn't understand. "What's his problem, is he stoned or something?"

"He's fine," Patty says. "I think he's just overwhelmed by the decision. Wouldn't you be?"

She is. She's been off welfare since her promotion a few years ago, and doing okay, but the money some of these places charge is ridiculous. Even a state school like Binghamton is asking way too much. She wants to know what's going on in Casey's head. Is he really interested in going to Elmira? If he isn't, then there's no sense applying there. All he'll say is "I've got to work on my list," like he can't take the time to think about it right now.

His spring break's in late March, the only time they can do the college tour. She pulls out the calendar and sits him down to choose. Together they've driven the Horizon to Clinton a dozen times; it'll get to Boston, if that's where he wants to go.

He does.

"That should make your father happy," she says.

And can they stop at Rensselaer in Troy? Also Amherst, halfway across Massachusetts.

When she checks the map, she sees he's thought it all out. The only long drive is the one home.

"What about Cornell?" she asks. "We could go up that Friday, just for the day."

He agrees, for her sake, just as, that fall, when it's time to apply, he applies to Binghamton as one of his backups. The full list includes MIT, Cal Poly, Carnegie Mellon, Rensselaer, Amherst, Cornell and Syracuse. Patty doesn't even have to look at the map: except for Cal Poly, all of them are closer than Clinton. And yet, the more she reads about Cal Poly, the more she's convinced that it's the best place for an independent kid like Casey. So she's not sure how to feel in the spring when he gets rejected. She says she's sorry, and though he tries to shrug it off, she knows he's hurt, and she wonders if he was depending on it, if that was his plan all along.

He doesn't make it into MIT either. Tommy doesn't understand—he's got straight A's.

Everywhere else, he gets accepted. Now he has to choose. They can get state aid to go to either Rensselaer or Cornell, but she makes it clear to him that it shouldn't influence his decision. Wherever he goes, it's going to be expensive.

Tommy's rooting for Cornell, since it's good *and* close. Patty is too. When he picks Rensselaer, she congratulates him as if she's happy with his decision. Troy's only three hours across I-88, she says, as if it's convenient. She doesn't have to say it's right on the way to Clinton.

SWEET TOOTH

SENDING CASEY OFF THAT FALL, SHE REMEMBERS HOW DIFFERENT his first day of school was, how he cried and made himself sick so he could stay home. All summer he's been preparing to leave, winnowing his CDs, choosing what to take from his room. He packed his car last night, pointed toward the road, so all he has to do is kiss her mother goodbye, and then her.

"Be good," Patty says. "I love you."

"I love you too," he says, but normally, like he's going to hang out with his friends and he'll be back for dinner.

She can only wave as he pulls out, the tailpipe of the loaded-down Tercel scraping the drive. He's busy shifting, crossing the long flat at the end of the yard, but then his hand appears in the window, flailing in their direction. He keeps it up even after the engine complains, until he's swallowed by the line of weed trees at the edge of the meadow.

"You should be proud," her mother says inside, because she can see from Patty's expression that she's lost. The feeling stays with her all morning, pursuing her through the empty house. She has food shopping to do, so she gets her list from the fridge and pokes through the cupboards to see what they need. With just the two of them, their grocery bill should be tiny.

She feels weird at the store, not picking up the usual three gallons of 1%. No Diet Dew, no Fig Newtons, so she splurges on some mint Milanos, as if they might console her, and has them with a cup of coffee, watching some awful sci-fi movie.

Later, straightening up his closet, she finds a stash of candy bars in a shoebox. KitKats and Snickers, Mr. Goodbars. There must be twenty bucks' worth. She can't tell how old they are. Over the years, they tried all kinds of diets to help him slim down. She remembers the expensive shakes, the vitamin supplements that came in the mail. She caps the box, sets it back in its place.

She could find worse things, she thinks.

The house seems quieter without him, though she knows it's not true. If he were home—which he wouldn't be, Sunday afternoon—he'd be in his room with his headphones on. The most they'd hear from him would be footsteps, maybe the toilet flushing.

She misses him most at meals, and in the morning, the daily scramble to get out the door. Some nights she still waits for the sound of his car in the driveway, the sign that he's finally home from work.

He's busy, and doesn't call as much as she'd like. Sometimes she feels like it's purposeful, as if he's punishing her. He sounds okay on the phone. His classes are interesting; there's a lot of homework. As always, she wishes he was more enthusiastic, but that wouldn't be him. The difference between talking to him and talking to Tommy is almost funny, one so glum, the other so interested. Because she and Tommy know how to use their minutes now.

Every time she talks to Casey, she has to resist asking him to come home for the weekend, to come with her up to Clinton to visit. Instead, she writes him letters he doesn't answer and doesn't mention, or only when she brings them up. She doesn't remember him taking so much of her time, except now she finds herself faced with even more empty hours. She tries to read but ends up watching TV, clicking through the channels when nothing's on or playing his handheld Yahtzee. One night she cleans the stove and while she's waiting for it to bake off the gunk, wipes down the miniblinds. Her mother tells her she needs a hobby.

"Like what?" Patty asks.

"I don't care," her mother says. "Pick something."

The next day at work, Patty signs up for an after-hours computer class. She already uses one to make the monthly schedules, but she really ought to know more. It passes the time, and some of the stuff is actually fun. Now when Casey tells her about what he's doing, she almost knows what he's talking about.

Fall break, he comes home for the week. Patty has piled up comp time, and takes off work to be with him. She does his laundry, makes chocolate chip waffles. She expects him to be different somehow, changed, more mature, but except for being ten pounds heavier, he's exactly the same. He keeps his door closed and barely speaks. He sleeps till noon, then heads over to Adam's, stops back home for dinner, then stays out late, cruising around town with his friends.

After a couple days of this, Patty can't hold back. She ambushes him at dinner, hoping he'll see how selfish he's being. "Look," she says, "I know you want to see your friends, but I took time off to be with you."

"I didn't ask you to."

"You don't have to ask people you love to do things for you. They just do them."

"I'll stay home tomorrow, okay?" He makes it sound like he's been wronged, but she doesn't want to argue. Later, when he comes home that night, she gets him to sit with her in the kitchen and they both say they're sorry.

It's the best conversation they have. Sunday he leaves, saying he probably won't be back till Thanksgiving.

It's okay, she says, to him and to herself. It's only six weeks. That's not so long.

MEDIUM SECURITY

JUST BEFORE HALLOWEEN SHE GETS A LETTER THAT SAYS TOMMY'S being transferred to a medium security facility. It's standard procedure with long-term prisoners. He'll be reassigned in late November, five years in advance of his first parole date. She's tried not to look that far ahead. Getting excited will only make the time go slower.

They're hoping for somewhere close, like Cayuga, at the bottom of Owasco Lake, just south of Auburn. There are dozens of mediums all over the state, half of them built since Tommy went in, part of the War on Drugs. There's Gowanda and Wyoming over by Buffalo, and Oneida and Mohawk up near Syracuse. Even Wallkill or Otisville down in the Catskills wouldn't be too bad. Almost anywhere would be closer than Clinton.

DOCS won't tell her anything—for security purposes. She relies on Prison Families to fill the gaps. Like maxes, not all mediums have an FRP, and mediums are actually more dangerous. With so many inmates doing short bids, their populations aren't as stable.

They have a last visit the Friday after Thanksgiving, all three of them, Casey driving most of the way up. The weather's warm and there are tons of buses, but it's not as bad as it will be Saturday. It amazes Patty how little changes. After twenty years, there's still the fear, going in, that they'll be turned away on some technicality, that he's been transferred early and no one's told her, that the whole place will go on lockdown, but no, they're on the list, Casey's college ID works, everything's cool.

Tommy's been there so long they've graduated to the honors visiting room, with regular tables like at Auburn. They can hold hands and play footsie as long as they're discreet. Casey sits quietly to the side as she tells Tommy everything Prison Families told her. Tommy reassures her; wherever he goes, he'll be fine. He's made it this far.

"So how's it going?" he asks Casey, touching his arm. "I hardly ever get to talk to you anymore."

"It's going good," Casey says, nodding, and tells him about

his classes, ignoring the second half of the question. There's a phone in his suite but he's got two roommates who wouldn't understand why he's getting collect calls from his father. He couldn't pay for them anyway. As much as Patty's worked to make sure Tommy's a part of his life, she can't force Casey to give him the number.

It's hard to leave, not knowing when and where she'll see him again. She takes Casey's hand as they move between the checkpoints, and he suffers it. Their stamps glow a toxic lemon-lime under the ultraviolet lights. As they cross the lot, the main entrance at her back, she has an attack of nostalgia. This is the last time she'll ever be here. She won't miss the giant white fortress or its dumpy gray town. She won't miss the six-hour drive or the claustrophobic bus ride through the pines. So why, driving away, does this sadness grab at her?

The long weekend ends. Casey goes back to school; she goes back to work. Riverview's growing so fast they're having serious understaffing problems, and she's been given the job of recruiting new employees on top of her usual duties. She likes being a supervisor. The beeper is annoying sometimes, going off while she's driving or in the middle of dinner, but it also makes her feel appreciated. With no distractions at home, she's able to concentrate, and has gone from just trying to keep busy to actually being good at her job. Sometimes, like the week after Thanksgiving, she accuses herself of hiding in her work. It's not a bad thing, necessarily. Like the waiting, the uncertainty never gets any easier.

It's Friday when he finally calls from Bare Hill.

The name of the place hits her like a verdict. Ever since she found out he was being moved, she's been studying the different mediums. Bare Hill is forty miles northwest of Clinton, even farther in the middle of nowhere, and like a lot of the mediums, doesn't have an FRP.

"Fuck," she says.

"Yeah," he says. "What you said."

UPSTATE

THERE ARE TWO NEW PRISONS SEPARATED BY A CROSSROADS OUT-side of Malone, and a third going up right beside them. At the crossroads stands a brand-new mini-mart and the only stoplight for miles, the concrete that holds up the aluminum poles it's hung from still raw and white. The land has been cleared for farming, and wind sweeps over the plateau. Every time Patty gases up here and grit sandblasts her paint job, she wonders what state senator sold DOCS on this location.

Tommy says it's not bad. She knows he misses his little black-and-white TV, even if he says he'd rather have more package privileges anyway. Instead of cells, they have open dorm rooms with bunkbeds. They have a lot of windows, a lot of light. And it's well insulated; he doesn't complain about the cold half as much as he did at Clinton. It's quieter, and clean, and everything works. Patty can verify that from the near-sterile neatness of the visitors' center; instead of a bus station, it feels like a hospital waiting room.

On the whole, the place is less oppressive than the old maxes they're used to. The walls aren't solid, just two silver stands of chain-link fence topped with razor wire, a gravel road running around the outside. Instead of long, massive cellblocks like factories, the housing units are groups of low, red-brick barracks, with softball diamonds and basketball courts scattered here and there among them, a football field inside a lined running track. Someone driving around lost could almost mistake it for an army base or community college. Franklin, the other medium half a mile down the road, looks exactly the same, making it seem even more impersonal. Over time, she realizes this lack of personality has something to do with the fact that it's out in the middle of nowhere. As ugly as they are, Auburn fits Auburn the way Clinton fits Dannemora. Bare Hill's just *there*.

Visiting is strictly weekends only. With no FRP, she doesn't look forward to it as much as she used to. Malone's an hour farther than Dannemora, and the county roads are a nightmare in winter. It's one reason she finally gets rid of the Horizon and buys a used Subaru. She still ends up missing visits when they get any real weather.

She misses more visits—and work—the next fall, when she strains her back mucking out the gutters. She can't sit for more than a couple of minutes without having spasms. There's nothing the doctors can do except prescribe rest and anti-inflammatories. She lies on the couch while her mother waits on her. Having spent so much time around patients, Patty's aware of how demanding they can be, and tries not to complain.

"Isn't this supposed to be the other way around?" her mother needles, delivering her grilled cheese with pickles. "I'm the old lady here. When do I get to be sick?"

Tommy tells her she shouldn't have been up on the ladder in the first place. Where the hell is Casey?

"I'm not going to ask him to come home just to do the gutters," she says. "I've been doing them for twenty years. It's no big deal."

"It wouldn't have happened if I was there."

"Don't be stupid," she says, though she's had the same exact thought about a million things over the years. "I'm out of shape and I tried to do too much, that's all. I'll be fine."

It's true, but she needs to be careful. Later that winter, getting out of her car in Eileen's icy driveway, she slips and only saves herself by grabbing the door, but twists something doing it, and for weeks she has to use her father's old heating pad. Now when she wants to lift or move something heavy, her mother makes her wait until Cy can come over.

It must be the age, because the years Tommy's in Bare Hill are full of changes for all three sisters. Eileen is diagnosed with breast cancer and has a lumpectomy, losing her hair and forty pounds to the chemo. When she recovers, she and Cy split up, and then, after Cy goes through rehab for his drinking, they get back together again. Since Kyra and Randy are already gone, Shannon and Marshall take advantage of his early retirement package and move to a condo in Hilton Head. Every year her mother invites them for Thanksgiving, and every year the answer's the same: they'd love for her to come down.

Patty's changes aren't as dramatic, but they seem big to her. When Carol Henry leaves Riverview, she takes over as full supervisor. For the first time in her life she has her own office. Semester after semester, Casey makes dean's list. She likes to believe he owes at least some of his consistency to her own steadiness, her determination to keep things together.

On his end, Tommy's been writing to Cy, and though he hasn't had a drink since that night, in sympathy he enrolls in a substance abuse program that will look good on his record.

His work assignments at Bare Hill are different. Since it's a medium, he's actually allowed out. He's part of a supervised crew that helps renovate Malone's ice rink, and in the spring of '98, when a huge ice storm knocks out power from Albany to Montreal, they're tapped to provide emergency services, turning the visitors' center into a shelter. Besides his work assignments, he's taking vocational training. As Casey's preparing to graduate, interviewing with GE and IBM in a beautiful suit she picked out for him, Tommy's piling up certificates—even one in computers.

He's so proud of Casey getting job offers. Over the phone, he laughs that everyone in his unit is sick of listening to him brag about his genius of a son. Patty says she's the same at work. She updates him on which way Casey's leaning this week. All of the places seem far away, but she trusts Casey has a plan. She and Tommy agree: it's his life. They don't want him staying home to babysit her. They discuss the possibility all that spring, so when he eventually accepts a job in New Mexico, she can't say she's shocked.

It rains the day of his graduation, and the pictures come out dark, but there's a nice one of the two of them smiling, showing his open diploma. Beside him, she seems tiny. She makes a copy for Tommy and frames the original. The big console TV her father and Tommy used to sit on is long gone; she and Casey join them on the sideboard in the dining room. Walking through, she sometimes stops to admire the resemblances and ends up brooding on Casey going away. Looking at Tommy and her father, she thinks it makes sense that she'd lose him too.

Casey stops home for a few days on his way west. She can't believe he's really leaving, that he won't be back to work summers at the Parkview, that Adam won't be cruising by to pick him up. It's a great job, and they're paying for his grad school, so she can't argue with his choice, but in many ways he still seems like a teenager.

"When am I going to see you again?" she asks as he's gathering his things.

Tommy tells her to look at it logically. He can't come back for both Thanksgiving *and* Christmas, the plane tickets are too expensive. She needs to invite him for just one.

Christmas is longer, and Casey has time off. He flies into Syracuse and rents a car and spends the week visiting his friends around town. They're supposed to go up to Bare Hill, but it snows, so he heads back on New Year's Eve without seeing Tommy.

Casey's private about his life, like in high school, his silence over the phone a closed door. He's not allowed to talk about his work, which frustrates her. He's got an apartment and a car, he has friends at the lab, but he never mentions girls or dating. Weekends he likes to hike and camp out in the national forest around Santa Fe. He says he's getting better at cooking. She worries that he's lonely. At the end of their calls, she says she misses him, and he echoes her, but dully, just to get her off the line.

"He's so unemotional," she confides to Eileen. "That's not how he used to be. Remember when he was a kid, he was so sensitive."

"I think he's fine," Eileen says. "That's just the way he is."

"I don't know if he'd even tell me if something was wrong."

"Of course he's not going to tell you if something's wrong. He's a guy."

Her mother agrees with Eileen, so does Tommy. She has to learn not to worry about him so much. It might be that she's grown too used to constantly fearing for Tommy, not knowing what's happening inside. That's going to have to change when he gets out. She can't be worrying every time he runs to the store.

She tries not to get too excited, but their initial parole date's coming up. Tommy's automatically enrolled in the Transitional Service Program. He's been meeting with his facility parole officer, working with him to put together his file for the board. Even people who don't know him have to admit he's done good time. He's never been written up for any kind of discipline, and his work assignments and program certificates will count in his favor. So will their marriage, and Casey, and that he's got a place to stay. The only thing he needs help with is a job, and that's easy: Patty has enough friends in personnel that she can guarantee him a position at Riverview. With all that going for him, she doesn't see how the board could possibly turn him down. While everyone else is gearing up for the millennium, she's focused on November.

It's not that simple, Tommy warns her. Hardly anybody gets parole their first time. He's learning how it works in the prerelease class he's taking. It's not about how he's become a better person. The first thing the board will ask him about is the murder. He'll have to answer their questions without a lawyer present. It's like a trial except he doesn't have any rights. Since he's presumed guilty, they'll want him to take responsibility and show remorse. If he doesn't, that's it, so it's either lie or be denied right off the bat. They have to rate his crime using a point system. The more forcible contact there was with the victim, the higher the score, and they're allowed to consider aggravating and mitigating factors, so Mrs. Wagner being old and blind will hurt him just like it did at the trial. He'll do okay with the prior criminal history score, but on top of the scores there's the victim impact statement. Patty thinks it's not fair. The family can say anything they want, but she's not allowed to testify on his behalf. She's not even allowed to be there.

If he does make parole, he still has to report to a local parole officer every week. Because he was drunk that night, he can't drink—at all—and because he's a convicted felon, he can't be bonded for certain jobs, like being a security guard. At Riverview he can clean up after patients but can't take care of them. He has to pay taxes but can't vote or own a gun, or even a knife. His parole officer can come to their house and search it without a warrant, or check in on him at work unannounced and demand a urine sample. Tommy can't get a driver's license without getting permission, can't leave the state without permission, can't change jobs without permission, can't change residence without permission, and on top of all that, he has to pay the state a fee of thirty dollars a month.

"Thirty bucks a month to have you home. Sounds like a good deal to me."

As the hearing nears, they make the necessary preparations; they just have to go ahead and assume he'll be approved. The class he's in has a long checklist he needs to take care of before he's release-ready, things she wouldn't even think of, like renewing his driver's license. She's amazed at how organized they are: he can apply right there.

He has his records together. They've even located their original defense attorney to give a statement. All that's left is the hearing.

She has no idea who's on the board. Supposedly it's only two or three people. Again, she feels helpless, putting their lives in the hands of complete strangers. After everything that's happened to them, it's hard for her to believe, and that day—so mild she eats her lunch by the river—she keeps busy, tries not to imagine him in the bright room, facing the table of judges.

He calls that night and says it went well enough. Elsie Wagner did send a statement, but the defense attorney said if Gary hadn't squealed, Tommy would have probably gotten manslaughter.

"He's still saying that," Patty says. "What did you say?"

"I said I was sorry for everything that happened."

"But you didn't do it."

"I was there," Tommy says, as if it's the same thing.

They'll send him a letter in a couple of days. If he's being released, they'll give him a date; if not, they'll explain why they turned him down. She's used to waiting—she's made an art of it—but the rest of the week seems endless. She smokes too much and upsets her stomach. She's scattered at work and hides in her office, goes home and watches TV and then can't sleep.

When he finally calls Friday night, there's no drama; she can hear the disappointment in his voice. Because of the age and the physical condition of the victim, the board has given him the maximum, two more years. She tries to convince herself that she knew this would happen. She's been living on faith for so long, she can't just suddenly turn it off. She swears she won't make the same mistake next time.

AT LAST

THE MILLENNIUM COMES, AND 2001, UNBELIEVABLE, TERRORISTS knocking down the twin towers, war in Afghanistan. The big event in Owego is the demolition of the Court Street bridge, there as long as Patty can remember. With a couple of puffs, it crumples into the river.

She turns fifty-five before his next board, older than her mother was when he first went in. Some days when it's damp and her back's bothering her, Patty feels her age, but she's still in decent shape, considering. She's been lucky healthwise, not like Eileen, still undergoing chemo and having mammograms every six months.

They prepare for the second board the same way, which makes no sense to Patty, since they're hoping for a different outcome. There are only three possibilities: the board can give him two more years, one more year, or they can let him go. Since his sentence is twenty-five to life, he can never max out; they can keep giving him two years forever. If they give him one year, that's good—they can't go back and give him two years again. But they can keep giving him one year. There's no logic to it that Patty can see.

He gets one year. This is supposed to make her happy.

The year that she waits for his next board seems longer than all the others—but they all seem long. It never gets easier. Bare Hill is worse because there's no FRP to look forward to, making the time he's been there feel unbroken, a long swim underwater.

She still goes up, but not as often, taking the bus from Elmira because the drive's hard on her back. The other women in the visitors' center are young and mistake her for someone's mother. Tommy's working as a gardener that summer, his arms tan. Every week he completes another module of the pre-release course, building life skills, filling out a monthly budget like a farmwife. He makes fun of it, but she can see he's tired.

The board meets as U.S. troops are massing in the Kuwaiti desert for another war in Iraq. The panel is all-male; Tommy's not sure if that's better or worse for his chances. He submits his usual stack of documents and answers their questions as honestly as he can. He can't tell if he's getting better at it, but by now he knows what to expect.

For some reason Patty will never understand, this time Elsie Wagner doesn't send a victim impact statement. Three days later, Tommy gets a letter from the state.

He's somber when he calls. He doesn't tell her what they said right off, he just reads the letter. "'Dear Mr. Dickerson,'" he says, and pauses—too long, teasing—and she doesn't have to hear the rest of it.

CONDITIONS

OF

PAROLE

NEVER DID BELIEVE IN MIRACLES

BUT I'VE A FEELING IT'S TIME TO TRY

FLEETWOOD MAC

GATE MONEY

SHE STAYS AT THE ECONO LODGE ON THE GRUNGY EDGE OF MALONE
and wakes up early so she can be there when he's released. The coordinator told her sometime between seven and eight. They try to
get people out before the day's in full swing; they don't like to dis-
rupt the routine. Patty gets up at five in the cold box of the motel
room to put herself together and checks out while it's still night
outside. In the backseat she has a bag of new clothes for him in
case he wants to change, a grocery bag of snacks, a fresh hardpack
of Marlboros, and a cooler she just restocked from the ice machine. It's like they're going on a road trip.

She's already on the right side of town. She drives north, skirting the blue runway lights of the airport. The shifts must have just
changed at the prisons, because there's traffic coming the other
way. It's not far and she's early, so she stops at the mini-mart for
a coffee, then sets up by the main gate.

It's strange not checking in at the trailer—closed, since it's a
weekday. Hers is the only car there, a little creepy, with the blinding lights on either side of the gate throwing shadows across the lot.
She keeps her parking lights on and the defrost on low so she can
see, though there's no way he could sneak by her. Slowly the sky
brightens, revealing the motion detectors and cameras poking
over the fence. At the bottom the grass is frosted a solid white. The
dash clock passes seven, seven-oh-five. In the mirror the sun's com-

ing up over the mountains, rising like a balloon. Once it clears the tree line, the floodlights inside click off. The coordinator did say the front gate; Patty has the letter with her but doesn't have to check it. She expects she'll have to wait till eight o'clock, maybe later— legally they can keep him till midnight tonight—and then she sees two figures approaching the fence, one in front of the other.

It's him. She can tell by the way he walks, rocking slightly forward as if he's watching his feet. She forgets the car's on and jumps out, the open-door signal dinging, then silenced as she shuts it behind her and heads for the fence. Tommy spots her and waves.

He's carrying a cardboard box and wearing the lined army jacket she bought from a catalog. Closer, she can see he's got normal khakis on, but still has his chunky black brogans. "Your shoes!" she jokes, pointing through the fence, but he just smiles and shrugs, who cares. She doesn't even feel the cold as she follows along outside.

She stops when they stop. He stands aside as the C.O. cracks the lock and pushes the chain-link door open for him. Tommy steps over the threshold, bends to drop the box on the ground, and then she's in his arms and there's nothing at all between them.

He picks up the box again, and she takes his elbow, bumping against him as they cross the lot. She can't stop looking at him. She wishes she'd brought a camera.

"Nice car," he says, but then she has to help him push the seat all the way back and recline it a notch so his head's not touching the ceiling.

For a minute they kiss like kids parking, then he says, "Let's get out of here."

"Put your seatbelt on."

"Why, are we going to have an accident?"

"We're not getting a ticket your first day out."

He clicks it closed, then says "Whoa" and braces a hand on

the dash as she swings the Subaru over the empty spaces. "Good thing I've got my belt on."

She thumbs at the bags and the cooler in back, asks if he wants a coffee from the mini-mart. No, he just wants to go. The road's clear, the day's bright, and she shifts into fifth.

"How fast are you going?" he asks.

"Sixty."

"It feels like a hundred."

"Want me to slow down?"

"No," he says, but she eases off.

He keeps a hand on her leg as he smokes, watching the lakes and hillsides flash by. He seems especially interested in the few ratty asbestos-shingled houses and boarded-up hunting camps, chains slung across their driveways. He sits up and follows them as they pass, as if he knows the owners.

The first town they go through is Bellmont Center, a bare crossroads where the one gas station is pumpless and dark. A rotting barn leans in a field. Across the road sits an abandoned trailer, its windows broken out, curtains fluttering.

"Nice," Tommy says.

Patty laughs. "Just wait. We're not even to the good part yet."

The only way back to the interstate takes them straight through Dannemora, right by Clinton. She apologizes in advance. As they ride along the massive white wall, he's on the side away from it and ducks down to get a better look. The visitors' center is busy. There are buses, even on a weekday.

"It's hard to believe," he says.

"What?"

"It's even uglier on the outside."

Dannemora's not that big. The speed limit changes at the edge of town and they put Clinton behind them. Up ahead is the collection of chain-saw bears that marks the taxidermy shop. "Fins, Feathers and Fur," Tommy reads off the hand-carved sign she's seen a hundred times.

"You know what's funny," he asks.

"What?"

"I couldn't sleep last night."

"I know," Patty says. "I was the same way. The bed being a rock didn't help."

"I haven't slept right since I got the letter."

"You'll sleep tonight," Patty promises. "I'll make sure."

All the talk about sleep must be getting to her, because once they're on the Northway she feels tired. She needs something to eat, and she could use a bathroom. He says he's already had breakfast but might have a coffee. She's lucky she knows the road. There's a McDonald's in Peru; after that there's nothing for miles.

"It's on me," Tommy says, showing her the two twenties the state gave him. "I'm loaded."

It's a nice surprise. She can't remember the last time someone paid for her.

As they're walking across the lot, a black Lincoln Navigator with tinted windows and gold rims rolls past, the bass from a rap song vibrating the air. Tommy watches it an extra second. "I've seen them on TV," he says, "but that thing's huge." And all she can say is "Yep."

He makes a point of opening the door for her. It's rush hour and loud inside, people three deep at the counter, amplified voices from the drive-thru mixing with piped-in pop.

"I'm going to use the restroom first," she tells him.

"I should too," he says, and follows her down the window-less hall.

She's always taken longer than him. She expects him to be

scanning the menu when she comes out, but he's waiting for her in the hall like Casey used to.

When they join the crowd out front, they're displayed on a security monitor to the side—and that's the camera they can see. Behind them, a dark globe watches from the drop ceiling. He sticks close to her the whole time, and she can't blame him. The place must seem strange and new, with its flat-screen menu, the last panel flashing a commercial for the new Harry Potter movie. Half the guys in line are on their way to work, wearing jeans and flannel shirts and Timberlands, hooded sweatshirts and field jackets. Tommy could almost fit in except for the shoes.

"You want something besides coffee?" she asks, but he's still trying to decipher the menu, as if there are too many choices. "I'm having a sausage biscuit with egg."

"That sounds good," he says.

He lets her order everything, hanging back while she returns the server's volley of questions: medium, cream and sugar, to go. He gives her the money to pay and they wait for the sandwiches to come out, stand marooned on the far side of the register before they finally make their escape, and then outside Tommy almost gets run over when he steps in front of a mail jeep.

"Are you all right?" she asks him in the car.

"Just out of practice, I guess," he says, but she can see he's embarrassed.

She can eat and drive at the same time, but she's used to having the passenger seat for a table. She waits till they're cruising on the interstate to take her first bite. By then Tommy's almost done with his, cheeks stuffed, nodding at how good it is. When she can't finish hers, he wolfs it down.

"Am I nuts," he asks, "or is this coffee really good?"

"It's pretty good," she admits.

"I think I ate too fast," he announces a few miles down the road. When she looks over, he's grimacing, holding a hand to his stomach. She should have realized, he's used to oatmeal.

"Are you going to be sick?"

"No, but if you see a rest area, I could use one."

She speeds up to her normal ten miles above the limit, scanning the median for cops. It's the end of the month, and some of the towns around here balance their budgets with tickets.

"How are you doing there?" she asks.

"I'm all right for now."

"Another five minutes and we'll be there."

"Sounds good to me."

She's been through the same thing with Casey, she's even done the same thing herself on this road, the long exits making her hold it. The whole thing would be funny if it wasn't for the timing.

There's the sign advertising the rest area ahead, and less than a minute later the area itself, a low concrete block building and some picnic tables, a couple raccoon-proof trash cans. She runs the car all the way up to the handicapped spaces and drops him off before finding a spot.

She doesn't need to go, and sits there with the engine off, wondering what's in the box in the backseat. Pictures, she expects. She hopes he's kept her letters, though the box doesn't look big enough. His take up the whole top of her closet, a wall of shoeboxes.

She's debating whether she should go in and see if he's all right when he comes out. He stops by the water fountain to take a look at the laminated map on the wall, then steps back to gawk at the little satellite dish on the corner of the roof. She wants to call to him to get back in the car, as if he's in danger just standing there. She doesn't know what she's afraid of—that he won't know what to do if a stranger approaches him. The parole officer who did their home visit told her it wouldn't be easy for someone who'd been away for so long, to not expect too much from him at first. She resented the way the man talked about Tommy, as if she didn't know him at all. The guy had never met Tommy in his life, and here he was trying to tell her what he was going to be like. She listened to him and let him leave her a folder, she even shook his hand at the door, but she didn't believe a word he said. Now she wonders if she was wrong.

He bangs his head as he gets in.

"God," he says, rubbing it, "can they make this car any smaller?"

She doesn't tell him it's regular-size, just asks him if he's all right.

"The bathrooms haven't changed," he says, "that's for sure."

With Casey she'd joke and ask if everything came out all right, but she's afraid he may be sensitive.

After they get going again, she tells him her mother's staying the night at Eileen's.

"Get out," he says.

"I didn't even have to ask."

"That's pretty nice of her."

"Just make sure you thank her," Patty says.

"I will." He's overwhelmed by it, because a few minutes later, out of nowhere, he says, "Wow."

"She's done a lot for us," she says.

"I know," he says, just as serious.

With so many miles alone together, they can't avoid the chewed-on topic of finding their own place. For everything her mother's done for them, Tommy doesn't want to live with her, and Patty can understand that. She's had fantasies of renting their old house on Spaulding Hill, as if they can start all over again. She's got enough money to go almost anywhere in the county, but her mother's stood by them for so long. Patty can't abandon her. She's in her late seventies, and doesn't drive after dark. She jokes that pretty soon Patty's going to have to get her into Riverview, but really she's terrified of the idea. Maybe if they could find someplace close by.

Near Schroon Lake, they're in the middle of discussing exactly what counts as close when—too late—she sees the cop hiding behind the rocks in the median. They're flying downhill and in her concentration on Tommy's argument she's let the needle creep up to eighty.

"Fuck," she says, and takes her foot off the gas. They're already in the right lane, so there's nowhere to go. She doesn't turn her head to look at the mirror, just flicks her eyes to the side. Has he moved? All she can think of is the cop looking in the window and noticing Tommy's shoes.

"How fast were you going?" Tommy asks.

"Fast enough."

She risks a look, turning her head an inch, and finds the cruiser, still lurking in the median.

"He's just sitting there," she says.

"Don't tell me we actually caught a break."

It does feel like luck. She doesn't push it. They're done with the fast part of the Northway anyway, hitting local traffic around Glens Falls and down through Saratoga Springs. They come into Albany around lunchtime, passing within a few miles of Troy, and Rensselaer. Tommy's never seen the college; if they had more time, she'd detour across the river and show him Casey's old dorm. As it is, she just lets the sign float by.

She wanted Casey to be a part of the celebration today. She even offered to pay his plane fare, but the project he's in charge of is way behind schedule and running round the clock and he has to be there if something happens. He'll be home for Christmas. It's only three weeks. When she broke the news to Tommy, he said he completely understood. Patty doesn't, and thinks it will be a long time before she forgives Casey—or Tommy, for not expecting better.

The tricky interchange with its swooping ramps makes her pay attention. The Thruway's always crazy. Tommy doesn't like the chaos of the toll plaza, or the curves, or the way people trade lanes like slot cars. "Is that legal?" he asks about a FedEx double trailer rig. They're both hungry but the only service area's on the wrong side. She's almost glad—those places can be madhouses.

She waits till they're on the quieter I-88 and she needs gas, combining the two stops. Tommy's surprised at the high prices. He gets out to pump but is stumped by the screen asking for payment information. Patty shows him how to use the Speedpass on her keychain.

They do the drive-thru at a Wendy's and get back on the road. It's only twelve-thirty but she needs to keep an eye on the time. Tommy's got to check in with the parole office in Elmira, so they're going there first. Her mother's expecting them around five-thirty. Patty's made his favorite lasagna ahead of time. She has fresh strawberries and pineapple chunks waiting for him, and Boston cream pie. She's bought new towels and flannel sheets and cleaned the whole house, emptying it of alcohol like the parole officer told her. She's even had Cy and Eileen help her resurrect Tommy's old recliner from the basement, wiping down the cracked naugahyde with mink oil. She can't wait to see his face.

The temptation on 88 is to blast it because there's no traffic. For miles there's nothing but forest, a dusting of snow highlighting the rocks and deadfall. She sets the cruise control eight miles above the limit and flexes her foot inside her shoe. Her tailbone hurts from sitting in the same position for so long, and she shifts her weight.

"Want me to drive?" he asks. "I've got my license."

"I'm all right," she says.

"It's pretty," he says a few minutes later, meaning the gray woods.

She doesn't tell him this, but the drive seems to take longer with him in the car. By herself, she'd space out to the radio, her attention on the road dipping in and out with the songs and talk, the miles and sights passing without comment. She's gotten used to that kind of waking trance, letting the hours slide by, her mind emptying until she can really think. She shouldn't miss it, not with him right beside her. As if to prove her point to herself, she reaches over and takes his hand.

81 funnels them into Binghamton.

"Wow," he says as they shoot through Johnson City, "this place has really built up."

They're getting closer, and he's noticing everything that's still there, everything that's changed, everything that's gone. Even the road is different; Route 17's slowly been switching over to Interstate 86.

"That's weird," Tommy says.

"It's just the signs," she says. "They've still got the stupid stoplights at Horseheads."

Past Apalachin with the massive Citgo plaza he's never seen, past the new exit. The Amish farmers' market's gone. At least the chicken barbecue is still there, and the soft-serve.

The biggest shock is coming up, as they near the main Owego exit, closed due to construction. The approach to the new Court Street bridge goes right over the road. Above them, a crew in optic yellow sweatshirts is working on the railings, and she wonders if Russ is at the house yet. It bugs her: Casey couldn't make it because he says he's busy, but Russ found the time to come all the way from Texas.

"Holy shit," Tommy says, looking across the river. The new

bridge is almost done, lined with quaint, fake gas lamps. The pilings of the old bridge poke out of the water like stepping stones.

"It took them three years."

"That's just nuts."

He's quiet, processing it, until they pass the new Best Buy warehouse going up across from the truck stop.

"I've heard of them," he says. "What do they sell?"

Patty's never been in one, but she knows from their flyers in the Sunday paper that they're an appliance store. She can't believe he hasn't seen their commercials, but doesn't call him on it. She doesn't mind being his guide. It actually feels good having the answers to his questions.

In the same way, she tries to help in Elmira, when they sit down with his parole officer, a tall guy in his early thirties with the bullet head and rigid posture of a marine. He has an inch-thick file on Tommy he spreads on his desk, the old mug shot stapled to a corner of the folder. He wants to double-check his information, and Tommy turns to her for the address and phone number of Riverview, his hours, the name of his supervisor. Patty has it all.

The officer talks to them like they've just been arrested—calmly threatening—going over the rules one by one from the handbook, pausing to make sure they understand. Possession of illegal drugs or drug paraphernalia or any controlled substance without proper medical authorization constitutes a violation. Patty's got a copy of the book at home, and knows it by heart. Tommy's not allowed to be out past nine unless he has to for work. He needs a travel pass if he's going to leave the state (even though, technically, they just crossed the PA state line where 17 makes that little dip south of Waverly). If he fails to report, or to report a change of address or employment, that's considered absconding. By law the officer will have to issue a warrant.

"And believe me," he says, "that's the last thing I want to do. The better you do, the happier I am."

To Patty, he sounds false as a politician, especially when he sends Tommy into a closet-sized bathroom right behind him to produce a urine sample. Throughout his time inside, Tommy's been strip-searched and forced to give urine samples hundreds of times, but she's never had to see it. Now when he comes out of the bathroom with the lidded cup half filled with beer-colored pee, she's angry and ashamed for him.

"That wasn't so bad," Tommy says when they're in the car again, and she has to agree. It's a relief to be out of there, done with their one obligation. He has to register with the Owego police, but that can wait till tomorrow.

She crosses the river at Nichols so they don't have to backtrack, and takes him into town the way they used to come from their old place, along the train tracks, past the cemetery and the speedway. There's no avoiding the courthouse—completely restored, floodlights showing off its repointed, steam-cleaned brick. She turns up North Street, leaving it behind, dips under the railroad bridge and past the blocks of ratty townhouses and the Open Door Mission with its thrift shop.

"Hasn't changed much," he says.

"Not this part."

A couple miles out of town, they come alongside the new Public Safety Building—the county jail—long and low and lit up like a factory, curls of razor wire glinting in the dark.

"Mighty fancy," he says.

"It cost enough."

The turnoff's not much farther. She's probably going too fast, but she knows the roads, and she's tired of driving. She just wants to get home.

"Thanks for coming to pick me up," he says as they head into the hills, because these are their last minutes alone together before they have to face everyone. It's silly—what was she going to do, make him take the bus?—but she knows what he's saying. He doesn't mean just today.

"You're welcome," she says.

And then, a minute later, they're there, turning into the driveway, her headlights catching the handmade banner hung from the porch roof—WELCOME HOME TOMMY. The front door opens before they can get out, and Eileen and Cy and Russ and her mother swarm the car, hugging Tommy and patting him on the back, taking their bags, whisking them inside where the food is laid out buffet-style on the dining room table. Her mother says their timing's perfect, she just took the lasagna out of the oven.

Tommy can't believe Russ is here. He laughs at the recliner with the big bow on it; Eileen takes a picture of him testing it out. While they wait for the lasagna to cool, Russ catches him up on the old crew. Shawn's still in Elmira, but most of them are gone. Perry's in Florida and has his own motorcycle shop—which leads to the story about the time Perry spent the whole winter building the ultimate dirtbike and then broke both wrists the first time he jumped it. Patty sits on the couch, sipping a Coke for the caffeine. The house is too bright, too loud. She feels like she's still moving. She must be crashing from the drive, because all of a sudden she's mad at Casey for not being here. She wants to call him and put Tommy on, except she knows he's working late, and with the time difference he won't be home for hours. She's tempted to leave a message: I guess we missed you. I just wanted to let you know: your father's home.

They eat off of their laps, gathered in the living room, passing the basket of garlic bread. Getting seconds, Tommy compliments her mother, and Eileen cracks up with her mouth full of salad.

"*I* made it," Patty says. "She just turned on the oven."

"It's the best thing I've had in years."

"I think there's going to be a lot of that tonight," Eileen says.

"I sure hope so," Patty seconds.

Before they cut the pie, Tommy gets serious, standing and thanking them for believing in him, and for helping Patty and Casey all these years. He says he knows he's got a lot to make up for, and that he'll do his best. He raises his glass of soda and toasts them. "I wish this was champagne."

"So do I," Cy jokes, and Eileen smacks his leg.

Her mother serves coffee with dessert, and they kick back and tell stories, letting the dishes sit. Looking around the room, Patty thinks her world has gotten so small. She misses Russ. She has friends at work, but she's had to keep her distance. The tactic has become a habit, and she wonders if that might change now. She's grown so dependent on those closest to her.

And on Tommy. It's hard, now, to share him with everyone else, to not follow him to the bathroom. While he's gone, she steals his recliner just to get his attention, like a little kid. She barely contributes to the conversation, and feels selfish, wanting everyone to leave so they can be alone. Russ has come so far, but Tommy can see him tomorrow.

"Well," her mother says during a lull, "I'm sure you've had enough excitement for one day."

Eileen picks up on her cue, and gathers Cy. Russ follows them to the front hall, where they all pull their coats on. Her mother whispers something in Tommy's ear as she hugs him, and then they're on the front porch, waving them away.

"What did my mom say to you?" she asks as they're cleaning up.

"Nothing," he says. "She said to be good to you."

Patty shakes her head. "I swear, she'll never get it. You already are."

"I know what she meant," he says.

They close up the downstairs—or she does, going from the front of the house to the back while he stands there with his box of stuff. He wants to take a shower, giving her a chance to peek at the contents: her letters—at least some of them—old pictures of her and Casey, his course certificates, a wad of birthday and Christmas and Father's Day cards, a cloud chart Casey sent him when he was at Bare Hill, then just shirts and pants and underwear, a few rolled pairs of socks in the bottom, some stray pencils, a single tennis ball. She closes the flaps again, strips and joins him in the shower.

It's been eight years since they've been together, and since she's had a desk job she's put on weight. He's thicker too, and gray in places, but still strong. The three scars on his back have magically disappeared.

They barely towel off before slipping into bed.

"Your hair's freezing," he says, but he doesn't want her to leave. The flannel sheets slowly warm them.

"It's so quiet," he says.

They make love, then agree to sleep. It's been a long day, so many miles behind them, the jump from one world to another. He still sleeps on his side, she still fits him. He drifts off first, and she listens to him breathe. She almost can't believe it. For so long this is all she wanted. Now that he's finally here beside her, she swears that no one will ever take him away from her again.

HOUSEKEEPING

HE HAS TO START FROM SCRATCH. HE'S NEVER HAD A REGULAR DOC-
tor, and he has to take a physical to qualify for her insurance. His
name's still listed on their bank account, but he needs an ATM
card. He's never used an ATM before, or a beeper, or a cell phone.
He's got a certificate in computers but he's never been on the In-
ternet. The first time he e-mails Casey he sends the message three
times because he's not sure it worked.

She's added him to their car insurance, but she has to push
him to drive. He's still timid of other traffic, going too slow, balking
at stop signs. He says he's not comfortable, that her car's too small.
He's also not good with keys, forgetting his every morning, as if
he doesn't need them. It's easier if she just chauffeurs him to work.

At home he won't answer the phone. The ringing drives her
mother crazy. He wakes up every day at six o'clock sharp, no matter
how late he stays up, takes an eight-minute shower and has their
bed made before Patty can dry her hair. The top of his dresser is
empty except for his watch and wallet, returned to the same spots
every night, lined up square with the edge. His drawers are just as
neat, the piles precise, his rolled socks all in a row. If she didn't
know better, she'd think he just got out of the Marines.

Because he's so regimented, she expects him to do well at Riverview, where there's a set daily schedule. She doesn't have to be in
till nine, but goes in an hour early to make sure he's on time. They

split in the parking lot and don't see each other the rest of the day, trying to defuse any gossip. Like every new hire, he's on ninety-day probation, but his supervisor's Holly, a friend of hers. Patty's told her that he's a good worker, and motivated. He shouldn't have any problems.

He won't get his first check until the end of the month, and has to ask her for pocket money, something neither of them is used to. Her mother warned Patty that he might have a problem with her making so much more than him. He hasn't said anything, but every morning she's aware of how they must look to someone driving beside them—her in a business suit, him in a workshirt and jeans. She tries to tell herself it doesn't matter, just as she doesn't dwell on the fact that he's doing a job she was done with twenty years ago.

What surprises her most these first weeks is how quiet he is, not like the Tommy who used to sing along with the radio or holler from the other room for the fun of it. It's unfair comparing the two, but it worries her. She finds herself observing him, looking for clues. When she sees him watching the Bills without even commenting on a long touchdown run, she wonders if the changes are permanent. She sits down beside him and folds laundry on the coffee table, talking back to the TV, and while he finally joins in, he's not as excited as he should be, as if the game doesn't matter.

He's still not good with crowds. Their Christmas shopping at the mall lasts about five minutes. In the car he says he's sorry, but doesn't offer to try again. Patty understands; he needs to build up to it.

He likes to be outside. He'll go and smoke on the back porch for the view even though it's freezing. They take walks in the woods, following the Indian trails past Casey's old lean-to, fallen now, a sopping magazine trapped under the leaves and debris. It's easier talking to him here, away from the world. He says he feels weird.

He thinks everybody can tell that he's been in prison just from looking at him. He wonders if it would be better if they moved.

He looks unsure when Patty laughs, as if he's said something stupid.

"No," she says. "It's just that I used to think the same thing."

"But you never did."

"I wouldn't have had the help I needed somewhere else."

He still thinks they should have their own place, but he's willing to wait. Maybe in the spring, when things are more settled. Right now he needs to get his bearings.

The best way to do that, Patty thinks, is to get out more, go to the grocery store, go ice skating. He's not going to catch up to the twenty-first century by setting up their old stereo and playing records all weekend like a teenager. At the same time, she can't be angry with him. She needs to be patient. She thinks it's lucky she has practice.

The one place they're making up for lost time is in the bedroom. He expects sex every night, and even when she's not in the mood she can't deny him. It's not the romance she dreamed of when he was inside, not the long-awaited celebrations of their FRPs, but how could it be?

He's with her now almost constantly. They're only separated at work, and even then they're in the same building. At first she couldn't let him out of her sight; now she's glad to have a few hours' privacy. She's grown so used to being alone, to following her own schedule and having her own space, that at times she feels cramped. It's just the power of habit; she really wants him here.

He's doing okay, according to his parole officer. He reports once a week, a convenient opportunity to practice some highway driving. On the way home is the only time she sees him seriously angry, calling the guy a prick. "I'm fifty-seven and I'm cleaning up old people's diarrhea, and he's lecturing *me* about reality? Let's see him walk into Auburn for five minutes and see how long he lasts."

"I didn't know you hated your job so much," she says.

"I'm just saying the guy doesn't have to be an asshole. It's bad enough I have to listen to his regular shit."

"You know, I did that job for six years."

"I'm sorry," he says. "I don't hate the job. The whole thing just gets to me."

He means parole, but obviously he doesn't love the job either. Maybe it was a mistake thinking they could work at the same place. Maybe her mother's right. Patty consoles herself with the idea that it was only supposed to be temporary. She doesn't want him emptying bedpans and mopping hallways any more than he does, but he has to start somewhere.

He's just frustrated, he says. Everything's harder than he thought it would be.

It's exactly what the parole officer told her that first home visit, but she can't say that. She needs to be positive, and tells him what she tells herself. Be patient. Things will get better.

And then, with two weeks till Christmas, he gets sick. There's been a flu going around, and he spends half the night in the bathroom. Because he's on probation, he doesn't have any sick days yet, and wants to go in so he won't get docked. He can't—not until his fever's gone. Patty almost takes the day off to take care of him. She explains the situation to Holly, who says it's no problem.

"How's he getting along?" Patty asks.

"All right," Holly says. "Did he tell you about Lainie?"

"No."

"I guess they got into it over something she asked him to do. You know how she can be when she's in a hurry. Otherwise he's been fine."

When Patty asks Tommy his side of it, he says he doesn't have to take Lainie's shit. She's not his boss.

"She's part of the nursing staff," Patty says.

"She's a fucking bitch."

"Maybe she is, but you're going to have to learn how to work with her."

"I have," he says. "I stay the hell away from her."

"Why didn't you tell me?" Patty asks.

"I didn't want you to get mad."

"You didn't think I'd find out?"

"I didn't think it was such a big deal, but obviously it is—like it's my fault she's a bitch. It's all right for her to talk to me like I'm a piece of shit, but when I walk away from it, I'm the bad guy. How does that work, huh? I didn't even say anything. I used my conflict resolution, and I'm the one who gets in trouble."

She doesn't want to argue with him—he already feels like no one's on his side. And he's sick, he's miserable. Instead of going downstairs she stays with him, sitting by his bedside and watching a rerun of *The Simpsons*.

He's out for three days. She notices that she doesn't worry about him as much, knowing he's at home.

The next week, she gets it, and he has to drive in by himself. It reminds her of when Casey first got his license. She just has to trust that he'll be all right. He should be coming home around five-thirty. One night he's late, pulling in a few minutes after six. She's ready to smell his breath and ask him where he's been when she sees the bag he's trying to hide—from Conti Jewelers, her Christmas present.

She thinks things are back to normal when she returns to work. He helps put up the big tree in the lobby. It's the busy week before

Christmas, parties and lots of visitors. Patty's asked Holly to keep an eye on him and let her know if he has any problems. She doesn't expect any, since Lainie's working swing shift through New Year's—a scheduling move Patty has nothing to do with.

Thursday morning before coffee break, Holly calls and asks if she's seen Tommy. He was supposed to be helping Janice turn over a vacancy on three when he took off. They have people looking in the locker room downstairs and the men's toilets on each floor. Holly thought he might be headed for Patty's office.

"What happened?"

"I don't know," Holly says. "Janice said he just left."

"Shit," Patty says when she gets off the phone. She paces to the window, trying to think, and looks down at the picnic tables by the river, the bare trees on the far bank, the dark hints of trails. He'll be outside, she realizes, and grabs her jacket.

Her first guess is correct. He's at the car—locked—standing there because he doesn't have his keys. She has to cross a long open stretch to reach him, walking hard in her pumps.

"What are you doing?" she asks him, aware of the whole nursing home at her back.

"I quit," he says.

"What?"

"I can't work here. I'm sorry, Pats, I can't. It's too depressing."

She's been at Riverview so long that she hadn't thought of that at all. He says the patients remind him of lifers, the way their rooms are set up like cells. He hates emptying their dressers and boxing their things. He hates the way the nurses leave them in their wheelchairs in the hallways.

"I don't see how you do it," he says.

"You can't quit," she says. "You're not allowed to."

"I can get fired."

He's serious, and she wonders if this is what was behind the Lainie thing, if she told him to do something he couldn't stomach.

She wants to reason with him, here in front of everyone. Why is he throwing this chance away? Doesn't he know how hard it is to find a job in this economy? Doesn't he care how much trouble she went to, arranging this for him?

Unlike her twenty years ago, he thinks he has a choice.

"Fine," she says, "you're fired," and hands him her keys.

THE GIVING SEASON

SUNDAY MORNING PATTY PUTTERS IN THE KITCHEN IN HER APRON and sweatpants and slippers, her hair tucked under a scarf. She's finished with her shopping and is dedicating the whole day to cookies. So far her plan's working perfectly. Her mother took off early for church; Tommy and Casey are outside, stringing lights. The sticks of butter she left out last night are just the right softness. She has the oven warming and the bags of flour and sugar ranked on the counter, the carton of eggs, the bowls of sprinkles. It's so quiet that she feels funny talking herself through her recipes, as if someone's listening.

Rinsing her hands at the sink, she looks out over the backyard, bare and brown. The sky's white, solid clouds. They're predicting a big storm for Christmas, just like in *Rudolph*—a nightmare for scheduling shifts, but still, Patty's excited. It's been an early winter, cold, snow cover all month until last Friday, when the temperature shot up to fifty, melting everything. After weeks of pretty, drifted fields, the world seems drab.

While the first sheet of sand tarts is baking, she slips into the gray living room and secretly peeks through the window at Tommy and Casey, untangling the green strings on the porch. Traditionally it's been Casey's job, saved for him ever since she had her back problems. Tommy doesn't see why they had to wait, he can climb a ladder just fine, but Patty wants Casey to be a part of this Christmas, not just a visitor. It takes two people anyway, one to go up the ladder, another to hold it.

The timer dings, reeling her in. She trades baking sheets, swapping new rows of raw diamonds for the done ones, then resetting the timer. Her mother's stove is old and doesn't keep the heat well. She has to overshoot with the dial and rely on a thermometer hooked to the rack. Since she's baking all day, eventually the stove will catch up, so she has to keep an eye on it.

She lays a sheet of waxed paper under the cooling rack and sprinkles the first batch of sand tarts with glassy cinnamon crystals, recycling the ones that fall through. Over the years, she's gathered a fair-sized collection of Christmas cookie tins in addition to her mother's. Some are ugly, or rusted along the seams, but she never gets rid of any. She lines a small one with waxed paper and piles the sand tarts in. By the end of the day, all the tins will be filled. She'll have enough to take a big assorted tin to work tomorrow and another for her mother to take to church Christmas Eve. It's just the beginning, but with each sheet that comes out of the oven, she feels like she's getting something done.

The front door opens. It's Casey, letting in a chill. Maybe it's her imagination, but he seems thinner this year, fitter. He says he's been walking a lot—doctor's orders. Now he's sweating in his jacket, his bangs matted.

"How's it going?" she asks. "Is your father helping you?"

"Oh yeah," he says, a joke, and rumbles down the basement stairs. A minute later he comes up with an orange extension cord.

He's made it clear in their phone calls that he thinks she shouldn't have let Tommy quit his job. Patty doesn't expect Casey to understand. She's told him flat out that she's not his father's keeper, and that her mother wasted a lot of good years trying to make her feel the same way.

They all need to find a new way to be with each other. This Christmas is their first try, and she doesn't know what to expect. She knows the temptation is to make up for all the Christmases they've missed, a kind of super holiday FRP. Though she hates to admit it, it would have been a hell of a lot easier if Tommy could have just waited one more week to quit.

She does the snickerdoodles next, hoping the cream of tartar from last year is still good. She doesn't even like them; they're Eileen's favorite. Patty will make a little tin just for her and take it by after work tomorrow.

The door opens and shuts and Tommy comes in with his Bills hat on. They have to beat Green Bay today or they're eliminated, and they're playing at Lambeau.

"Think you'll be done by gametime?" she asks.

"I'm hoping," he says, and goes downstairs, returning with a pair of needlenose pliers.

Patty lets the door close behind him before creeping into the living room.

While Casey holds the string for him, Tommy uses the pliers to unscrew the base of a bulb that's broken off in the socket. Tommy sets the jagged neck on the porch rail and waits for Casey to find the next one. Their mouths move, steam leaking out. Patty wishes she could hear what they're saying. She watches them do two more that way before the timer calls her.

Is it a good sign that Casey's letting him take the lead, or is he just putting up with him, the way he's always put up with things? He can be so distant, as if he still has that passive teenager hiding inside him. Considering how long they've been apart, she has to laugh at what she's hoping for: she doesn't expect them to suddenly become close, just to love each other.

She mixes the dough for the pinwheels and splits it between two bowls, stirring melted chocolate into one, then refrigerating them so they'll roll without bleeding. She checks the list she put together at work. She still has lemon squares to make (Shannon's specialty, if she were here), and candy cane cookies, and gingerbread snowmen. There are no bourbon or rum balls this year, and she's only making a small batch of the date-nut bars, since no one eats them but her mother. And though there are no children to decorate them, she'll make some plain bells and Christmas trees and whip up four bowls of powdered sugar icing using the food coloring that hasn't been touched since Easter and gob it on thick.

The timer goes off, and the clock says it's past noon, less than an hour till gametime. She goes out to check on their progress.

This time she doesn't hide, but they don't notice. They're sitting on the top stair with their backs to her. On the porch floor behind them, as if cast off, lies a string that's had all its bulbs plucked out.

They both look back when she opens the storm door. Between them they've got one of the other strings hooked to the extension cord. It should be on, but it's not, and they're going through the bulbs, replacing them one at a time from a box of extras.

"Case says we've had these for a while," Tommy says. "How long would you say?"

"I don't know," she says. "A long time."

"I think it might be time for some new ones."

"They didn't just go bad," Patty reasons, because she's attached to them (and because, through the years, she's become cheap). They're old, the outdoor-only kind, the bulbs bigger than the ones on the tree. Originally she had six strings and did the whole porch and the bushes and the dogwood. They used to blink.

"I had problems with them last year," Casey says.

"Those two are okay," Tommy says, "and I'm hoping we'll get this one going, but that one's shot."

"Three strings aren't enough to cover the front," Casey points out.

How can Patty argue when they're united against her? It's almost worth it to send them off to Wal-Mart. Casey says he has money, which is ridiculous. Tommy tells him he can drive. Patty doesn't remind him that the game's starting, just watches them off in the rental car and goes back inside. The last batch of snickerdoodles is almost done.

As she spreads the gooey filling of the lemon squares over the dough, she times the drive to Vestal. Twenty minutes there, fifteen in the store, then twenty back. Nearly an hour. It's probably the longest they've ever been alone together. Greedily, she wants to be there, hidden in the backseat, listening. She wants to see what the greeter at Wal-Mart sees coming through the doors—two big guys with stooped shoulders, obviously father and son.

For now, the house is hers, sweet with the smell of vanilla. The tins are filling. She's made a decent dent in the list, and the Bills will be on soon. It's supposed to snow for Christmas. In the quiet, she finds herself whistling "Rudolph the Red-Nosed Reindeer" over and over, happy, as if she's won something.

OPENING DAY

THIS TIME, WHEN THE TROOPS INVADE IRAQ, THE WEEK OF CASEY'S birthday, Patty has someone to complain to about the yellow ribbons. She flips the channel whenever she sees a story coming up about soldiers who've spent two weeks as POWs being called heroes. Tommy says it's natural and that it doesn't bother him.

He's working at Best Buy, driving a forklift, thanks to the job bank at the parole office. He's got a used Ford pickup, just like before, making the monthly payments to build his credit. With two checks coming in, they've been able to put some money away. He hasn't bugged her about a house, but it's the season. Once the weather turns, the realty signs will pop up like dandelions.

Winter lingers into April. It's still cold Opening Day when they go out with Eileen and Cy. Though she drives over Owego Creek twice daily, it's been years since Patty's been down to the water, probably not since their father took them fishing. The flats below the Talcott Street bridge are packed, a gauntlet of rods. Cy has a pair of waders for her, but she begs off, sticking to the rocks like Eileen. Cy and Tommy slosh across and claim a sandbar, giving each other room to cast. Eileen has to show Patty what to do. When the fire siren sounds to officially start the season, she sends her line out over the water in a long arc that makes Tommy smile.

She doesn't expect to catch anything, it's more of a ceremony. The whole town's out, and after the claustrophobia of watching the war, it feels good to be doing something normal. Tommy and Cy are a good match, like her and Eileen.

They're talking about her mother going down to visit Shannon for Easter when Patty's line snags on something. The current's taken it toward shore where there's a snarl of black branches among the rocks. She tugs—it's stuck. She moves a few steps downstream and tips her rod back, hoping to clear it, and with a high-pitched whizzing, line begins stripping off her reel.

Her first reaction is to grab the handle to keep it from spinning, but she can't stop it cleanly.

"I've got something!" she calls.

"Let him take the line if he wants," Eileen says.

"How do I do that?"

"Just don't let go."

She wants Eileen to do it, but people are watching—Tommy and Cy laughing and hollering encouragement.

Eileen has her play the fish, reeling him in and then letting him run, like that might tire him. Somehow it does. Patty can see the sleek torpedo shape of him drifting in the shallows, powerless, as Eileen wades in with the net. They've gathered a crowd of little kids and their parents.

"Brown trout," one of the men says before Eileen even lifts it out, curved in the web of the net.

"Wow," a kid says.

"Oh, he's pretty," an older woman says. He's as long as Eileen's forearm, with muddy speckles and a yellow belly. His gills open and close.

"Want to keep him?" Eileen asks.

"No," Patty says, "let's let him go." But before she does, she holds him up so Tommy and Cy can admire him.

They stay until Tommy gets his limit of five. Cy and Eileen

take four each. Patty had just the one, but they all agree, hers was the prize.

IN THE DARK

IT'S A HUMID NIGHT IN JULY. THE WAR'S OVER. THE BRIDGE IS FIN-ished. It's been a good day: work, an easy commute, then dinner, TV. Boring, normal life—exactly what she wanted for so long. They've switched off the news and gone to bed at the regular time. They're both too tired to read so they turn the light out and have a last sip of water before settling in.

They've gotten past having to make love every night and gone back to their natural haphazard schedule. He starts out facing her, then rolls over. She rolls with him, spooned and then spooning, her knees tucked behind his, an arm flung over him so they can hold hands, and soon he's gone, his breathing raspy and jagged. He sleeps so easily.

She's awake, for no reason she can think of. The bed's too hot, or maybe it's the full moon, tracing the crosspiece of the window over the curtains, as if she's left the spotlight on out back. In the woods, the peepers are calling. It reminds her of Auburn, the canal just beyond the wall. For years, lying here, she used to imagine herself there with Tommy, in the old trailers. She'd fly to him through the night like a witch, over the dark lakes and forests, the sleeping towns. Now all she has to do is reach for him.

She knows from experience that anything can happen, but he's been so good. Even her mother's impressed. Casey will take longer, and honestly, he may never understand.

Tommy shifts, and she rolls with him, takes his warm hand in hers and presses it to her chest. He's asleep, she's awake, yet they're together here, and she dares to believe the long pause that's kept them from their real life is finally behind them. It's over. He's home. They made it.